Rain of Ruin

Mark Kelley

DEDICATION

To Marty, my partner in life

CONTENTS

Mark Kelley

Rain of Ruin

FOREWORD

This work of fiction is based on a true story. Many of the events described, including some of the most horrific ones, actually happened and many of the characters actually existed. In some cases, names have been changed to preserve the privacy of the individuals. In other cases, events have been created to enhance the narrative. But this remains certain: I could not alter the awful truth of this story, even if I wanted to.

Mark Kelley

Orono, Maine

PROLOGUE

On Monday, August 6, 1945, at 11:00 AM Eastern Standard Time, sixteen hours after an unprecedented explosion destroyed much of Hiroshima, Japan, President Harry Truman issued the first public statement about the U.S. atom bomb program. The release provided some background on atomic energy and the United States' great achievement, but much of it was directed at the Japanese government, urging them to surrender or face unimaginable destruction.

If the Japanese did not give up, Truman said, the United States was prepared "to obliterate more rapidly and completely every productive enterprise the Japanese have above ground in any city." The President continued, "If they do not now accept our terms, they may expect a rain of ruin from the air, the like of which has never been seen on this earth." Truman intended the "rain of ruin" to descend only on our enemies; what he and so many others did not know at that moment was that the apocalyptic device they had created would bring a storm of suffering on the heads of thousands of their own kinfolk. Agnes Jenkins Flaherty was one of those people.

Mark Kelley

CHAPTER ONE

"This isn't right. Take another look at the map. If we'd taken the right road, we'd *be* in Intercourse by now. I think we screwed up turning onto PA 897, on the other side of this ridge."

Ben Roth tightened his grip on the wheel of his rental car as he wandered, lost, through the lush, green landscape of Pennsylvania's Amish country. His wife, Sarah, pulled on her reading glasses and peered down at the dog-eared atlas they'd used for years whenever they headed out on one of their excursions. Practically everyone they knew was punching buttons on a GPS to get from Point A to Point B these days, but they remained loyal to the printed book. They actually preferred the atlas and welcomed the challenge of finding their way with the help of cartographers rather than the digital voice of the GPS.

What they both knew very clearly right now was that they weren't approaching Intercourse or Paradise, that other renowned village here in Pennsylvania Dutch country. But they wanted to. They'd told their friends in New York they intended to live out the old saw about having to go through Intercourse to get to Paradise. Ha! Ha! But they couldn't honestly say it yet because they hadn't found either of the darn towns, Instead, three hours after braving the Schuylkill Expressway to get west of Philadelphia, Ben was steering along a country road they didn't know the name or number of that meandered between three foot high embankments crowned by plowed fields and pastures full of grazing cows.

Sarah looked up from the map.

"Have you seen a road number yet? If we knew what we're on, I'll bet I can get us where we want to be. I have a feeling we're close." She generally served as navigator on their adventures; Ben thought she was at least as good as a GPS, and he liked her voice a lot better.

He scrutinized the shoulder of the roadway as he negotiated yet another ninety degree curve. These were amazing roads. He was convinced the early settlers must have let the horse find its way home from the tavern at night, and then paved over the path and called it a road. As they rounded the turn, he saw a small white sign reading "PA 135." A short distance beyond that he saw houses on the side of a low ridge. The houses were spaced in even rows that climbed, in parallel, up the hillside. Near the first cluster of homes, a green sign with a gilt edge and gold lettering welcomed them to Dillerville.

Ben glanced down at the map.

"Is Dillerville on there? And, if it is, where the hell is it and where are we?"

Sarah had just seen the name Dillerville in the atlas; she scanned the map again to find it.

"Oh, yes. It's a real place. Not too big, though. It's a black dot town, not a circle or a yellow patch." She held the booklet up so Ben could see where her finger was pointing. "And over here is Intercourse, but I'll be darned if I can figure out which of these back roads is going to get us there. They all just seem to wiggle around."

"No shit."

Entering Dillerville from the south, the first thing PA 135 did was climb up the side of the ridge. Just before the road tilted up, Ben noticed a street off to the left. He hit his turn signal and slowed down.

"So near and yet so far, babe. I'll bet somebody on this street can point us in the right direction."

The street had houses only on one side. A four foot grassy shoulder on the other side sloped into a cornfield. Ben slowed the car to a crawl and scanned the well-manicured front yards for signs of life. A few houses down the street, he saw a day-glow pink poster tacked to a telephone pole announcing a yard sale at 215 Orlon Street. The sign at the corner had said Orlon--a strange street name in the eyes of a stranger from New York, but meaningful to the natives who knew the local silk mill built the homes on this street and the one above it so their workers would have a place to live. Less than a hundred yards down the street, both the curb and the shoulder on the opposite side   were lined with cars and trucks. As they drew closer, they saw that a lawn on the curb side was laid out with what looked like typical yard sale offerings. Ben eased in behind the last car in line, switched off the ignition, and removed the key.

He turned to Sarah. "You okay checking out the merchandise while I find someone who can help us out?"

"Do I ever turn down a chance to cruise a yard sale? I'll be looking around. Don't leave without me." She smiled and hopped out of the car, as Ben stepped out on his side.

The yard in front of the one-story, frame house at 215 Orlon overflowed with stuff, racks of clothing, old wooden furniture, a sixties style love seat and chair with chrome arm rests and bright colored seat cushions, a set of barbells coated with a patina of rust, and several folding tables holding what looked like house wares and baskets of smaller items. Sarah waded in; she always seemed to find something of value at these things. Ben sized up the scene before stepping onto the grass. He didn't like shopping in any form, and he especially tried to avoid yard sales. Pawing through someone's personal items, objects that bore the wear-and-tear, the marks of their life, seemed like an invasion of privacy. It made him uncomfortable, especially if the owners were right there watching him sift through their worldly possessions.

Off to the right, behind one of the tables, he spotted an old man, wearing a baseball cap with a very straight brim, not shaped like a face-down "C," the way most people wore them now. Cross-stitched fish--they looked like rainbow trout--leaped over each other on the front of the hat. Beneath them, just above the brim were the words Promised Land. Ben figured if anyone could tell him how to get to Intercourse this old codger could. He sat low in a nylon-webbed lawn chair. From the way his knees jutted up toward his chin, Ben guessed he was a fairly tall man, but he seemed shriveled and drawn into himself, which made him appear smaller than he might have once been as he strode through the world. He wore brown slip-ons with argyle socks, brown slacks, and a light blue spring jacket that he hugged to himself, as though he were chilly, even though fall had yet to push the temperature south of 75 degrees.

Ben would have bet these were his belongings, or his wife's. If the old guy was out here selling them, maybe he needed the money. Ben really didn't intend to buy anything; he just wanted directions. As he approached the table, the old man kept his head down, scowling into his lap. Ben didn't want to startle him, so he walked up to the table and looked into the baskets of trinkets. It was mostly what he expected: old ball point pens with advertising on them, small boxes of paperclips, pencils, some sharpened, some not, a couple of bottle openers, lots of big spring clips for holding stacks of business papers together, and one basket nearly filled with those finger-shaped rubber things secretaries used to use to dig through a stack of documents.

Ben felt no urge to buy anything until he looked in the third basket. There, on top, was a cursive capital letter "A," about three inches high and an inch and a half wide at the bottom, dark brown with a glossy finish. He picked it up for a closer look. It was made of wood, but he couldn't tell if it was hand-carved or the product of clever machine work. Attached to the back, with very fine screws, was a brass pin. It was obviously jewelry. Ben had never seen a decorative pin made of wood. It felt heavier in his hand than he expected.

As he gazed at it, the old man stirred behind the table. When Ben looked toward him, he was pointing a thin, bent finger at the letter and yelling in a thin, reedy voice. His slurred speech was unintelligible, but his dark eyes flashed as they connected with Ben's. He grew more and more agitated. Ben held up the pin.

"Do you know about this pin, this letter "A"?

The old man grabbed the arms of his lawn chair, rose unsteadily to his feet, and tottered to the edge of the table. He kept pointing at the pin. Now Ben could make out what he was saying; his voice got louder every time he spoke.

"She was so naïve, she didn't know anything. Hell, she thought that thing meant "A" for Agnes. Shoot! Didn't mean any such thing. She was just too dumb to know that. Christ, after while I didn't listen to a thing she said. "A" for Agnes, my ass."

Ben smiled at the old man and racked his brain for something he could say that might calm him down a bit.

"So this belonged to a member of your family?" he asked, extending the pin to the old man, who backed away and launched into his rant again.

"'A' for Agnes, my ass. She could be so damn dumb sometimes. I couldn't make sense out of most of what she said." The old man's voice had risen to a shrill screech.

Just then Ben felt a hand on his arm, and he turned to see a very attractive, blonde haired young woman, probably in her twenties, standing there. She smiled and spoke quietly to Ben.

"It was my grandmother's. Her name was Agnes, but she didn't really think it stood for her name. She just told my dad that as a joke when he was growing up. But since the Alzheimer's set in, Granddad doesn't remember the real story."

She moved around the table to the old man.

"Come on, Granddad. It's okay. Why don't you sit back down and stand guard over all of these valuable things we're trying to sell today. Remember, we're having a yard sale?"

The old man turned to look at her with age-clouded eyes. The consternation drained away and his face brightened.

"Oh, hello there cutie. Come to see what the old dog is up to, did ya'?"

The young woman gripped his arm gently and started leading him back to the lawn chair. She looked toward Ben.

"He hasn't known any of our names for quite a while now, not even my dad's. He seems to realize he knows us, but I'm not sure he could tell you whether I'm his granddaughter or some woman he used to work with."

She turned back to the old man.

"Here you go, Granddad. Just settle in there. Aren't those the lawn chairs you and Grandma used to take to the Poconos on vacation every summer?"

The old man looked down at the chair as he lowered himself into it, and then back at the young woman, but he seemed unable to respond to her question. He sank down, taking on the same shrunken appearance Ben had noticed when he walked up to the table.

"That's all right, Granddad. I'll bet you remember." She smiled at the old man, leaned down and kissed him on the cheek.

The old man responded to the kiss.

"Whoo! Whoo! I like that!"

"I'll bet you do," the young woman told him and patted his shoulder. The old man dropped his head and sank back into his scowling reverie. The young woman walked around the table and rejoined Ben on the other side.

"We've been losing him a little at a time for ten years now. He was a shy, gentle man before Alzheimer's started taking him away from us. By the way, my name's Karin."

"Mine's Ben. It's nice to meet you." He still held the carved letter in his hand. He looked at it and then at the young woman.

"I didn't mean to set him off. I just noticed this pin and picked it up. It has an unusual quality to it."

"Don't worry about it. My grandfather got rid of most of my grandmother's possessions shortly after she died a long time ago. I didn't even know that pin was still around. Considering how little my grandfather remembers at this point, I'm a little surprised he reacted so much when he saw it just now. I remember seeing that pin in my grandmother's jewelry box when I was very young, but she never told me anything about it. She died when I was seven. I agree with you, the pin is beautiful, but the real story of how my grandmother got it isn't, really." Her expression grew somber and sorrow filled her light blue eyes.

"I'm sorry you lost your grandmother so early. She must have been young."

"She was fifty-nine. I know that's not so young, but it was way too soon for a woman as wonderful as she was. I would love to have had more time to get to know her."

"Was her death related to the story of the pin?"

Karin looked up at him, a look of pain in her young eyes. For a moment, he thought his curiosity might have led him to invade this family's very private space. He was relieved when Karin nodded slowly and replied.

"Yes, it has everything to do with her death. I don't know the details as well as my father does, but the short version is that my grandmother, Agnes Jenkins Flaherty, worked for the Manhattan Project during World War Two. It was her first real job out of school. And it killed her." She reached over and lifted the pin from Ben's hand. "And this beautiful carved pin, this wooden "A", doesn't stand for Agnes, it stands for atom, as in atom bomb. It was a gift from the people she worked for. And the bomb killed my grandmother as surely as it killed all those people in Japan."

Earlier, she had spoken to Ben and her grandfather in a bright, lilting tone of voice. This summary she delivered almost in a monotone, her eyes reflecting the pain and loss she felt over her grandmother's tragic experience. Ben felt real sympathy for this young woman and her family. But alongside that--and he felt a little guilty to be having these other thoughts at the same time--he was thinking about what a powerful story he could tell as an independent filmmaker, which is what he did in his non-vacation life back in New York. He tried to phrase his response to Karin in a way that would retain an opening for what he knew he needed to ask her.

"I'm so sorry. Was your grandmother a physicist or some sort of engineer?"

"No, she was a clerical worker who just happened to land in the Washington offices of the Manhattan Project."

That left Ben confused.

"So how could the atomic bomb kill her there?"

"That you'll have to ask my father."

Ben waited a moment before he spoke.

"Karin, I need to tell you something. I'm an independent filmmaker working out of New York, and I'm always looking for stories to tell. Do you think there's any chance your family would tell me this one? I assume your grandfather isn't able to do that anymore." He gestured toward the old man, who sat with his head down, mumbling into his lap. "Is your father willing to talk about all of this?" He looked around the yard. "Is he here today?"

"No, he's not. We're doing this because my grandfather needs to move into a place where they can deal with his Alzheimer's. He almost set the couch on fire a month or so ago while he was trying to light his pipe. My dad said he just couldn't bear to stand around and watch people truck away all the pieces of his parents' life. He lives in Maine. He's planning to be here to move what's left to Granddad's new place."

"And, to answer your first question, I'm not sure if he'd be willing to talk about it. He's always said Grandma wouldn't say much about what happened to her, maybe he'd feel the same way. But you could ask him. I can give you his phone number and email. I know my brother and I would like people to know this story. We're pretty much anti-nuclear. And we're a bit resentful that the atom bomb deprived us of our grandmother. So, if you want our blessing to work on this, you have it. My dad you'll have to see about."

She handed the pin to Ben, lifted a ballpoint pen out of one of the baskets and tore a corner off a sheet of paper lying on the table. While she was writing, Ben looked at the pin. If he could just get the right pieces together, this might be one hell of a story to tell. It was no secret that his earlier work, although fairly well-received critically, had never caused much of a stir at the box office. This one might be different.

Karin finished writing and tossed the pen back into the basket. She handed the slip of paper to Ben.

"I put my phone and email on there, too, in case you have trouble reaching my dad. Are you really going to do this story? Would anybody really want to know the story of my grandmother, a simple girl from Pennsylvania, who filed paperwork in Washington, D.C.?"

Ben looked at the pin and then into her earnest face.

"Yes, if your family's willing to work with me, I will tell this story, or try to. And for a whole bunch of reasons, I think people will want to see it." He held up the pin. "Of course, I'm going to need this to tell it. How much do I owe you?"

Karin shook her head.

"No, if you're willing to do all of that for my grandmother, and that pin will help, you can have it." She looked across the lawn to where three little boys were tumbling over each other and laughing. "In the meantime, those three are mine. I'd better check up on them. It was nice to meet you, Mr. Roth. Good luck with the story."

Ben found Sarah in the process of buying a light blue lamp shade with dark blue fringe ringing the bottom edge.

"You ready to go?"

"Yep, my record is intact." She held up the lamp shade. "I have never left a yard sale without buying something. How do you like it?"

Ben looked at it and smiled.

"I can't imagine where that's going to fit in the apartment, but I think I like it." He held out the carved wooden pin. "I got something, too. What do you think?"

Sarah took the pin in her hand and traced the smooth contours of the letter "A" with her fingertip.

""It's lovely, but it's not my initial."

"I know. It's not really for you. It's a great story idea I just found here."

"Really? This close to Paradise?" She grinned at him.

He motioned toward the car.

"Doesn't really have anything to do with Paradise. In fact, maybe just the opposite. Let's bag the visit to Intercourse and head home. I'd like to get started on this."

Sarah looked at him intently.

"And how will you pay for this one? We're still in the hole from the last project."

Ben smiled at her and started walking toward the car.

"Let's jump off that bridge when we're a little closer to it. C'mon. Let's get home."

CHAPTER TWO

By the time they reached Allentown and set a course for the George Washington Bridge, Ben had explained to Sarah what he'd learned from Karin and the meaning of the wooden pin. As she listened to him, she detected a familiar tone in his voice. She had seen him grow excited over story ideas before, only to see the energy leak away, like helium from a balloon, when he discovered the story was too thin or unimportant, or, as was generally the case, they couldn't put together the finances to actually make the thing happen.

They'd made three movies up to this point, working on them part-time and holding down what their parents called "real jobs" full-time, to pay the day-to-day expenses. Sarah believed in Ben's vision as a filmmaker; his kind-heartedness drew him to stories about real people, people he came to care about as much as his own family. He especially embraced ordinary people who battled great odds or found themselves caught up in events for which they paid a great price. What he'd just told her about Agnes Jenkins Flaherty certainly seemed to fit his mold.

"But, Ben, how can you make the movie when you don't know the whole story?"

She turned to look at him as she steered the rental car east on I-78.

""I know. This one, if it happens, is going to take a lot of research. I think I'm going to have to dig up the details and basically write the book about Agnes Jenkins Flaherty and her dance with the nuclear devil before we can make a movie. Heck, maybe we can get that published and make some money on it."

Sarah took her eyes off the road again to look at him. She appeared slightly exasperated.

"Oh, sure. We'll just get that in print and on the best seller list, like we did the other three books you've written." She paused a beat, then added, "Not!"

Ben laughed.

"Hey, stranger things have happened. I mean, the more I think about it--and I haven't had a whole lot of time with this idea, at this point--the more I think this may be the strongest one we've ever tackled. It's got the Everyman thing, with Agnes, it's got the war thing, which should stir some hearts, and it's got the nuclear thing, which used to scare the hell out of everybody, and there was Three Mile Island and Chernobyl, and now even Obama is pushing for more nuke power plants around the country. That's a lot to deal with, I know, but it also might make Agnes's story appealing to a lot of different groups."

"Can we really afford to get into another film right now?" She didn't look at him, but he heard the concern in her voice.

"We don't need to get into all of that right away. Let me do some digging first. I've never seen any coverage of the little people who worked on the bomb; it's always about Harry Truman or Robert Oppenheimer or that Groves guy who led the Manhattan Project." He had started jotting things in a small notebook he always carried with him. "I promise not to create any serious expenses until we both agree this one has legs, okay?"

Sarah held up her hand for a high five. Ben's first attempt to smack her palm missed, intentionally. It was a little inside joke they always shared in high-five moments. His second attempt was right on target, and their hands met squarely. Before he pulled his hand away, Sarah slid her fingers between his and their fingers interlaced. They squeezed each other's hands for a silent moment before they pulled their hands apart and hers returned to the steering wheel and he picked up the notebook. Ten minutes later they crossed the G-W and headed for Brooklyn.

As soon as they reached the apartment, Ben pulled out the phone number Karin had given him for her father and dialed it. A resonant, baritone voice came on the line. Karin had said her father was in TV news in Portland. Just in the way he answered the phone, Ben thought he sounded like a news guy.

"Hello?" The speaker did not identify himself.

"Hello, this is Ben Roth. I'm trying to reach Matt Flaherty, is he available?"

"This is he," responded the voice, with elegant enunciation and grammar.

"Mr. Flaherty, I just met your daughter a few hours ago, down in Pennsylvania. You know, at the yard sale?"

The line went silent for a couple of beats. When Flaherty responded, the professional sheen had slipped from his voice; he spoke more slowly, his tone softer.

"Yes. The yard sale was today, wasn't it?"

Ben eased into the reason he was calling, trying not to sound too aggressive, like some pushy, New York media type.

"Yes, sir, it seemed to be going pretty well. There were lots of people there, and they were buying a lot of the items."

"Ben, did you say your name was?"

"That's right, Ben Roth."

"If you don't mind my asking, Ben, how did you come to be at my father's yard sale?"

"Well, it's a little embarrassing, but my wife and I drove down to P-A for a weekend excursion. We wound up in Dillerville by mistake when we were trying to find Intercourse. You know, the old

Intercourse to Paradise routine?" He chuckled a bit at himself, and waited for Flaherty's reaction. Flaherty did not share the joke.

"Yes, I know the old saw. You can't grow up in Pennsylvania Dutch country and not run into a zillion people, most of them from Jersey or New York, who find the whole place fairly amusing."

"Guilty on all counts," Ben said, still unsure how he was doing with this guy.

"But that's not why I'm calling you this afternoon, Mr. Flaherty."

"Ben, I'm not that old, at least I don't admit to it, anyway. If you're acquainted with our beautiful daughter, that's good enough for me. Please call me Matt."

"But I still don't know why getting lost in Lancaster County should occasion a call to Portland, Maine. What's up?"

Ben launched into his explanation. He told Flaherty about his film work, and then told him about finding the "A" pin. He finished with the encounter with Karin's grandfather and subsequent conversation with Karin about her grandmother. Flaherty wanted more.

"Okay, you now know our family's tragic secret. Why are you calling me?" His voice had taken on a harder edge. Ben took a deep breath.

"Well, Matt, when I heard a little bit of your mother's story, and realized she was directly involved in creation of the atomic bomb, I got an idea to make a movie, with her as a central character, that tells the story of how we got to this terrible state of things where the whole nuclear thing continues to threaten our whole existence. I don't mean to speak out of school, but I'm definitely anti-nuclear."

Flaherty cut in.

"I agree with you. But my mother didn't invent the bomb. Why would anyone want to see a movie about a file clerk?"

"It wouldn't just be about a file clerk, it would be about a young woman who got caught up in something so much bigger than all of us, who had a front row seat on one of the most awful chapters in human history. I think people would definitely want to know that story. At the very least, depending on your point of view, she's one of the unsung heroes. From the other vantage point, she's an unsung victim, who was sacrificed along with so many others, to achieve goals she probably had no hand in setting."

The line went silent again for a few seconds.

"How much of my mother's story do you actually know, Ben? Karin couldn't have told you too much, because she doesn't know too much."

Ben sensed the opening he'd hoped would come.

"That's just it, Matt. She didn't tell me much, but she told me enough to make me think this is a very important, untold story. Not a very happy one, I know. But one I think people should hear."

"Ben, my mother was a wonderful woman, a real saint. I have been singing her praises all my adult life. But I'm not sure about putting her out there in the public sphere we have going on today, where God knows who can twist and turn the details and dishonor her memory. Are you thinking in terms of a documentary here?"

"No, Matt. What I'd like to do is fictionalize it, keeping pretty close to the real story line about your mother, and factor in reasonable characterizations of the major players in the nuclear story, with whom she lived her life during that time."

"I don't know, Ben. My mother was a very private person. She hardly told me the details of her work with the Manhattan Project. I'm not sure she'd want anyone spreading them all over the big screen, especially with a few narrative curlicues thrown in."

"Matt, I certainly understand your reservation about this, especially coming out of the blue. But I really believe this story would work." He paused before the dash to the finish. "So-o-o-o-o," he drew it out while he decided how to ask for what he wanted. "Let me make this request: Would you be willing to sit down with me, there in Maine, and talk at greater length about your mother and her experience, and then decide whether or not to let me follow through with the idea? I know this is all rather sudden and intrusive, but the more we talk about it, the more convinced I am that this movie must be made."

He stopped and listened to silence again. Then Flaherty spoke, in the softer tone he'd adopted earlier. He began with a sigh.

"Ben, it's been a long time since my mom died, but the pain of losing her is still as intense sometimes now as it was back then. Part of me doesn't want to dredge all of that up again. But another part of me says this could be a way to honor Mom and send a message about this tragic thing--the bomb--that I really do believe killed her, along with all the others over the years."

He sighed again.

"Man, I don't know you from squat. But after trying to talk people into doing news stories with me all these years, I know how it feels to have a great idea that people resist letting you do. If you're willing to pay the freight to get up here, I'd be willing to sit down and talk some more. When would you like to come?

Ben breathed a sigh of genuine relief.

"Matt, I really appreciate this. I could be up there next weekend, if you're not busy."

"No, we're not tied up with anything important. We've got some leaves to mulch before it snows, so we'll be around the house working on Saturday. Why don't you give me a call when you get into town, and I'll tell you how to find us. Our phone's not listed to keep wackos who see me on the air from hassling my family. Does that sound O.K.?"

"Mr. Flaherty, that sounds just great. Thank you so much. I'll see you in a week."

"O.K., Ben. See you then." The line went dead. Ben clicked off his phone and went looking for Sarah.

Ben borrowed a friend's car to keep the first of what turned out to be three appointments in Maine. He made contact with the Flahertys as soon as he exited I-95 at Forest Avenue. A few minutes later he pulled up to the house to find, as promised, Matt and Louise out raking. After the introductions, Ben offered to help them finish up. They accepted.

Matt Flaherty looked to be in his fifties. He had the chiseled good looks common among TV news anchors, with white, carefully styled hair and green eyes. Ben guessed he was about six feet tall. Flaherty and Karin's mother, Louise, a petite woman with only a trace of gray in her brown hair and vivid blue eyes, lived in a modest home near Portland's Deering High School. The conversation Ben had come for began over lunch and continued through the afternoon into the evening. One of the first things Ben learned was that Flaherty had actually wanted to write his mother's story so generations to come would know who she was and what she did. They spent a lot of time that first visit looking at old family photos: relatives, vacation shots, Agnes Jenkins Flaherty with friends in D.C. during the war, and Agnes and her own family at home, with family during holidays, and Agnes and her sons on vacation in the Pocono Mountains.

The second and third visits consisted mostly of Matt talking and Ben recording his comments and taking copious notes. Matt also entrusted Ben with documents his mother had saved from her time in Washington, including an autographed picture of General Leslie R. Groves. In a stylish hand, Groves thanked Agnes for her hard work over the many months it took to create the bomb.

By the end of the third session, Ben had a lot of leads to follow up, and a lot of reading to do to understand the big picture of the Manhattan Project and Agnes Jenkins's connection to it. In the months that followed, whenever he could get away for a couple of days, he visited Agnes's home territory in Southwestern Pennsylvania, tried to track her life in Washington, and arranged for a guided tour of Ground Zero in New Mexico, where the fruit of Groves and company's labors had erupted into a brilliant, terrifying light unlike anything anyone had ever seen before. When he couldn't think of anywhere else he should go or anyone else he should talk to, Ben sat down to write the story of Agnes Jenkins Flaherty.

CHAPTER THREE

Republic, Pennsylvania was a company town, that is, it was a town of, by and for the Republic Coal Company that built it and stocked it with men willing to burrow deep into the earth in exchange for less than adequate pay. Republic wasn't quite as bad as some company towns, where management owned the houses where miners lived and the store where they bought life's necessities, at prices that cost more than they earned, creating a cycle of perpetual indebtedness, virtual slaves of the company. Republic permitted independent merchants to set up shop, not that it made that much difference.

Most of the men and many of the boys still trooped off each morning for the ride down a mile long shaft to spend days and nights, depending what shift they worked, blasting and clawing coal from a vein that snaked through the countryside, underground, till it finally crept under the streets and houses and back yards of Uniontown, more than five miles away. Those who avoided the mine and the wicked lift operators, who sent the cage hurtling down the shaft at breakneck speed to terrify the new men, did not avoid the dust and filth that coated this mountainous coal country. If they didn't have to dig in the depths, they bent their backs to the task of shoveling coal into round-topped, brick ovens that baked it into coke to feed the voracious, glowing maws of the steel mill furnaces in Pittsburgh.

Agnes Jenkins Flaherty drew her first breath of life in Republic in 1924, filling her clean, pink lungs with the polluted, sulfur-saturated air, common in bituminous, soft coal territory. It would not be the last time she put herself at risk the first time she did something. Agnes was the second daughter of Neil and Irene Jenkins. Their first, Naomi, was biologically Irene's, but not Neil's. How Irene acquired her, before she and Neil were wed, was never exactly clear to Agnes or her two younger brothers. Or, if it was clear, they chose not to share it with their own children when they came along. Neil and Irene's grandchildren never knew. In any case, Neil adopted Naomi and raised her as his own.

Neil stood nearly six feet tall, with a build people used to refer to as "big boned." He was sturdy, reasonably attractive, and, by middle age, a natty dresser when he wasn't in the mine, who drove expensive Packards and liked women. He was, for his time, a self-made man. He ran away from a brutal father at thirteen. People said he worked in the circus somewhere in those years. He told stories of riding the rails with the hoboes for a while. He gave the army a shot, during World War One, but didn't like it and got out. The only evidence of his time in uniform were the elaborate, blue, patriotic tattoos permanently imbedded in the pale underside of his forearms from wrist to elbow.

Eventually, he descended into the mines, where he was working when he met Irene. With her coaching, he passed the tests to rise above the ranks as a foreman, which meant he still had to work by the light of carbide lamps and arrived home blackened by coal dust, but it wasn't as bad as swinging a shovel or hoisting wooden timbers, bigger and heavier than railroad ties, to keep the roof of the mine shaft from caving in. When she wasn't helping Neil study for his exams, Irene ran an independent general store owned by an Italian named Bertuli.

It was actually something of a surprise to Neil and Irene that they ended up together. She was many things he was not. Her family had money and land. Her four brothers made even more money building some of the finest homes in Uniontown. Three of them got married and had families, one didn't. All of the Howards, including Irene, were known to be very smart. The family supported that assertion about Irene by pointing out that she earned a high school diploma at the turn of the twentieth century, a time when most children, like Neil, were lucky to make it past sixth grade before they were put to work.

The Howards were never all that keen on Irene marrying Neil Jenkins. The hard feelings smoldered as Irene and Neil started their family and finally erupted when the matriarch of the Howard clan died and left all of her money to Irene. That goaded the brothers into action. Apparently assuming that Neil had somehow managed to convince their mother to leave it all to Irene, they raced up to Bertuli's store and sat there honking their horn until Neil stepped outside.

Still in the car, their heads extended out the open windows, all four of them snarled at Neil, threatening to beat the hell out of him. Neil, long since battle-hardened by life, stood his ground and offered to take them on, one at a time or all at once. He swore he'd kill every one of them on the spot, if he had to. He made his point. The brother behind the wheel threw the car into gear, and put some serious distance between them and Neil, who stood in the yard spewing a stream of obscenities after the ever-diminishing automobile. Three of the brothers never came close to Neil again, not even when he and Irene attended their oldest brother's funeral.

Along with their smarts, Irene's family exhibited a certain mental instability. It was there in their father, along with a streak of meanness. The Howards raised their children on a wooded mountainside outside of town. Their father clung tenaciously to his land and his money, even at the expense of his children. By the time Agnes's children came along, people still told the story of old man Howard, the meanest man on Dunbar Mountain. His own daughter told the story of the day the old man took himself to town and returned sporting a brand new pair of brown shoes. When his sons finished admiring them, he vowed that the first one up the next morning could have the shoes. The boys, eager to win the new footwear, rose at the crack of dawn. They pushed and shoved their way down the narrow stairway looking for the shoes and found the old man rocking contentedly in his chair, the shiny, new shoes laced tightly on his feet.

The strain of craziness eventually surfaced in three of Irene's four brothers. In the middle of very successful careers, they abandoned work and family and took to the hills, back to Dunbar Mountain and the old home property. By the time Agnes took her sons to visit her uncles, they were three, withered, old men, crowded into an abandoned, one-room schoolhouse, the schoolyard outside piled high with thousands of used tires and one pretty good looking Pierce Arrow, *sans* engine. Traces of intelligence still glimmered in the quizzing they gave their grand-nephews. But it would be only a few more years before they trooped into the schoolhouse for the last time and locked the door. They told anyone inquiring about their well-being that their children were conspiring to take away their land.

For months they refused to come out. The standoff lasted until one of them died and the children finally forced their way into the building. Besides two bent and scrawny old men, they found dirty cups and plates, filthy clothing, and garbage strewn everywhere, except for a three-by-six foot clearing in the center of the room. There, lying face up, was their dead brother, with a chicken clucking softly on his chest.

Irene avoided her brothers' version of madness, but life with Neil was turbulent enough to trigger two breakdowns. Agnes remembered the second one, most likely precipitated by another of Neil's philandering episodes. As she described it years later, Neil and Irene started shouting at each other in the middle of their recently repapered parlor. Irene's sharp tongue pricked Neil's volatile temper. Unable to find the right angry words, he grabbed a nearby cup of coffee and, in a long, arching motion, flung the contents across the pristine, papered ceiling. Irene raced to the front door, yanked it open, and fled down the front walk. Neil lurched into the doorway and, in a roaring voice, ordered her to get the hell back in the house.

When Irene paid no heed, Neil piled Agnes and her siblings into the Packard and headed down the road after her. Agnes recounted, in heartbreaking detail, the scene the neighbors witnessed: Irene, a short, plump woman, no more than five feet tall, stomping along the road, energized by anger and fear, with the Packard rolling slowly alongside, the children reaching out the windows, pleading tearfully for her to come home. After a quarter mile or so, Irene stopped walking and climbed in the back seat with the children, and Neil drove them all--in total silence--back to the house. Not long afterwards, Irene went away for a while. She returned with dark circles under her now dull eyes, graphic testimony to her struggle with depression and sorrow.

Agnes came along when her older sister, Naomi, was two. One brother, Neil, Junior, arrived two years after that, but Carl didn't make his entrance until nearly ten years later, perhaps another surprise for Irene and Neil. All of the children inherited the Howard family's braininess. The younger three got their physique from Neil's side. That translated into fine, big-boned boys, more than capable of defending themselves in a scuffle, which, like their father, they occasionally had to do.

Agnes was big-boned, too, but with a beautiful face and a smile that could light up a room when she flashed it, which, as years went by, she didn't often do. In school pictures, where most children appear grinning like idiots, Agnes, her dark brown hair cut in the popular page boy style, looks into the camera with soulful, dark eyes and a serious, almost sad expression on her face. As an adult she always enjoyed a good laugh, but there would also be, especially in her later years, hints of the melancholy that haunted her mother.

Not that life in the Jenkins household was interminably tumultuous. The Jenkins kids had good friends and a relatively comfortable life, materially. Neil always had work, right through the Great Depression. The older children all knew that. And they knew other kids in town had it much worse. Agnes told her sons stories of classmates whose fathers fell on times so hard they often sent their children off to school with little or nothing in their aching bellies.

Naomi started first grade when she was six, the usual age, and Agnes, who was only four but already a bit precocious, went along with her. By this time the family had moved a few miles south of Republic to Smithfield, and Neil had gotten work in the Crucible Steel Company mine nearby and Irene managed another store for the Bertulis. The girls walked to the little two-room Tobin schoolhouse, rain or shine. Naomi focused on the work assigned to the children in her grade; Agnes did that work, then proceeded to learn the lessons for the older grades, as well.

Religion was not a central element of the Jenkins household. But early on Agnes made it part of her life. Perhaps it was a reaction to the behaviors she witnessed in her father and others in their small town--she used to tell her sons that their grandfather had no morals-- no one was ever quite sure of the reason. Whatever it was, Agnes began rising on Sunday mornings and marching across the road to the Free Methodist Church opposite their house. Her presence there was so regular that she was awarded a lapel-full of perfect attendance pins. They also gave her a Bible, which she cherished and read faithfully every day of her life.

Agnes absorbed a fair amount of fundamentalist values from the Free Methodists: alcohol never touched her lips, no one ever heard her utter one syllable of the profanities both her father and mother indulged in during heated moments, and, to her dying day, she lived by the motto--"If you can't say something nice about someone, don't say anything." Obviously, her comments about her father's moral behavior were the one exception to her rule. Otherwise, she adhered to it as faithfully as she did her program for reading through the Bible every year. Her ability to keep her mouth shut, and reputation for it, would prove extremely useful in just a few short years.

But she wasn't entirely a stick in the mud. Yes, she seemed a bit plain and reticent compared to Naomi, who was strikingly attractive, with her jet black hair, cute-as-a-button face, and more delicate figure. Naomi knew how to flirt and that translated into an endless series of boyfriends through high school, all of whom Neil despised and considered nowhere near good enough for a daughter of his, biological or otherwise. If there were dances or pep rallies during high school, Naomi was there, with big, shiny earrings, bright red lipstick, and penciled on eyebrows. Agnes sometimes tagged along, but managed to complete her entire secondary education without a single formal date.

She was more likely to stay home and help her mother with the store or do homework or simply read. She eventually took to wearing earrings--the clip-on kind that didn't require the more worldly piercings Naomi eagerly underwent--and some lipstick. But her fashion choices remained as conservative as her faith. When Naomi started prancing around in halter tops, Agnes did not. The situation was made more challenging by her tendency to gain weight, which limited her wardrobe options. Right up to the point where she got her first job--in the big city--she wore mostly simple dresses and sensible shoes. Her friends in the city encouraged her to experiment with a trendier line of clothes, and her job, at least for a while, helped with the weight problem.

CHAPTER FOUR

When the Nazis ascended to power in Germany in 1933, making Adolf Hitler their chancellor, Naomi and Agnes, sixth graders at the time, did not notice. It's unlikely most American children paid attention. They were much more concerned with reading and writing and recess. But by the time they entered junior high, history teachers had begun tracking the relentless Nazi march across Europe. Eventually, the grim reality of it would have been hard to avoid. The Uniontown Gazette carried banner headlines tracking Nazi occupation of one sovereign nation after another, first the Rhineland, then Austria, and on to Czechoslovakia, Poland, Denmark, Norway, then France, Belgium, Luxembourg and the Netherlands. There were rumors, reported only briefly in the paper, that the Nazis were also carrying out a pogrom against the Jews, but most Americans, and certainly American teenagers wouldn't know the vicious truth of that until much later.

By the time Naomi and Agnes finished up in the clerical curriculum at Georges Township High School, in June, 1940, they were well aware of what was happening. They read of the horrible events unfolding across the ocean, heard Ed Murrow on the radio, reporting from the rooftops of London as the German blitzkrieg rumbled overhead, indiscriminately destroying ancient buildings in the city's center as well as homes along the city's crowded, winding, residential streets, as British men, women and children huddled underground, hoping to survive. The Jenkins family, like most Americans, had little desire to go to war. Neil's experience in the Great War was enough to convince all of them that such conflict yielded mixed results at best, especially for ordinary people. But they all knew it would be hard to avoid. And Neil, Junior was already fourteen.

While not yet at war, the nation was already inching toward getting into it. The first real sign of that in Fayette County, at least for the Jenkins household, was the day Naomi came home waving an application for a job in Washington, D.C. In anticipation of the challenges to come, the military was expanding its civilian staff and needed hundreds of well-trained, clerical workers. They'd put out the word through the most logical channel--high school business teachers. Naomi applied the day after graduation. A week later, her teacher called to say the civil service office was investigating her.

Two weeks after that a letter arrived, offering her a job in Washington. In two days, she boarded a train for D.C. She was assigned to the new Pentagon building, across the Potomac from most of the other federal buildings. It was an innovative design, built to withstand attack by enemy forces, under the direction of a colonel in the Army Corps of Engineers, Colonel Leslie Groves, a man Naomi did not encounter after she reported for duty; that would not be true for her sister. The Howard genes served Naomi well. Within six months, she had risen to office manager in her section.

Agnes kept busy that summer helping her mother run the store and looking after Carl, the family surprise, who was four by now. Her church friends, who knew as well as anyone how bright she was, urged her to go on to college in the fall. They offered to help cover the cost if she'd enroll at Roberts Wesleyan, a fundamentalist school in upstate New York. Everyone knew she would do well in a good, Christian environment like that, not one of those godless schools like Penn State or the University of Pittsburgh. One after another, the elders took Agnes aside after Sunday services or Wednesday night prayer meeting, and tried to explain what a blessing she could be if she went off to college and trained to be a school teacher or a nurse. She could even do mission work among the heathen people in Africa. But no one in her family had ever gone to college before, except a distant uncle on the Jenkins side. And no one at home got behind the idea.

Irene took no position on the proposition; Neil made it clear that he didn't see why his daughter needed that kind of education to get on in the world, he certainly hadn't. Agnes, at the age of sixteen, with little experience of the world beyond Fayette County, found the prospect of separating herself from her family, especially her mother and Naomi, more than a little intimidating. With that serious look on her young face, she thanked her Free Methodist friends for their offer and quietly, gracefully rejected the college option.

She couldn't know it then, of course, but it was a fateful decision. Her life turned a corner in that moment, and headed in a direction that would eventually lead to her destruction. If she ever regretted her decision, if she ever thought, *what if I'd just gone to college*, she never told anyone. As she always said, if you can't say something nice, don't say anything. Like her Lord's mother, she chose instead to ponder such things in her heart.

But she was very interested in Naomi's experience in Washington. In the age before the telephone had become the standard mode of communication, the sisters corresponded regularly. Naomi provided detailed accounts of life in D.C., written in the elegant cursive style the girls had been taught in school:

"July 12, 1940

Dear Sis,

Hope all is well with all of you back in PA. I miss everyone a lot. I'm living in a boarding house filled with young women; all of us work for one government agency or another. Our house mother, Emily Sisko, runs a tight ship. We have to keep our rooms tidied up and she expects us to be in for the night no later than 9:00. D.C. is just beautiful this time of year. It can be hot sometimes. I remember Mom saying it really is a southern city. Well, it feels like it. With so many things to do here like bowling and eating out, a curfew sometimes feels a little restrictive. We do lots of things together after work. And everybody dresses so well, which you know has always been important to me. I'm enclosing a picture of a bunch of us outside our house in Chevy Chase. They're all wonderful girls and the soldiers and civilian workers in our offices have certainly noticed. I've met a couple of young men already who seem decent and are quite good looking. I'm having a great time dolling up for a night on the town. Which reminds me, could you ask Mom to send me that little jewelry box in our bedroom. If I was ever anyplace where pierced earrings look great, it's here.

My job is going well. I do secretarial work for a couple of officers and fill the rest of my time filing. The army certainly has a lot of paperwork. But I'm staying on top of it. My boss, Major Dovey, gives me a lot of compliments. Maybe it will lead to a promotion one of these days. How are you doing? Did you decide what to do about college? How is Mom's knee doing? Does Dad think the miners will go on strike again soon? That was so awful the last time, when he had to cross the picket lines to get to work and all of his men stood there calling him a scab. Does he still have that cough? I guess I will close for now. Give Carl a big smooch for me. He is so cute. He'll slay some young hearts one of these days, I know. Take good care of yourself, Sis. I miss you and love you tons.

Your loving sister,

Naomi"

When fall rolled around, Agnes had just turned seventeen, and had no real prospect of finding a job in Smithfield or even Uniontown. Her mother suggested she might want to go back to school. That was a novel idea; most kids were only too glad to be done with school. But Agnes, with her agile mind and love of learning, took it seriously and paid a visit to the high school principal. He knew Agnes and had been impressed all along the way that someone so young had handily succeeded in classes aimed at students at least two years older than she was. He also knew her reputation for being a responsible, mature teenager. When he put the two together, he quickly agreed to have Agnes audit another year of high school. He knew she'd enjoy learning new things, and he counted on her to be a stabilizing influence on the behavior of her classmates. He arranged for her to work as a student assistant in some of the clerical courses she'd already taken. Agnes enjoyed it immensely. It wasn't college, but it gave her a way to use the good brain she'd inherited.

Agnes was reading Naomi's latest letter and listening to a radio drama called "Inspector General" on NBC's Blue Network when she first heard about Pearl Harbor. She was still reacting to Naomi's announcement that she'd fallen in love with a soldier from Minnesota named Franklin Worthy, and she was pretty sure this was the one--a declaration she had made many times before--when the network interrupted the show to report that a massive Japanese attack had destroyed the American naval base in Hawaii. It was 2:30 in the afternoon, December 7, 1941.

Agnes clasped her hands together, closed her eyes, and prayed that God would protect her family and her country. Thoughts flashed through her mind. Surely this meant war. And Neil, Jr. was pushing fifteen. Naomi was in Washington. Surely that would become a more dangerous place. Maybe she should come home. But she'd just fallen in love, with a soldier who'd already told her that if we got into it, he'd be shipping out. If we go after the Japanese, will we go after the Nazis, too?

Her life up to that moment had been fairly calm and safe. Now, for the first time, she felt fear, and her intuition told her this wasn't a feeling she could pray away, no matter how much time she spent on her knees. She finished Naomi's letter and sat down to write a quick response, in which she pleaded with her sister to just come home, where she'd be safe. The U.S. declared war on Japan the next day.

Naomi came home a few weeks later, but not to stay. She arrived for Christmas, all "dolled up," as she liked to call it, in pierced earrings and the stylish wardrobe she and her friends sported in Washington. The sisters talked for hours about Naomi's new friend. Agnes, always the sensible one, reminded Naomi that she'd fallen pretty hard a few times before, but after a few minutes, it was obvious that with this young man it was different. Naomi was head-over-heels crazy about Franklin. She already had a picture of him in her wallet. He was wearing his uniform in the picture. Agnes could see why Naomi found him so attractive. He was tall and handsome with wavy, dark hair and a charming smile. Naomi said he loved to laugh and have a good time. He'd grown up on a farm and done a couple of years in college before he enlisted. She said they saw each other almost every night; they talked for hours. And, yes, they'd already used the word marriage. But they knew they couldn't really do that until after the war was over.

By the time Agnes returned to the high school after Christmas, the ranks of military age young men in Fayette County had thinned considerably. Dozens of them signed up the day after Pearl Harbor, eager for a chance to fight the filthy Japs. When the U.S. started shipping troops to Europe in January, 1942, even more joined up. A couple of months later, Neil, Jr. and his buddy, Allen Flaherty, fifteen by now but still too young to enlist, trained in as plane spotters. They memorized the profiles of all the German and Japanese aircraft and spent hours on a makeshift wooden tower scanning the skies for signs of an enemy attack, feeling very patriotic as they protected the country on the home front until they could put on a uniform and fight for real. They both wanted to be pilots. Allen bought a leather bomber jacket and a white silk scarf to strut around in so he could look like a fly boy.

Naomi came home again to visit over Easter. She didn't bring Franklin, partly because he had taken the train home to visit his family in Minnesota before he shipped out for England, and partly because Neil had made it plain during her last visit that he didn't give a damn who this man was, he wasn't nearly good enough for any daughter of his, and he didn't want him setting foot in his house, and he sure as hell didn't want her getting married at the age of nineteen. Irene would like to have met Franklin, but after her last breakdown, she just didn't have the energy to make Neil back off.

What Naomi did bring with her was an application for a job with the government for Agnes. With war underway, the Pentagon and other Washington offices needed even more support staff. Naomi had told Major Dovey, her boss, about her younger sister, and, largely because he was so impressed with Naomi's work, he'd encouraged her to have Agnes apply, which she did. It took a while for the paperwork to make its way through the complex bureaucracy, but shortly after Agnes turned eighteen, a letter arrived offering her a position in the typing pool at the Pentagon. Naomi came home again for Fourth of July, and Agnes, heavy suitcase in hand, boarded the train with her when she returned to Washington. Irene and Neil took them to the station. Neil gave them both a relatively unemotional farewell; Irene hugged and kissed them with tears in her eyes, and waved her handkerchief, the one she'd been using to dab away tears, to say goodbye to her two, bright daughters as they smiled and waved at her from inside the train.

A few hours later, the sisters rode into in a city at war. Men and women in uniform hustled through the train station, and walked along Washington's broad avenues on a sunny, wartime Sunday. Naomi guided Agnes, whose urban experience was limited to a few trips to dingy, industrial Pittsburgh, through the crowds to a bus stop, where they caught a ride to Chevy Chase. Naomi had arranged a room for Agnes in her boarding house. Agnes felt anxious about what lay ahead, but she was also excited to be on her own, in the city, tackling her first real job and doing her part to support her country as it battled the Nazis and the Japs.

They arrived just in time for dinner, where Agnes met some of the young women who would become life-long friends. When they finished eating, the other girls proposed a stroll down their tree-lined street before dark. Agnes noticed that even in casual moments all of these young women dressed well, as Naomi always had, and paid close attention to their hair and make-up. She complimented her new friends on their attractive wardrobes and vowed, to herself, to adopt the same stylishness, which she did. Pictures surviving from those days show a crowd of attractive, smiling, well-turned out young women, including Agnes. She turned in that first night smiling to herself, happy to be in the city with new friends.

The next morning, all of the girls boarded the same bus for the half hour ride into the city. Some got off in Washington; Naomi and Agnes continued on to the Pentagon, where Agnes and Naomi would now be working in different offices. The route ran past Rock Creek Park, where Agnes would spend many happy hours in the years to come, strolling and enjoying the natural scenery that reminded her of her favorite spots back home. They could see the

Pentagon sprawled out on its vast acreage as the bus crossed the Potomac into Virginia. Agnes had never seen it before, but Naomi had described it as the biggest office space in the world. As they approached the sparkling, new structure, Agnes could see two of its five sides angling out to the right and left. She was fascinated by its novel design.

"Why did they build it with five sides, Naomi?"

"Because there were five roads around the property they decided to build on. I guess once they had that figured out, they just kept using the number five. It's not completely finished yet, but when it is, it'll have five sides, with five rings of offices inside and five stories. That's why they call it the Pentagon. It's got ten corridors running out from the central courtyard, like spokes on a wagon wheel, and courtyards between each of the rings to give it more light. Wait till we get inside. Sometimes I feel like a rat in a maze, trying to get from one place to another."

"Why'd they build such a gigantic thing?"

"Oh, I think they wanted to put as much of the war department in one place as they could. Right now, with the war build-up and all, we're in seventeen different buildings all over the city."

"How much space is there now?"

"When it's all done, it'll have something like six-and-a-half million feet--that'd be thirty-four acres back home--just for office space. And the hallways run more than seventeen miles. The mailroom guys actually ride bicycles to get around." She paused before she opened the door for Agnes. "Are you scared?"

Agnes took a deep breath and smiled.

"I'm a little nervous," she admitted. She took another deep breath and exhaled slowly. Then she set her jaw and the serious look she always displayed in her school pictures came into her eyes. "I'm ready," she said.

Naomi gave her a quick hug, opened the door, and the two sisters from rural Pennsylvania joined thousands of soldiers and civilians flooding in to do their duty. Agnes was assigned to the typing pool in Major Blaine's offices on the third floor in the B ring.

Naomi worked on the second floor in the A ring with Major Dovey.

After Agnes had been introduced to her co-workers, her office manager took her in to meet Major Blaine. He explained what he expected her to do--typing and filing work--and then asked her to sign a confidentiality agreement, promising not to share any of the information she worked with. Agnes signed in her elegant hand and got to work. In her first few hours on the job, her co-workers gained respect for the speed and accuracy of her typing. At lunch time, she joined the other girls in the courtyard between the A and B rings, where they all ate the bagged lunches they'd brought with them.

The girls came from all over the country--Kansas, Wisconsin, Maine, Texas, and California. They were all young, many, like Agnes, came from small towns and rural communities. But those who had been in D.C. for a while had adopted the same stylish professional apparel that Naomi loved. Agnes thought they were all very pretty, in the way most people are attractive while the fresh glow of youth still lights up their faces. She enjoyed listening to them kid around and was a little shocked by what struck her as their quite forward attitude about the men they were meeting and spending time with in the city.

Agnes, at eighteen, was the youngest girl in the typing pool, but the other girls didn't know that. Her generally serious demeanor and no-nonsense approach gave the other girls the impression she was older and probably more mature than most of them. But that didn't put any significant social distance between them. She was a good listener and always had sensible things to say, and her brilliant smile and hearty laugh convinced them all that she was going to be a good friend.

Naomi came by at the end of her first day.

"Hey, Sis, how'd it go?"

Agnes smiled and took her arm as they started down the hall.

"Naomi, I absolutely love being here. Everyone in the office is so nice." She stopped walking and turned toward Naomi. She took Naomi's hand and her eyes welled-up. "Thank you for helping me get here. This has already been the best experience of my life."

Naomi squeezed her hand.

"I'm so happy to hear you say that. I've been having a really great time down here, what with meeting Franklin and all, but I know it's going to be even better with you here. We're not doing too bad for a couple of country girls, are we?"

"No, we're not. I have a feeling there are lots more good times to come." She took Naomi's arm again as they moved to the stairway and out of the building. "Shouldn't we be getting back to the house? I wouldn't want to miss supper."

They both laughed as they stepped into the late afternoon sunshine and headed for the bus stop.

CHAPTER FIVE

In early 1943, six months after she started working at the Pentagon, Agnes was summoned to Major Blaine's office shortly after she returned from lunch in the cafeteria. When she walked in the room, Major Blaine introduced her to Jean O'Leary. O'Leary identified herself as the administrative assistant to newly minted Brigadier General Leslie R. Groves. Agnes recognized Groves' name; he was the Army Corps of Engineers officer who built the Pentagon. He'd been assigned that task by his superior, Lt. Col. Brehon B. Somervell, who had recently recommended Groves to head up the Manhattan Engineer District.

O'Leary, a young widow from New York, had come to Washington in 1941, less than a year after her husband's death, with her ten year old daughter to work in the typing pool in the Quartermaster General's office. Groves, who was assigned there, had been so impressed by her feisty spirit and her skills as a secretary and office manager that he had made her his assistant and then taken her along on his new assignment to the MED.

O'Leary told Agnes that Groves had set the same standard for staffing his new project that he'd applied in his past assignments.

"He told us to recruit the best people we can. We're looking for, as he put it, 'intelligent people with the ability to go a long way in getting the job done.' And we're told that you are that kind of person. This project was originally headquartered in New York, but General Groves moved it to Washington."

O'Leary, whose straightforward approach had appealed to Groves--a gruff, no-nonsense man himself--wasted no time posing the question.

"So, I'm here today Agnes to ask you if you would like to join General Groves' staff."

Agnes perceived Jean O'Leary to be a formidable presence but she wasn't ready to sign on for something she didn't understand. "Mrs. O'Leary, what is the Manhattan Engineer District?"

O'Leary frowned a little, but she answered the question.

"It's a munitions project assigned to the army by the President. I can't say any more than that unless you accept the position."

Agnes couldn't help blurting out her reaction.

"The President! What kind of project is it?"

"A highly confidential one. But one that means more to the war effort than almost anything else." She paused for a moment before adding, "Agnes, I can't tell you much more at this point, but I will share with you that when General Groves was given this assignment his superior told him, and I'm quoting now, 'If you do this right, it will win the war.' That's the kind of project it is. Can we count on you?"

Agnes's mind raced as she tried to understand what she might be getting herself into. It sounded deadly serious and very exciting at the same time. It sounded like a tremendous amount of responsibility, and probably a lot of stress that she would have to bind up inside, if it was all hush-hush and top secret. But she had always been good at keeping her mouth shut.

"Mrs. O'Leary, I would be honored to work with you and General Groves."

O'Leary smiled for the first time and extended her hand.

"You're a smart girl, Agnes, in more ways than one. I look forward to working with you."

She reached in her briefcase and pulled out a sealed envelope.

"Please report to these offices first thing Monday morning. We'll do the formalities and have you hard at work by nine o'clock." She turned to Major Blaine, who had stood by silently as the two women talked.

"Thank you, sir, for giving up one of your best workers. General Groves appreciates your cooperation."

Blaine shook her hand and ushered her out as Agnes walked back to her desk. Her typewriter clacked away at its usual rapid pace throughout the afternoon. At five o'clock, she turned off her desk lamp, pulled the cover over the typewriter, and found a small box for the few personal items she allowed herself to have in the office. A few minutes later, as the bus bounced across the Fourteenth Street Bridge into Washington, she told Naomi what had happened. Naomi wanted to know everything.

"Who does Jean O'Leary work for?"

"General Groves, the officer you told me built the Pentagon."

"And what's he doing now?"

Agnes squirmed a bit, deciding how to answer a question about something O'Leary had told her she couldn't talk about.

"Still government matters. But he has a new assignment."

Naomi, as inquisitive as she was fun-loving, insisted that Agnes give her more than that. She squeezed Agnes's arm.

"Yes, I could guess that, silly. *What* kind of government work is he doing? I have to guess it has something to do with the war, right?"

Agnes gave up, at least as much as she honestly thought she could in a conversation with her beloved sister. She lowered her voice and leaned closer to Naomi.

"Mrs. O'Leary said it's a munitions project. That's really all she told me. She said I'll know more after I report for work on Monday."

"Well that's a lot of help. What project in this city right now isn't some kind of munitions project? Did she say what you will be doing?"

"No, not exactly, but I guess they need someone for typing and filing. That's really all I'm trained to do."

"Did she say how they found you?"

Agnes, whose faith-fed modesty had prevented her from ever boasting up to this point in her young life, felt her cheeks growing pink with embarrassment as she remembered what O'Leary had told her.

"She said General Groves is looking for the best, most intelligent people to be part of his staff. And she said someone had told her I was one of those people."

Naomi put her arm around Agnes and hugged her.

"Well, if that's what they're looking for, I have to say they found it."

Agnes leaned her head on Naomi's shoulder. They sat side-by-side in silence for the next several blocks. Besides their considerable intelligence, the sisters shared an intuitive sense that told Naomi there was even more to be said about this new job.

"Sis, did Mrs. O'Leary tell you how this new project came about?"

Agnes was not surprised Naomi sensed there was more.

"Well, that's probably the most amazing part. She said the assignment came directly to the army from the President."

Naomi turned and looked at Agnes.

"My gosh, Agnes, that sounds very important." Her dark eyes sparkled as she continued on, "And what did the President ask the army to do?"

Agnes wagged her finger in Naomi's face.

"Nice try, Sis. But the honest answer is I don't know. Mrs. O'Leary didn't tell me. And if she does tell me on Monday, I won't be able to tell you. She made that very clear. This is some sort of top secret work that no one is supposed to talk about." She paused to let that sink in and to consider whether she should share the one other bit of information O'Leary had told her, the bit of information that had convinced her she should take the job. She tried to deliver it in a nonchalant voice.

"Oh, yes, there was one more thing. I don't know if you'll think it's important or not."

Naomi knew her sister too well to be fooled by her casual approach. She leaned in close and whispered in a conspiratorial tone.

"O.K, so what was the other thing she told you?"

"Well, she said when General Groves's superior gave him the assignment, he told him if he did it right it would end the war."

Naomi looked at her sister with admiration and concern.

"Agnes, what have you gotten yourself into?"

Agnes reached over and took Naomi's hand.

"I know, it does sound awfully serious, but I know things always work out for the good. And that makes me sure this is what I'm supposed to do." As she would many times in years to come, she pressed Naomi's hand between hers to reassure her; the younger, more somber sister consoling the older, more excitable one. They rode the remaining six blocks in silence.

* * * * * * * *

That night, after dinner, the girls in the house walked to the nearby bowling alley. They weren't particularly good at bowling, but it was relaxing and, most importantly to Agnes, it was a clean, decent place that didn't serve alcohol. Of course people smoked, but it was a time when Americans smoked almost everywhere. Free Methodism had instilled in Agnes a strong conviction against

41

drinking; smoking was a different matter. As the daughter of a coal miner, she'd been around it all her life, and didn't think less of someone just because they lit up. But she would never do either.

As the girls put on their shoes, three young men settled into the next lane. Naomi recognized two of them from the office next to hers at the Pentagon. She flirted with all of them as she greeted them, as she always did around young men, not that she was serious about it; her heart was in Europe with Franklin. Then she introduced them to Agnes and the others. It was all very ordinary, just a gang of young adults out for some fun on a wartime Friday night in their nation's capital. But all of them would remember one moment of that evening.

It happened during Naomi's introductions. She always made quite a show of such things. She introduced each young man to each girl individually, trying to say something witty about the girls and make everyone laugh. The third young man was Morris Racklin. The last girl to meet him was Agnes. All the others had greeted each other with a handshake and a smile, and then turned away to get ready to bowl. It was different with Morris and Agnes. Just as Naomi finished telling Agnes Morris's name, all other conversation stopped, and everyone turned to see Agnes extending her hand to Morris. What they all remembered was the look on the young couple's faces as their hands touched. Agnes was flashing her brilliant white smile, Morris looked a tad bashful, but his eyes sparkled. And their handshake lasted several beats longer than any of the others had.

No one in the group would have claimed to be an expert on love at first sight, but they all thought they saw it happen in that Washington bowling alley. Whatever it was, the attraction was so immediate and so strong that Agnes and Morris sat out the bowling and talked until it was time to go home. Before they parted, Morris took Agnes aside where the others could not hear what he had to say.

"Agnes, it has been a real pleasure to make your acquaintance this evening."

"That's very nice of you to say, Morris. I enjoyed meeting you."

Morris smiled at her for the thousandth time that evening.

"I'm awfully glad to hear you say that. I'm wondering if you'd like to visit the Smithsonian with me tomorrow."

Agnes's pale, white cheeks flushed rosy-red. She smiled, too.

"I'd like that very much, Morris. I need to do my washing and ironing in the morning. Would tomorrow afternoon be O.K.?"

Morris's smile was stuck in place.

"Oh, that would be just fine, Agnes." He said her name gently, as though it might break if pronounced with too much force. "That would be terrific. I'll see you tomorrow afternoon."

He extended his hand to her and she took it in hers as she looked into his eyes.

"Will you be O.K. getting home? D.C. can be rough sometimes at night."

"Oh, I think there are enough of us to stay safe. Thank you, Morris. I look forward to seeing you tomorrow. Good night."

"Good night, Agnes. Sweet dreams." The girls were heading for the door; Agnes waved to Morris and hurried to catch up with them. Morris turned back to his friends who were still removing their bowling shoes. When Agnes allowed herself a quick glance over her shoulder, she saw the two other young men slapping Morris on the back and punching him in the arm. He was still smiling.

The moment Agnes stepped out the front door of the bowling alley, Naomi slipped her arm through Agnes's and started whispering in her ear.

"Okay, Sis, let's have it. What do you think of him? What did you two talk about all evening? That grin on your face tells me something special happened here tonight. So give."

Agnes tried to suppress the smile that had spread across her face as she and Morris bid each other goodnight. But her feelings bowled over her attempts to restore her usual serious expression. She waited until the other girls had moved a little ahead of them, and then looked at her sister.

"This was a wonderful night. Morris is just the finest young man I've ever met. We talked about his home and my home and what we'd like to do in life, and it was all so natural, so pleasant. He has very good manners. And he spoke to me with such respect." She paused for a moment before adding, "And, by the time we said goodnight, I think I sensed some affection." She squeezed Naomi's arm with her hand. "Oh, Naomi, I've never felt like this before in my life. You know, better than anyone, I've never had a date before, and now I'm going to the Smithsonian with this handsome young man. I wouldn't tell anyone else this, not even Mom, but I think I'm in love."

By this time, Agnes's smile had spread to Naomi. She pulled her arm free and wrapped it around Agnes's shoulders, and pulled her close.

"Oh, Sis, I'm so happy for you. I always felt a little bad when I came home and raved on and on about my soldier boy, whom I adore, as you know. Nothing would make me happier than for both of us to find the man of our dreams here in Washington. Think what a great time we'll have getting married and having families after the war. And, if everything goes just right, we can live near each other and stay as close as we've always been."

Agnes took Naomi's arm again.

"I think we better slow down just a bit, Naomi. I've only just met this guy and you aren't engaged to Franklin. Maybe it's just a passing fancy for both of us, and we'll go home after the war and end up with a couple of coal miners."

"Agnes! You don't always have to be so sensible. Let yourself go a little, and believe it's all going to turn out for the best. That's what I'm doing."

She bumped Agnes gently, trying to jolt her out of her always cautious mindset. The problem, for Agnes, was that she had never felt like she did just now. Her lack of experience in romance left her feeling a little uneasy. She'd watched as Naomi fell for one boy after another, only to have her heart broken when he decided he was more interested in someone else. Agnes wasn't sure she wanted to go through that. But she knew what she felt in her heart after just a couple of hours with Morris. He seemed so gentle and kind and intelligent. They'd already discovered they had a number of common interests. And talking to him had seemed so natural. She took a deep breath and let it out slowly.

"Okay, Sis, I'm willing to believe this is all happening for a reason. And I sure do like Morris, more than I ever thought I'd like any guy, and I've only just met him. So, I'm just going to enjoy knowing him, for as long as I can. And if it leads to that wonderful life you just described, I will thank the Lord every night for as long as I live."

"Agnes, for being such a serious minded person, I think that's the most sensible thing you've ever said. I just know it's all going to turn out great."

Promptly at one o'clock Saturday afternoon the boarding house doorbell rang. Mrs. Sisko opened it to find a nattily dressed Morris standing there with a handful of flowers. Agnes had told her about Morris at breakfast. She greeted him with the solemnity of a house mother who was very solicitous of her young charges. She always insisted on meeting any man who came courting.

"Hello, may I help you?"

Morris smiled and held up the bouquet of roses.

"Hello. I'm Morris Racklin." He pointed to the flowers. "These are for Agnes Jenkins. Is she at home?"

Mrs. Sisko smiled and stepped back from the doorway.

"The flowers are lovely. And, yes, Agnes is here. She's just finished doing her laundry. Why don't you have a seat here in the front parlor and I'll tell her you're here."

Morris perched on the edge of a Queen Anne's chair just inside the parlor doorway. He smelled the roses and tapped his foot gently. Anyone who had looked in on him as he waited would have thought he looked very relaxed and self-confident, unless they noticed the tapping. A few minutes later he heard footsteps on the stairs, and then Agnes strode into the room. She was wearing a fashionable wool coat over a stylish blue dress. Her long brown hair was brushed to a sheen and held back on the side with silver barrettes. Her cheeks were slightly flushed, without the benefit of rouge. Morris thought she looked absolutely beautiful. He jumped to his feet as she came in. Agnes spoke first.

"Hello, Morris. It's wonderful to see you again."

"Not as wonderful as it is to see you, Agnes. I've really been looking forward to this afternoon."

"I have, too. I've walked past the Smithsonian lots of times, but I never made it inside. I love going new places and seeing new things."

"Well, let's get going. There's an awful lot to see in the Smithsonian."

Emily Sisko walked into the room as they moved toward the doorway.

"Just a moment, Mr. Racklin."

"Oh, please, call me Morris. Mr. Racklin sounds like my father."

"All right, Morris. I hope you and Agnes will have a pleasant afternoon on the Mall. What time can we expect you to return? Will you join us for dinner?"

"Oh, I'd like that very much. I would expect we'll be home around six. Would that suit?"

"Yes, that would be just fine."

She turned and walked toward the kitchen as Agnes and Morris headed for the front door. Fifteen minutes later they stepped off the bus near the Smithsonian. They had picked up the thread of last night's conversation as they left the house, and continued getting to know each other as they explored the "nation's attic." Agnes would always remember her first visit to the gem and mineral rooms, and coming upon one of the museum's most recent acquisitions, the Star of Artaban, a 316 carat sapphire with slender white rays radiating across its surface to form a six-pointed star.

"Oh, Morris, can you believe how beautiful it is? I read about it when I was a young girl. I never thought what it would be like to actually stand in front of it. Do you know the story?"

Morris gently put his hand on her shoulder and leaned in close to the glass case.

"No, I don't. It sure is beautiful. Where did you read about it?"

Agnes grew excited as she gazed at the gem.

"Well, there was a small book about it in the library at my home church. It was called *The Story of the Other Wise Man* by Henry Van Dyke. He wrote it a long time ago. According to Van Dyke, there were actually four wise men who came in search of the Christ child, not just the three we always talk about--Caspar, Melchior and Balthazar. The fourth was named Artaban. He was coming with three jewels-a ruby, a pearl, and this sapphire. It's a wonderful story."

"Will you tell me the rest of it?"

"Oh, yes, it won't take long."

She gazed at the brilliant blue gem as she spoke.

" It seems Artaban had almost reached the caravan where he was to meet the other wise men when he came across a very sick man lying in the road. Since Artaban was not only wise but a doctor of sorts, he helped the man, who was actually an exiled Hebrew. In thanks for Artaban's care, the man told him that the new king was actually to be born in Bethlehem, not Jerusalem, as the wise men had all thought."

" Artaban finally reached the meeting place, but the others had already gone on without him. He couldn't travel across the desert by himself, so he went back to Babylon and used the sapphire to buy a camel and other supplies so he could get to Bethlehem. He got there three days late, and both the wise men and Jesus and his family were gone. Artaban still wanted to find the child, but while he was there, Herod's soldiers came to kill the first-born sons of the Hebrews. Artaban was talking to a young mother when they arrived and he stepped into the doorway of her home and blocked the soldiers from coming in. He told the captain he was alone in the house and he offered him the ruby if he would go away and leave him in peace, which the captain did."

"Artaban finally set out in search of truth and he was still searching many years later. He found himself in Jerusalem, thirty-three years after his quest began, standing along the way when soldiers came down the street dragging a young girl, who told him she was a true believer also and begged him to save her from being sold into slavery to satisfy her father's debts. Artaban had only one gift left that he was still hoping to bring to the king. He pulled out the pearl and gave it to the girl, who used it to buy her freedom."

"At that moment, the city was seized by an earthquake and the soldiers and everyone else fled. Artaban and the girl tried to hide from the falling debris, but a roof tile broke loose and struck the wise man on the head. As the girl bent over Artaban to see if he was still alive, she heard a voice, but couldn't make out the words. Then Artaban spoke, as though answering the voice. He seemed to be disagreeing. He said he had not been faithful; he had not ministered to the Lord's hunger, or thirst or sickness. And the girl heard the voice tell Artaban that in caring for those he had met in life, he had done just that. A peaceful expression came over Artaban's face and he died. Isn't that a wonderful story?"

"Yes, it is, and told by a wonderful person." Morris had listened in absolute silence, mesmerized by the warmth of Agnes's alto voice. " If I could, I'd become Artaban and give you that sapphire."

Agnes spun around and looked into his eyes.

"Morris, we've only just met. I don't think we should be discussing things like that yet." She spoke in a stern tone of voice, but there was playfulness in her eyes, and she flashed her brilliant smile as she said it. Morris looked around to see if anyone was watching, then bent down and kissed her lightly on the cheek.

"Agnes Jenkins, you bowl me over." He took her hand and they moved on to the other displays. Agnes smiled at his punning reference to the place they'd first met, just a few hours ago. They strolled through many more rooms before they caught the bus back to the boarding house. Morris held her hand the whole way home, and only relinquished it as they entered the house and were greeted by the other girls.

Naomi caught Agnes's eye as they all moved toward the dining room. The expression on Agnes's face told Naomi that if Agnes had left the house that afternoon with any doubts about this young man, a few hours on the Mall had vanquished them. It was plain as day that Agnes Jenkins was in love, for the first time in her life. And, by the way Morris kept looking at Agnes across the dinner table, it was obvious that he had a pretty good dose of it, too. Naomi's eyes welled up with happiness for her younger sister, the sensible, level-headed one, who was finally plunging into the world of romance. Naomi wasn't as devoutly religious as Agnes, but she prayed, just the same, that this would all turn out for the good for Agnes.

CHAPTER SIX

At fifteen minutes to eight the following Monday morning, Agnes walked through the heavy doors of the New War Building, the 21st Street entrance, between C Street and Virginia Avenue, NW. As she entered the spacious lobby, she noticed a large mural on the wall to the left. She thought it must be at least thirty feet long. It was, in fact, twelve feet high and fifty feet long. She walked over to take a closer look at it. A small plaque at the bottom identified it as the work of Texas artist and architect Kindred McCleary, painted on plaster, the medium often used by famous Renaissance artists like Michelangelo. The title of the piece was "Defense of Human Freedom."

At the center of the mural, the artist had painted crowds of people rallying around orators exercising their American freedom of speech. On the right, another group of people gathered in front of a drugstore. To Agnes, it looked like people bustling about and doing business. The two central images were surrounded by soldiers, lots of soldiers, some wearing gas masks, as they had in World War I. Although the gas masks brought back unpleasant memories of stories Agnes had heard at home about local boys who fell victim to chemical warfare "over there," the overall impression was of a free people, willing to come together and defend their freedoms when the times called for it. Agnes thought it was totally appropriate for Kindred McCleary to paint such a picture on this wall in Washington, D.C. as the nation locked arms to battle another fearsome threat to our way of life. She felt proud to be part of that effort. She stood silently before the mural for a long moment, then found the elevator and rode up to her new job on the fifth floor.

She found Room 5120 without any trouble and walked in. It was filled with clusters of desks, ringed by filing cabinets. On the far side, a doorway led into a second room, 5121. The woman she'd met at the Pentagon, Jean O'Leary, stood there, looking at her watch. When she looked up, she saw Agnes and smiled.

"Good morning, Agnes. You are right on time. Did you have any trouble finding us? We're sort of tucked away here on the fifth floor." She moved across the room and extended her hand. "Welcome to the Manhattan Engineer District."

Agnes could see that O'Leary was all business, and she liked that. She shook O'Leary's hand firmly.

"Thank you, Mrs. O'Leary. I'm very pleased to be here. I only hope I can do my part to help with the work that needs to be done."

"Oh, I am fairly certain you'll have no problem doing that, Agnes. Now come with me, I want you to meet someone."

She turned on her heel and headed for the inner doorway. Agnes followed her. Inside Room 5121, she saw two desks, and a large safe. The desk lamp was lit at the first desk, but no one was sitting there. Agnes thought it might be O'Leary's. At the second desk sat a man in uniform, who stood as she entered the room. O'Leary handled the formalities.

"General, I'd like you to meet our newest staff member, Agnes Jenkins. She's from Pennsylvania." She paused and turned toward Agnes. "Near Pittsburgh, I think?"

"That's right. Fayette County, actually. A little town called Smithfield, near Uniontown."

"Right." O'Leary turned back toward the man in uniform. "Agnes, I'd like you to meet Major General Leslie R. Groves, the director of the Manhattan Engineer District."

Groves moved around the desk and shook Agnes's hand. He was nearly six feet tall, and, Agnes was surprised to see, a bit portly. He worked in shirtsleeves, with two stars on his collar, and his tie tucked between his second and third buttons. His uniform looked a bit tight around the midsection. Having always fought the battle of the bulge herself, Agnes was immediately sympathetic to the general's plight. She would learn later that he dieted constantly, but guaranteed failure on that front by consuming large quantities of caramels, peanuts and chocolates that he squirreled away in one of his two safes. Only a few people would ever know that Groves ordered his uniforms a size too big to try to hide his bulk.

Agnes thought Groves a handsome man, with his wavy, dark hair, blue eyes and pleasant smile, a smile he flashed sparingly at work. Most women who met the general found him quite attractive.

"It's good to have you on board, Agnes. Please sit down for a moment and let's talk a bit."

O'Leary pulled up two chairs in front of the general's desk and motioned Agnes to the one on the left as she settled into the one on the right. Groves returned to his desk chair. He sat forward, clasped his hands together, and looked straight into Agnes's eyes.

"Agnes, Mrs. O'Leary has already told you a little about what we're doing here. I'll try to tell you a bit more, but I think you already understand that we're working under unusually strict conditions in this office, so there's only so much that can be said. But, before we get to that, tell me a little bit more about yourself."

Groves had already scrutinized the security report on Agnes, but his attention to detail and security was so intense that he always examined new staff members in person to satisfy himself that they were up to the challenges of the assignment. Agnes had grown accustomed to addressing military officers during her brief time at the Pentagon, but Groves's presence was far more commanding and his aura of self confidence far greater than any of those men had been. She hesitated in responding, not sure where to start.

"What would you like to know, sir?"

Groves leaned partway across the desk, as though trying to peer into Agnes's soul. He waved a hand in the air dismissively.

"Well, I already know the facts of your life, where you were born, who your parents are, how many siblings you have, what schooling you've completed. What I want to know is what kind of person are you," he pointed to his chest, "in here, where it counts?"

Agnes thought she understood what the general was getting at.

"Well, sir, I've always tried to be a decent person. I don't drink, smoke, swear, play cards, gamble or carouse. I'm a church-going person, and have been for most of my life. I observe Sunday as the Lord's Day, and try to keep it a day of worship and rest. I believe in working hard and doing my best no matter what job I'm given to do." At that moment, her mind flashed on the mural downstairs, and she added, "And I love my country dearly. I am proud to be an American and, even though I'm young, I am more than willing to do my part to help us get through these very difficult times."

Groves sat back in his chair and smiled.

"Good for you, Agnes. I respect your commitment to living a decent life. You know, I'm a preacher's kid myself. My father was a Presbyterian minister and then an army chaplain for many years. He would often be off stationed with troops all over the world--places like Cuba, the Philippines, China-- while my brother and I stayed home with our mother in Vancouver, Washington. Despite the fact that he spent his time ministering to a bunch of pretty rugged, hard-drinking soldiers, my father was a tee-totaller all his life. I've been in the army since I graduated from West Point in 1918--just ten days too late to get into the Great War--and I've followed in my father's footsteps, as far as all the things you mentioned are concerned. I'm not a drinker or a smoker, and I try not to indulge in a lot of salty language."

Agnes could hardly believe she was sitting in this office having a personal conversation with this important, powerful officer. She was surprised and impressed that Groves lived by values so similar to hers. Her admiration for him began to grow in that instant; it would increase steadily over the years that she worked for him. She felt blessed to be doing her wartime duty under the direction of this good and decent man.

Groves was forming impressions of Agnes, too, impressions that might as well have been carved in stone; he was not a man inclined to ever doubt his judgment. He sensed in this young woman, barely eighteen years of age, the same strength and groundedness that Mrs. O'Leary had displayed when she came to the Quartermaster General's office. In O'Leary's case, that strength had led him to give her an ever- increasing amount of responsibility and authority in the project. And he knew, as he had known that Oppenheimer was the man to lead the work at Los Alamos the first time he met him, that this young woman was right for the task that she would be asked to carry out. It was time he and O'Leary told her what that task would be. But he had one more personal question to ask.

"Agnes, I don't mean to be indiscrete, but do you have a boy friend? Someone special that you spend time with?"

Agnes blushed; she feared her cheeks were glowing; she had not expected Groves to pry into that arena. Her voice quavered just a little as she answered the question.

"Well, sir, I don't know if you'd call him a boy friend. I've just met a young man who is quickly becoming very special to me. We've not spent a great deal of time together, having only just met last Friday night. But I think it might turn out to be a special relationship. "

"Good for you, Agnes. It's only natural that an attractive woman like you would find friendship. And I apologize if my question embarrasses you. I ask it only as a way of making a very important point to you. From this moment forward, you cannot share with this young man anything about your work here. I have an absolute rule about confidentiality. You won't necessarily know exactly what the secretaries and officers sitting at the next desk out there in the office are working on and they won't know your work, either."

"Secrecy is of the utmost importance here. I know your sister is also working here in the city. And you are very close to your family back home in Pennsylvania. To all of them I would encourage you to say what I said to my wife the day we were married. Grace, I said, don't ever ask me any details about my work. And she never has. People who know you back home told our investigators that you can keep a secret, that you are discreet almost to a fault. Do you think you can manage that with this young man, your friends, your sister and your family while we're all working together on this critically important project?"

Agnes was a bit intimidated by the seriousness with which Groves asked the question, but she didn't let it show on her face. She wrung her hands in her lap, but her voice was firm as she replied.

"Yes, General Groves, I can keep a secret. And I am certain I can make everyone understand that's the way it has to be. I consider it a privilege to work with you and Mrs. O'Leary on this important project. I would never do anything to jeopardize its success."

Groves was satisfied. He moved on to the task itself.

"Agnes, we are engaged in the most important quest of this war. What we do here matters more than anything you have ever been associated with in your young life. We are building a weapon of immense proportions, and we have only a limited amount of time to do it. You will soon learn that the pace of work here is very fast, indeed, and the work load weighty. From your evaluations," he gestured to the file on his desk, "I have no doubt you will be able to pull your freight as well as anyone."

"As I mentioned a moment ago, you will not share your work with anyone, not even those sitting beside you or across the desk from you. You will use your secretarial and clerical skills as Mrs. O'Leary directs you to. You will be preparing and processing thousands of documents. You will know things that hardly any American knows. And, for the duration of the project, you will share none of that information with anyone. Are we absolutely clear on that?"

Agnes nodded solemnly.

"Agnes, raise your right hand."

She did as she was told. Groves was obsessed with the need to keep the project secret until the time came to reveal what they had done. He now inducted Agnes into his small administrative band.

"Agnes, do you swear that you will carry out your duties with the Manhattan Engineer District to the best of your abilities and maintain absolute confidentiality for the duration of this work, so help you God?"

Agnes sat ramrod straight in her chair, her eyes pinned on Groves.

"Yes, sir, I do."

"All right, then, let's all get to work."

He reached across the desk and picked up what looked to Agnes like a telephone operator's headset and slipped it on his head. He turned to Mrs. O'Leary.

"She's all yours, Mrs. O'Leary."

O'Leary stood and took Agnes's arm to lead her from the room. Before they reached the doorway, Agnes heard Groves greeting someone at the other end of the phone line. Mrs. O'Leary glanced back and then leaned close to Agnes as they walked into the outer room.

"Yes, that is an operator's headset. The general is on the phone so much of the day coordinating things that he didn't want to waste time holding the phone in his hand."

By this time, most of the desks in Room 5120 were occupied, some by uniformed officers, the rest by well-dressed young women. In all, there were no more than a couple dozen people in the room. Agnes did a quick head count and turned to O'Leary.

"Is this everyone? The general talked about this huge project, but there are only a few people here."

O'Leary had fielded nearly the same question from each staff member as they arrived.

"Yes, this is the crew. Just a couple of dozen people who will provide administrative support for a project that already employs thousands and will touch thousands more before it's over. That's the way the general wants it. We're probably the smallest headquarters unit of any outfit in the city. He did the same thing when they were building the Pentagon. You need to remember that General Groves is an army man's army man. He thinks even this large a staff is too many."

She leaned closer to Agnes and spoke in a conspiratorial tone, but there was a twinkle in her eye.

"You see, his hero is General Sherman, the Union officer who commanded the troops that torched Atlanta and marched to the sea during the Civil War. Sherman managed to do all that with headquarters gear that fit in a single escort wagon."

"How big was that?"

"Oh, I don't know exactly. The general showed me a picture once. It looked to be about ten feet long, about four feet wide, and a couple of feet high, with a canvas top arching over it."

"And General Sherman carried everything he needed for the drive through Atlanta in just one of those?"

"Apparently he did, and it galls General Groves that he can't run this operation as economically as Sherman did." She smiled. "Still, considering what we're doing out of just two rooms, I think he's come pretty close."

They were now standing by a desk about fifteen feet from the doorway to Groves's office. Another desk butted up against it, and a small table stood alongside. All of the desks were gunmetal gray with a hard rubber working surface. A typewriter sat on a small stand to the left. The top of the desk held a large glass ashtray, a desk lamp, "In" and "Out" trays stacked on top of each other, and a small wooden rack with a rotating top that had rubber stamps clipped to it. Heavy steel filing cabinets with sturdy looking locks at the top and bottom lined the walls.

"Agnes, this will be your desk." O'Leary motioned to the desk facing Groves's doorway. "And your desk mate here is Eleanor Dewitt. Eleanor, this is Agnes Jenkins."

The young woman at the opposite desk stood up and extended her hand. She was a vivacious looking girl with dark brown, wavy hair that fell to her shoulders, lively dark blue eyes, and deep dimples that appeared quickly when she smiled.

"Welcome, Agnes. It's nice to meet you."

Agnes liked her immediately. She shook Eleanor's hand and flashed her own brilliant smile for the first time since she'd entered the office that morning.

"It's a pleasure to meet you, Eleanor."

O'Leary glanced at her watch and moved things along briskly.

"Agnes, I want you to concentrate on learning our filing system this morning, so you can start putting things in their proper place by this afternoon. Eleanor can fill you in on what's what. And while you're doing that, if any of the officers need something typed up, you can get right to that. Their needs always take priority. I'm counting on your speed and accuracy to help us get these letters and reports out on time. I think you'll be impressed by how much work gets done by this escort wagon crew." She gazed across the roomful of busy people. "I'll be in the office with General Groves, if you have any other questions."

She walked briskly back through the second doorway. Agnes hung up her coat on the rack by the wall, and sat down. Eleanor looked toward Room 5121, then leaned across the desk toward Agnes.

"She's not as tough as she seems. But she does expect us to do our work right. Sometimes you'd think she was an officer, she runs such a tight ship. General Groves trusts her more than anyone. Some of the officers have a hard time with that; they call her 'Major O'Leary,' and give her a little trouble once in a while. General Groves offered to make her a major in the WACs to quiet the officers, but she didn't want it."

"Anyway, it's awfully nice to have you join us. Where are you from?"

Agnes told her.

"Well, I'd like to know more about Pennsylvania. I've only ever driven through it, and that was on my way here. I'm a Kansas girl, born and bred. My dad is a farmer. What does your family do?"

"My dad is a coal miner, and my mom runs a general store in a little town called Smithfield."

"Well, that's sounds just fine, Agnes Jenkins. I think we're going to get along great." They did. Agnes came to love Eleanor as a sister; they visited each other off and on for years after the war. Whatever other thoughts she might eventually have about the Manhattan Project, she always thanked God for introducing her to this fine young woman from the Midwest.

They spent the morning getting to know each other as Agnes quickly mastered Mrs. O'Leary's filing system. She was ready to start handling documents by mid-afternoon. Many of them were quite technical, often dealing with procurement of materials, including uranium, an ore she knew little about, and development of work sites. Her high school science class had introduced her to the table of elements. The only thing she knew about uranium was that Madame Curie had experimented with it before she won the Nobel Prize in physics in the early 1900s. She knew nothing about radioactivity, but then neither did most Americans at that time. The ignorance was so universal that no one suggested, when Curie died, that there might be a link between her research and her death from aplastic anemia, which Agnes had read about in the paper in 1934, a death most likely caused by years of exposure to radiation.

For Groves's purposes, with his intense concern for secrecy, that ignorance was probably useful. Agnes did not, initially, understand the connection between Madame Curie's work with uranium and the munitions project underway in this office. But gradually, after O'Leary put her in charge of the only complete set of documents -- Groves's personal set of files--and document after document crossed her desk, this smart, young country girl began piecing together an understanding of what it was all leading to, an emerging awareness she could share with no one.

What Agnes also didn't know--and again she was in the company of most Americans not privy to the thinking taking place within the esoteric world of theoretical physics -- was how the project came about, other than O'Leary's comment that the President had assigned it to Groves personally. She, like most Americans, had heard of Albert Einstein, the smartest man in the world. But her high school science teacher had not tried to explain Einstein's theory of relativity, especially to clerical students like Agnes and Naomi. And few people knew about the work other scientists had begun after Einstein opened the door to nuclear energy with his famous $E=mc^2$ formula.

She was unaware that in 1933 a Hungarian physicist named Leo Szilard had conceived of a nuclear chain reaction--particles smaller than the already invisible atom slamming into other particles and releasing vast amounts of energy. Szilard and an Italian physicist, Enrico Fermi, had patented the idea of a nuclear chain reaction shortly after Fermi and his Jewish wife fled to New York to escape Benito Mussolini's anti-Semitic government in Italy. Then, in 1939, Neils Bohr, a Danish physicist, had identified U-235, a uranium isotope, as the central ingredient in triggering a chain reaction.

In August, 1939, Szilard had drafted the first of a series of letters to President Roosevelt, which he convinced Einstein to sign, urging the President to create a unified American effort to corral the known supplies of uranium ore around the world, support creation of the chain reaction theorized by Szilard, and tap its potentially vast destructive power in the form of an atomic bomb. The letter ended on an ominous note, based on information European scientists now in the United States had gleaned from their former colleagues on the continent:

"I understand," Einstein/Szilard wrote, "that Germany has actually stopped the sale of uranium from the Czechoslovakian mines which she has taken over. That she should have taken such early action might perhaps be understood on the ground that the son of the German Under-Secretary of State, von Weizsäcker, is attached to the Kaiser-Wilhelm-Institut in Berlin where some of the American work on uranium is now being repeated." In other words, the researchers wanted the U.S. to beat the Germans to the atomic punch, and they believed time was of the essence.

The President was listening. He formed a national committee, the National Defense Research Committee, to monitor developments. That group told him the same thing. NDRC member and Harvard University President James Bryant Conant told him "the possibility must be seriously considered that within a few years the use of bombs such as described here, or something similar using uranium fission, may determine military superiority." But Roosevelt looked to his chief science advisor, Vannevar Bush, a noted engineer and scientist, for guidance.

A tall, bespectacled man, thin to the point of Ichobod Cranishness, Bush had been listening, too. In fact, he had been suggesting to Roosevelt for some time that the United States needed to grab hold of the atomic issue. In October, 1941, Bush marshaled his arguments and sat down with the President. He made three main points: his conversations with trustworthy scientists informed him the a-bomb was a distinct possibility; a report from British scientists concluded that such a device was not only possible but could be constructed in time to help win the present war; and, from what he had been told, he feared the Germans would be able to build an atomic bomb. If Hitler managed to get his hands on such a weapon, he might well manage to enslave the world. That, for Bush and the other scientists, was the gravest concern of all. And, with the nation at war, Bush urged the President to put the entire project in the hands of the U.S. Army.

This time the President agreed to the idea of full-scale, coordinated research and planning for an atomic weapon, but no one was to actually build an a-bomb without his direct authorization. By the end of 1941, Bush was busy planning the facilities needed to produce the nuclear material required for an atomic bomb. Three months later, he pressed Roosevelt for the final go-ahead. He reminded the President that Germany was most likely already at work on such a device. Having the Germans reach the goal first would be, he said, "an exceedingly serious matter." And, for the first time, he predicted that American scientists and engineers could produce a bomb within two years.

The sense of urgency was building, and Roosevelt must have felt it. Two days later he set the process in motion, telling his trusted advisor, "I think the whole thing should be pushed not only in regard to development, but also with due regard to time. This is very much of the essence." Bush had permission to build an atomic bomb, and do it as fast as possible, before the Nazis could.

With the project officially approved, Bush, who had worked feverishly behind the scenes to bring it about, stepped back to let the newly appointed Secretary of War, Henry L. Stimson, run the show. Stimson, already seventy-three years old, was a wealthy, Republican, Harvard-educated lawyer from New York. Roosevelt overlooked his party affiliation and put him in charge of the Army-Air Force because of the tough public stance he had already taken toward the Nazis. During his five year tenure, he would expand the ranks of the U.S. military by twelve million and make sure America's troops got the war materiel they needed on the battlefield.

On direct orders from Roosevelt, Stimson handed the new bomb project to the army, and gave military leaders a blank check to cover what promised to be the exceptionally high cost of bringing this urgent project to completion in such a short period of time. To deter curiosity, he located it in New York and called it The Manhattan Engineer District, the MED. The army assigned it to the Corps of Engineers. They were the army's builders, after all, having just completed the Pentagon, the world's largest office complex. The costs, which started mounting almost immediately, were slipped into the Corps' budget under innocuous headings such as Procurement of New Materials or Expediting Production. It would prove to be the most expensive project ever undertaken by the U.S. military.

General Groves was actually the second officer assigned to lead the MED. In the very beginning, General James Marshall was in charge, but the powers-that-be grew impatient with Marshall's deliberate, research-oriented approach. They wanted a bomb, and they wanted it as soon as possible. The search for a replacement officer led to Groves, who had demonstrated only recently his exceptional leadership ability by completing the sprawling Pentagon project in record time.

Groves's direct supervisor, Lt. Colonel Brehon B. Somervell, informed Groves of the decision. Stimson and others had impressed on Somervell the importance of beating the Germans to the a-bomb. He made sure Groves understood how crucial the project was, telling him, in the words O'Leary had shared with Agnes that day at the Pentagon, "If you do this job right, it will win the war." Groves agreed completely with those who had chosen him; he knew he was the right man, probably the only man, who could get it done in time. The preacher's son had always intended to make a name for himself. He would do it by building the most devastating weapon in the history of the world. Shortly after Groves took over, on December 2, 1942, a pile of graphite bricks and uranium fuel, built by Enrico Fermi on a commandeered racquetball court under the football stadium at the University of Chicago, went "critical." Fermi had produced the world's first controlled nuclear reaction.

****

By the time Agnes arrived in Room 5120 in early 1943, many of the pieces needed to produce a bomb were falling into place. The documents she processed for filing referred to important work sites by code names that Eleanor had interpreted for her: S-50 was the code name for a project at Site X in Oak Ridge, Tennessee; Site W was in Hanford, Washington; and the most recently added was Site Y in Los Alamos, New Mexico. Over the next several years, as a river of paperwork flowed across her desk, Agnes watched the interconnected web of the project extend ever outward until it encompassed factories, labs and mines in thirty nine states, Canada, and Africa.

The volume of documents was so great that she couldn't read through them, even if she had wanted to, but she noticed they often made some reference to uranium or U-235 or uranium ore. Many, especially in the early years of her time in Room 5120, bore the name of Colonel John C. Healey, the MED's Personnel Officer. He oversaw the hiring of thousands of workers, staggering numbers, Agnes thought, and probably good news for a nation struggling to recover from the deep depression that had left millions unemployed.

Agnes used the rubber stamps in the wooden rack on her desk to classify the documents; most of them went into the file embossed with the word "Confidential" or "Secret." Later, as Groves's security concerns intensified, Mrs. O'Leary gave her a "Top Secret" stamp, a stamp visible on only a few other desks in the office. Her orders were to hand anything marked "Top Secret" to O'Leary for deposit in one of Groves's safes, where only Groves and O'Leary could reach them.

At five o'clock, Eleanor leaned across the desk to get Agnes's attention.

"Agnes. Agnes Jenkins."

Agnes was so focused on the papers in front of her that she didn't hear Eleanor speaking to her. The third time Eleanor spoke her name she realized someone was talking and looked up. Eleanor was smiling at her.

"You really are a hard worker, Agnes. I'm sorry to interrupt you, but I thought you might like to know it's time to go home. The officers often work later, especially Colonel Healey and Colonel Lansdale."

She lowered her voice to a whisper.

"He's a special assistant to General Groves for security." She glanced toward Lansdale's desk. "He's always here when the general is."

She sat up and continued in a normal tone of voice.

"General Groves and Mrs. O'Leary often stay later working on things. But most of us girls get to go home around five." She smiled again. "So, you've finished your first day with the Manhattan Project."

Agnes repeated her last words as a question.

"Manhattan Project? I thought this was the Manhattan Engineer District."

"Oh, it is. But everyone here refers to what we're all working on as the Manhattan Project. I mean, we're not just a branch of the military. We're actually working on a project. General Groves is building some new weapon. I don't know exactly what it is, but it's taking an awful lot of us to do it."

Agnes nodded her head in agreement. She started to mention some of the personnel documents she'd just processed that referred to thousands of new workers, but quickly remembered Groves's warning that she wasn't to discuss the matters that crossed her desk with anyone else in the office.

"Yes, it is a big undertaking."

Eleanor had gotten up to put on her coat. She handed Agnes hers when she came back to their desks. Agnes turned off her desk light, then stood up and took her coat from Eleanor.

"Oh, thank you." Eleanor's small gesture of thoughtfulness fit perfectly with the impressions she was forming of this young, Midwestern gal. The room was emptying quickly as they moved toward the doorway. Agnes looked back over her shoulder as they stepped into the hall. The lights still shone brightly in Room 5121. She could see Mrs. O'Leary leaning over the desk, discussing some detail with General Groves. Groves still wore the telephone headset he'd donned nearly eight hours earlier.

When they stepped out the front door, Eleanor said a quick goodnight and rushed to catch the bus to the apartment she shared with a group of young women on Connecticut Avenue. Agnes waved to her and moved to the side as dozens of men and women poured out of the building, eager to get home or meet friends someplace for dinner. When most of the crowd had passed by, Agnes turned around and gazed up at the massive, stone building where she now worked. It was so unlike any of the structures that had surrounded her in her world back home.

Everything here in D.C. was bigger, faster paced, and significantly more important in the great scheme of things than anything she'd ever been part of in her life. A simpler country girl might have been overwhelmed by it all, but not Agnes. Even General Groves, with his ultraserious demeanor and elevated rank, did not intimidate her. As he had no doubt about her ability to handle this task, neither did she. She believed, with all her heart, that God had brought her here to do a job, and by God's grace, she intended to do it. She smiled, buttoned her coat, and, in high spirits, hiked the short distance to the bus stop in record time.

She was still reflecting on how well her first day with the Manhattan Project had gone when the bus pulled up to the light at 34th Street. She heard a woman sitting two seats in front of her gasp and saw her pointing out the window. Agnes turned and looked. There, in an alley, she saw a man with a cap pulled down low over his forehead prying open a manhole cover. Another man lay motionless on the pavement beside him. Then, while the bus driver waited for the light to change, the man in the cap heaved the lifeless body into the manhole, jumped into a nearby car, and roared away down the alley. As the driver put the bus in gear and made the turn onto 34th Street, the passengers on the bus were deathly silent. As they moved away from the scene, a man in the front seat leaned over to the driver and told him what they'd all seen. The driver shrugged, said he hadn't seen anything, and continued on his route.

Shocked by what she had just witnessed, Agnes started to cry, quietly. She was still weeping when she got off the bus and walked the two blocks to the boarding house. She had dried her eyes by the time she reached the front door, but the girls who greeted her in the front hallway saw that her face was flushed and she looked upset. Naomi came down the stairs as the girls gathered around Agnes, trying to comfort her.

"Sis? What in the world happened to you? You almost never cry."

Agnes reached for her and Naomi pulled her into her arms.

"What is it, Sis? What happened?"

Agnes clung to Naomi for a few moments before she regained enough composure to tell everyone what she'd seen. Her description was enough to elicit from the girls the same gasps Agnes had heard on the bus. Mrs. Sisko pulled Agnes off to the side as the rest of the group trooped into the dining room.

"Agnes, I'm so sorry you had to see something like that. Is there anything I can do to help you?"

She had her arm around Agnes's shoulders. Agnes leaned against Mrs. Sisko and sighed.

"Oh, Mrs. Sisko. I was feeling so good about my new job and Morris and being here in the city. Now this. How can people be so dreadful?"

Mrs. Sisko patted her gently on the back.

"I don't know, Agnes. I really don't know. But it's always been with us. You know your Bible well. Think of all the terrible things that happen in there. I'm not sure we can ever expect men to behave in a truly civilized fashion, no matter where they live. But I am sorry you had to see it tonight."

Agnes pulled herself up straight and looked at Mrs. Sisko.

"You are right, Mrs. Sisko. And God saw the good people through those bad times in the Bible. And I know He will do the same for us here. Thank you for the caring words."

She turned and started up the stairs to her room. Mrs. Sisko called after her.

"Agnes, aren't you going to join us for supper?"

Agnes continued up the stairs.

"No, I'm really not very hungry tonight. I'm going to go to bed a little early. I'm sure I'll feel better in the morning."

"All right, Agnes, if you need anything, please let me know. Good night."

"Good night, Mrs. Sisko."

Mrs. Sisko stood at the bottom of the stairs as Agnes reached the top and moved down the hall toward her room. Just before she detected the sound of the doorknob turning, Mrs. Sisko thought she heard Agnes start to cry again, softly.

In her room, Agnes sat down and opened her Bible. She turned to her favorite passage, the Twenty-Third Psalm. Reading it always gave her a sense of peace, which she desperately needed at this moment. She felt especially comforted this night when she came to the fourth verse: Yea, though I walk through the valley of the shadow of death, I will fear no evil, for Thou art with me; Thy rod and Thy staff, they comfort me. She closed her Bible, laid it on the nightstand, and knelt down by the bed and prayed. When she finished, her spirits had already begun to lift. She sat down at the small writing table Mrs. Sisko had provided and wrote her weekly letter home.

"January 10, 1943,"

"Dearest Mom,

Greetings once again from our nation's capitol. I hope this letter finds you and everyone there in fine fettle. At this exact moment, I'm not completely up to par because of an experience I had earlier this evening. I was on my way home from work, on the bus, when I saw a terrible thing happening. A man pushed what I'm sure was the dead body of another man down a manhole, in an alley not more than five blocks from the White House. It was the most terrible thing I have ever seen. Others on the bus told the driver about it, but he just kept on driving. It upset me so much I was still in tears when I got home. Mom, it was just awful to watch it happen. I know people had said Washington could be a rough place at times, but I just never expected to witness something like that with my own eyes.

I just can't understand how someone could do a thing like that. It upset me so much that I couldn't even think of eating supper, so I came right up to bed. I've already prayed about it, and that makes me feel a little better. But I think it will be a while before I can get such a dreadful thing out of my mind. I'm not telling you this so you'll worry about me. And if you read this to Dad, don't let him jump in the car and try to come take me home. I'll be OK, I'm sure. I know Naomi will tell you about it, so I wanted to make sure to tell you first."

"But I have happy news, too. I started a new job today. I'm working in a government office downtown now, so I won't be able to ride the bus with Naomi anymore. It's a very exciting job, and an important one. But I can't tell you anything else, with wartime secrecy and all of that going on. I think I'm going to like it and I already like my co-workers. The woman who sits across from me is a Midwesterner and she's just a lovely gal. I know we're going to get along famously."

"There's other happy news, too. I've met a young man; he's a civilian worker, too. We've only just met, but we get along really well. He's a college graduate and he's from Minnesota. He does accounting work for the Treasury Department. He's tall and very good-looking and has a wonderful smile. He came here to work when the army turned him down for physical reasons, which he hasn't told me any details about so far. I hope to spend a lot of time

68

with him. If it gets serious, I'll probably want to bring him home sometime to meet everybody. But after Dad's reaction to Naomi's beau Franklin, I won't even suggest doing that unless there's good reason to."

"I guess that's all the news for now. Don't worry about me, I'm a big girl now and I can handle the big city, I'm sure. The Lord willing, I won't get hurt. Give my love to everyone, and give Carl a great big smackeroo from his big sister. Take good care of everybody and yourself. If we can, Naomi and I would like to come home for Easter. We'll let you know. Your loving daughter, Agnes."

By the next morning, Agnes felt calmer, but the experience left a residue of uneasiness that took some of the spring out of her step as she exited the bus and walked the short distance to the office. She found herself looking over her shoulder when footsteps sounded behind her, and she looked more closely at anyone coming toward her.

The incident still haunted her when she and Morris stepped off the bus downtown in early April. He had invited her to spend Saturday on the Mall, seeing the monuments and something else that he said was very special. Just being with him made her feel safer. They crossed Fourteenth and Fifteenth Streets to the Washington Monument, which Agnes saw jutting into the sky every day as she rode to work, but she had never really explored it. She wished they could climb the 896 steps to the observation deck more than 550 feet above them, but Morris convinced her that the elevator would get them there in much better condition. She squeezed Morris's arm as she gazed out of the windows; the day was so clear she was sure they could see at least the thirty miles promised in the brochure.

When they got back down, she took Morris's hand and they hiked along the Reflecting Pool to the Lincoln Memorial. Agnes admired Lincoln more than any other President. They climbed the massive steps up to the foot of the seated Lincoln statue. As Agnes gazed up at him, she remembered the story about how he'd acquired his beard. She smiled at the thought. She turned to read Lincoln's words, the inspiring oration he had given at Gettysburg, inscribed in the wall. As a country girl, who knew first-hand the struggles of rural life, she had always identified with Lincoln's determination and strength of character. She was thrilled to be standing in this massive memorial paying her own tribute to him.

Morris stood by quietly while she communed with the President, then gently took her hand and led her back down the stairs, but didn't tell her where they were going. They walked away from the memorial on Twenty-Third Street and turned east on Independence Avenue. Ahead of them, Agnes saw the Tidal Basin. When they were about a hundred yards away, Morris slipped behind her and put his hands over her eyes. Agnes stopped walking.

"Morris, what on earth are you doing?"

Morris kept his hands over her eyes as he answered.

"I want to surprise you with what comes next. I'll take my hands away but you have to promise to keep your eyes closed until I tell you to open them."

Agnes giggled.

"Morris, you are so silly. I promise I will keep my eyes tight shut, but you have to make sure I don't trip over something."

"Don't worry, dearest Agnes, I will take very good care of you."

They moved forward again; Agnes reduced her normal stride from the swinging gate she'd brought to the city from the rural countryside. Now she moved each foot forward tentatively, as though trying to dip her toe in the ocean without getting drenched by the wave as it broke on the sand. Morris tried to hurry her along.

"Agnes, I told you I'd take care of you. The pathway is very smooth ahead; you can walk at a normal pace."

Agnes stepped out more confidently, her eyes squeezed shut. She felt the warm rays of the sun washing over her face. After a minute or two, Morris stopped her. She could hear voices murmuring off to the left.

"Whoa! We're there. Are you ready?"

"Yes, I am."

Morris turned her forty-five degrees to the south.

"Okay, you can open your eyes now."

He let go of her shoulders as her eyelids slowly opened. There in front of her was the most beautiful, flowering tree she had ever seen. With the sunlight filtering through it, it glowed a wonderful pink color. She was so close that the reflected pink light colored her cheeks almost as if she were embarrassed. She took a deep breath and then turned around to Morris.

"Oh, Morris. Is this what Naomi has been talking about, the cherry blossoms?"

Morris's face broke into a grin at least as wide as the one Agnes had seen on his face that night at the bowling alley. His eyes welled up to see her so pleased. For a moment, his voice failed him. He looked at Agnes and nodded. She gave him a quick hug and spun back around to enjoy the view.

"Morris, thank you for this wonderful surprise. I just love them." She turned her head to the left to take in more of the scene.

"Oh, and they just go on around the Tidal Basin, an endless riot of color. Morris, this is the best part of Washington I've seen so far."

Morris pressed against her from behind, his hands squeezing her shoulders.

"I hoped you'd like them. In fact, I was pretty sure you would."

Agnes reached up and put her hand over his. Then she moved to the right, toward a plaque next to the tree. On the bronze marker, she read:

"This is the first Yoshino Cherry tree planted along the Tidal Basin. It was a gift from Japan in 1912. Thousands of visitors from across the nation and around the world now come to Washington to observe the rite of spring and bask in the explosion of color presented by this tree and the many others that now line the Tidal Basin."

When she finished reading, Agnes stepped back with a jolt. How could the nation that had staged such a tragic attack on Pearl Harbor be the same people that bequeathed such splendorous beauty to the nation's capitol? She turned to Morris, who was reading over her shoulder.

"Does it seem right to you that the Japanese would give us this gift and then attack us in a war?"

Morris wasn't sure what to say. He pushed his wire-rim glasses up onto his nose and cleared his throat.

"I don't know, Agnes. That was a much different time, 1912. And this war won't last forever. Maybe we'll be friends with the Japanese again someday."

Agnes's brow remained furrowed.

"Well, it just doesn't seem right, somehow."

She was lost in thought for a long moment. Morris watched her, then put his arm around her waist.

"Come, sweet Agnes. Let's not let the troubles of the times deny us the pleasure of this beauty right now." He nudged her away from the plaque and the tree.

"Look down there." He pointed along the Tidal Basin. "Have you ever seen anything more beautiful in your life? Let those other thoughts just drift out of your pretty mind."

Agnes looked at him and realized, again, that she was truly in love for the first time in her life.

"Thank you, Morris. You are so good to me. This is a beautiful place and it's a beautiful day. You're right. Let's enjoy it."

They walked along the edge of the Tidal Basin, arms around each other, marveling at each burst of color they came upon. The inspiration and beauty and affection of the day worked together to push the ugliness of the bus ride and the war into the background, at least for a few hours.

CHAPTER SEVEN

Eleanor Dewitt was the only person in the office Agnes had told about that day on the bus. The two of them had begun palling around together from the first day they met. Eleanor's heart had gone out to Agnes as she listened to the story of her new friend's awful experience. In the days that followed, she paid special attention to Agnes, and thought she saw a new sadness draped across Agnes's usual somber brow. When Agnes walked into the office after her April weekend on the Mall, Eleanor could see that the veil had lifted, at least a bit. She leaned across the desk as soon as Agnes sat down.

"Good morning, sunshine. You look absolutely radiant this morning. Did you have a good weekend?"

Agnes smiled broadly and sighed.

"Oh, yes. It was a great weekend. Morris and I visited some of the monuments on the Mall, and then he surprised me by showing me the cherry blossoms by the Tidal Basin."

Eleanor grew excited.

"Aren't they magnificent? I read in the paper this is one of the best years ever. They said Saturday was supposed to be the peak of the season. You picked the right time to see them."

"Give Morris credit for that. He has a wonderful way of knowing things."

She sighed again, the bright smile still on her face. Eleanor sensed there was more to it than cherry trees.

"Agnes, I know the blossoms are beautiful, but is that all that it took to chase away the gloom you've been under for weeks?"

Agnes's eyes twinkled, and she giggled.

"No, dear Eleanor, it's more than just pink cherry blossoms. It's just that as I stood there looking at the wonderful show, with Morris's strong arms around me, I knew beyond a shadow of a doubt that I am truly in love. He is such a nice, decent man, and he's so good to me. I think it was the first time that I really allowed myself to think we could have a future together. It really is very exciting."

Eleanor leaned farther across the desk, took Agnes's hand and squeezed it.

"Good for you, Agnes," she said, her dimples flashing as she broke into a broad smile. "I don't know anyone, and I mean anyone, who deserves to be happy more than you do." She pressed Agnes's hand again. "I truly pray that it all works out for you."

The two young women were so engrossed in their celebration that neither of them had noticed the arrival of Mrs. O'Leary, who now cleared her throat to get their attention. Eleanor released Agnes's hand and sat back in her chair, and they both looked up at O'Leary.

"Girls, I'm sorry to interrupt your personal conversation. But Colonel Lansdale needs someone to type up a report for him. Eleanor, would you be so kind?"

"Of course, Mrs. O'Leary."

She grabbed her stenographer's pad and walked toward Lansdale's desk.

O'Leary called after her.

"Thank you, Eleanor."

She looked down at Agnes.

"And congratulations to you, Agnes, on whatever you girls were so excited about."

A quick smile crossed her face before she turned on her heel and marched back into her office.

The report Eleanor typed for Lansdale crossed Agnes's desk a few days later. It dealt with the new counterintelligence assignment given to the Manhattan Project to explore persistent rumors about German bomb research. Lansdale had named the project Alsos, a Greek word that meant sacred grove, to hide the true nature of the task. In his official orders to Lansdale, General Groves expressed his great displeasure over learning, through a Swedish newspaper, that the British had destroyed a German heavy water plant in Norway.

Agnes had no idea what heavy water was or how it affected the Manhattan Project. But she would read in a subsequent report that Groves had orchestrated a second attack on the facility by more than 170 American B-17 bombers. According to the report, the bombing had killed twenty-two people, eight men and fourteen women and children. Agnes felt sad that mothers and their babies had to pay such a price in the war. Groves had no such regrets. In the days before the second attack, he had ordered Lansdale to start looking for other German facilities. He was adamant that the Americans should be the first to know about any wartime projects the Germans were working on.

As 1943 wore on, Groves spent much of his time in the Washington office, but he began making more and more trips out of town. In those days, he traveled mostly by train and occasionally commercial planes. In a country that had yet to build interstate highways, both modes of transport were much faster than a car. Eventually, toward the end of the project, Secretary Stimson gave him his own plane.

The general's work load remained so heavy that he would sometimes take Mrs. O'Leary or other aides along to the railroad station and have them ride along with him on the first leg of the journey, so he could dictate letters or instructions. O'Leary and the others would get off at one of the stops down the line and return to Washington while Groves continued on to his destination.

Agnes knew the places Groves went most often from the reports that crossed her desk before and after his trips. He paid many visits to Wilmington, Delaware to confer with DuPont officials. Agnes knew from O'Leary's transcriptions of Groves's many phone calls that DuPont was in charge of the work at Hanford, Washington.

Groves would often stop first at Oak Ridge, Tennessee, where uranium was being purified by thousands of workers who had absolutely no idea what it would be used for. Thanks to Groves's compartmentalization of the project, the Hanford workers, who would eventually number upwards of 130,000, were generally as clueless as their counterparts in Tennessee. Agnes knew from the documents that the uranium was shipped, mostly by railroad, under armed guard to Hanford for processing in reactors that produced an enriched variety known as U-235. It was U-235 that yielded the isotope Bohr identified as the key to triggering a nuclear reaction. Agnes still didn't know what an isotope was.

The men and women who helped create U-235 didn't know anything about isotopes, either, nor did they know what it would be used for when it arrived at its shipping destination, Site Y. What they did know was that they weren't supposed to talk about what they were doing. Posters, taped on the plant walls, reminded them, in bold letters hard to miss, that there should be "NO LOOSE TALK" and to "ZIP YOUR LIP." In the offices, additional warnings asked: "IS YOUR SAFE LOCKED?" Even in Rooms 5120 and 5121, few people knew how uranium could be used as a weapon. Agnes certainly didn't, but unlike the scattered thousands across the country, she knew it was all leading to an immensely destructive tool. But she didn't dwell on the details that crossed her desk. She simply thunked the documents with the appropriate rubber stamp and made sure they landed in the right filing cabinet.

Some of the first documents she filed when she arrived dealt with Site Y, which Eleanor and Mrs. O'Leary had told her was Los Alamos in New Mexico. The reports had been filed by Colonel John

O'Brien, who headed up the project's real estate branch. Shortly before Agnes's first conversation with Mrs. O'Leary, O'Brien and company had evicted the residents of the Los Alamos Ranch School and taken over some fifty thousand acres of land. O'Brien confirmed Groves's preference for the site, repeating the general's conviction that the location would keep their work away from the prying eyes of the public, and, as Groves had already pointed out, it would keep the scientists and engineers hired to work there away from anyone who might want to know what they were up to so they could share it with the enemy. From the outset, Groves instituted a censorship system to guarantee that no secret information got out.

Construction had already begun, and the director of the Los Alamos work was pulling together the people he needed to do the job. According to one of the letters Agnes classified for the file, "The laboratory will be concerned with the development and manufacture of an instrument of war, which we may designate as Projectile S-I-T." *So,* Agnes thought to herself, *this is the weapon we're all helping to build. But what kind of weapon needs a laboratory? And why would you need uranium and not gunpowder to make it?* She had the jist of it, but still had no knowledge of the weapon's radioactive core.

In late April, a slender man wearing a pork pie hat and a slightly rumpled suit walked through the outer doorway. Mrs. O'Leary rushed out of Room 5121 to greet him.

"Dr. Oppenheimer, it's good to see you. We've been expecting you. The general is waiting."

Oppenheimer removed his hat and smiled. He looked directly at O'Leary, never once glancing around the room. She took his arm and ushered him quickly into Groves's office and closed the door. Agnes recognized the name from O'Leary's phone transcriptions. This was her first look at the man in charge of Los Alamos. Somehow she had thought this brilliant son of a wealthy, New York, Jewish family would be bigger, more physically impressive. Oppenheimer was slight, so thin it would take almost two of him to make one General Groves. The intelligence reports she'd seen had identified him as the preeminent theoretical physicist in the country. On the strength of his own judgment and the recommendation of Colonel Lansdale, his top security officer, Groves had hired Oppenheimer, even though some of his men thought Oppenheimer had been too close to communists or communist sympathizers in the past to be trusted with this critically important project. Lansdale had reported to Groves that he believed Oppenheimer's high opinion of himself and his burning desire to make his own mark on history would easily override any socialist tendencies he might carry from his earlier days. Groves approved him immediately, writing in the hiring orders that Oppenheimer was absolutely essential to the project.

Oppenheimer was a scientist, not a munitions expert. Agnes didn't understand this part of the plan, either. But she told herself again that she wasn't supposed to. Just stick to your knitting, Mrs. O'Leary would often say, quoting General Groves. Still, there was something exciting about being part of this and watching it come together. She thought, for the umpteenth time, how glad she was to be here. *These may be the most significant years of my life,* she thought to herself. They were, but not for the reasons she had in mind that day.

****

Shortly after Thanksgiving, Morris escorted Agnes from the boarding house in Chevy Chase, and treated her to a cab ride downtown to do some Christmas shopping. Agnes wanted to buy presents at Garfinkel's Department Store to take home to Smithfield for the holidays. Morris loved seeing Agnes excited as she was this day, her cheeks flushed with anticipation and her eyes sparkling; although he thought her normal alabaster complexion seemed a bit pale when she greeted him at the house. But her spirits were as high as ever. They talked and laughed in the cab all the way into the city, then got out a few blocks from the store so they could get some exercise.

While they were still some distance from Garfinkel's, Morris heard Agnes draw a quick, sharp breath. She clutched his arm tightly for a moment and then collapsed onto the sidewalk. As he knelt down beside her, he could see she was unconscious. Other pedestrians gathered around them to see what had happened. Morris looked up, a panicked expression on his face.

"Help! Can someone please call an ambulance? She's passed out and I have no idea why!"

His voice cracked with emotion as he pleaded with the bystanders for assistance. An elderly woman standing near Morris rushed into a nearby jewelry store and told the young clerk behind the counter to call for help. She paused long enough to explain that a young woman had passed out on the sidewalk, then rushed back out and took charge of the scene. Agnes was coming to as the Good Samaritan reached her. The woman bent over Agnes, then reached down and took her hand.

"How are you doing, my dear? Can you hear me?"

Agnes raised her head and opened her eyes. She focused on the woman. When she spoke, her normally rich, alto voice was little more than a whisper.

"Oh my, I don't know what happened."

The woman patted her hand and spoke soothingly to her.

"That's all right, dearie, you just probably had a spell. I used to be a nurse. We have help on the way. You just take it easy." To Morris and another man whose arm she grabbed, the nurse said, "Here, it's not right to let her lie on the cold pavement. Help her up and let's get her inside the store where it's warm."

The other man knelt down on the other side of Agnes; he and Morris gently helped her sit up. Morris leaned close to Agnes, his face creased by deep concern.

"Dear sweet Agnes, are you okay? Do you feel strong enough to stand up? We're going to take you inside to wait for the medics."

Agnes was fully conscious by this time. She managed a weak smile.

"Yes, Morris, I think I'm okay. I don't know what happened to me."

Morris took her hand as he steadied her.

"Don't worry that pretty head of yours, my dear. We're going to get you to a doctor and make sure you're all right."

He looked at the young man across from him.

"Thank you for helping out. Let's see if we can get her on her feet."

They each gripped one of Agnes's arms and slipped their other arm around her back. Agnes tried to help by pulling her knees up toward her chin and positioning her feet flat on the sidewalk. As they raised her up, a stabbing pain shot through her abdomen. Morris saw her wince.

"Are you in pain, Agnes?"

"Yes, a little. But I'm sure it will pass."

Once she was on her feet, the pain receded. Morris and the stranger guided her carefully into the store, with the nurse clearing a path through the small crowd that had gathered around them. The clerk brought a chair from behind the counter, and the nurse helped Agnes sit down. A sheen of perspiration spread across her forehead. The older woman put her hand on the back of Agnes's neck and held it there for a few seconds.

"Yes, my dear, I think you are running a fever. Maybe it's the flu or something. Let's just get you to the emergency room and they can find out."

Agnes took the woman's hand and looked up at her.

"You are so kind. Thank you. I'm a little embarrassed by all of this. I hate to make a scene."

The woman patted Agnes's hand.

"There, there, my dear. That's what I'm trained to do. I've only been retired for a year or so. I'm glad I could help."

The undulating wail of a siren penetrated the store.

"And there's help right now."

An ambulance screeched to a halt outside and two attendants jumped out. They flung open the back doors and pulled a gurney onto the street. The nurse opened the front door of the store and beckoned the crew inside. They had Agnes stand and remove her winter coat, and then helped her onto the gurney. All the while, they kept up a humorous patter, hoping to relax the look of fear on Agnes's young face. With their patient securely strapped in place, they rolled the gurney to the curb, slid it into the ambulance and, after one of them had climbed in beside Agnes, the other secured the rear doors and hustled to the driver's seat. With red light flashing and siren wailing, the ambulance roared off. Morris hailed the next cab he saw and headed after her.

By the time he reached the hospital, Agnes was in an examining room. The E-R nurse invited him to have a seat in the waiting area while Agnes was with the doctors. In the examining room an elderly physician leaned over Agnes, who had already been asked to exchange her dress for an airy, open-backed hospital gown. The doctor smiled at Agnes and reached toward her abdomen.

"You say you had a pain around this area."

Agnes raised her head and looked where the doctor was pointing.

"Yes, but it doesn't seem so bad now."

The doctor laid his hands on her lower abdomen and palpated the area. Agnes felt the sharp pain again. The doctor didn't have to ask her about it; he saw the instant reaction on her face. He moved his hands to the other side of her abdomen and thumped there. Agnes felt the slight pressure of his touch and some pain, but nothing like the first area the doctor had checked. The doctor looked to the nurse standing beside the examination table.

"What did you say her temperature was?"

The nurse consulted the chart in her hand.

"We're looking at about 101."

The doctor took Agnes's hand in both of his, and looked into her face.

"I think that clinches it, young lady. You need to have your appendix out."

Agnes grew flustered. She had never been seriously ill in all of her eighteen years. Her eyes welled up.

"When do I need to do that?"

"As soon as we can get you into the O.R. Unless I miss my guess, your appendix burst out there on the sidewalk. We need to get it out immediately."

Two hours later, the E.R. nurse asked Morris to come over to the desk. The wait had seemed like an eternity.

"Yes, ma'am, do you have word about Agnes? How is she?"

"Yes, Mr. Racklin, I wanted to let you know Agnes just had her appendix removed. Everything went very well, but she'll need to stay with us a few days before she'll be ready to go home."

"That's good news. Can I see her?"

The nurse smiled patiently.

"I'm sure you would like to see her, but she's not going to be ready for visitors until tomorrow. Right now she's in recovery and she's pretty groggy. But she's just fine. She's a good, sturdy, young woman. Let's give her a chance to rest up a little after a rough day. We'll be sure to tell her you were here. Shall I say you'll be back for visiting hours tomorrow?"

"Oh, yes. I was so worried about her. She's very special to me, you know. Yes, tell her I'll be here as soon as visiting hours start."

He turned and walked toward the exit, wringing his leather gloves in his hands. The nurse leaned over to a colleague behind the desk and pointed toward Morris.

"Ain't love grand?" she asked, with a smile.

The other nurse smiled and sighed.

"Yes, it certainly is."

Morris arrived moments after visiting hours started the next afternoon to find Naomi already at her sister's bedside. Agnes looked tired but not quite as pale as the day before. Morris tapped softly on the open door. Naomi turned and saw him standing there with a bright bouquet of roses clutched in his hand. She turned back to look at Agnes whose eyes had already met Morris's. Agnes was flashing her most brilliant smile. Naomi stood up and motioned for Morris to come in.

"Hello, Morris."

Agnes kept smiling as Morris approached her bedside. When he reached her he bent down and softly kissed her cheek, then held out the roses.

"These are for you. I thought they might brighten up this sterile, old hospital room."

Agnes's voice reflected the weakness she still felt after her surgery.

"Oh, they're lovely, Morris. What a thoughtful thing to do." She took the flowers in her hand and brought the bouquet to her face and inhaled. "Oh, they smell just wonderful. Thank you so much." She looked around the room and then at Naomi.

"Sis, would you please try to find a vase for these. We should get them in some water right away."

"Sure, I'll go ask at the nurses' station. I'll be right back." She winked at Agnes. "You two behave while I'm gone."

Agnes and Morris laughed. Agnes patted the side of her bed, inviting Morris to sit down. He accepted the offer and took her hand in his.

"I was so worried about you, Agnes. Out there on the sidewalk, you just dropped like a stone. Thank God for that nurse who just happened to be there when we needed her."

Agnes slid her hand free and gently caressed Morris's.

"You were wonderful, Morris. Basically, from what the doctor just told me, you and that kind woman saved my life. Apparently, my appendix had burst and when that happens all sorts of nasty stuff gets into you and it can kill you if they don't do something right away. The doctor said I must be able to stand a lot of pain not to have noticed it before yesterday." She patted Morris's hand. "Thank goodness you were there. You're not just my friend anymore, you're my hero."

She smiled up at him, her cheeks rosy with embarrassment. She had never expressed that sort of feeling to a man before. Morris colored a bit, too.

"I'm not a hero, but I do care very much for you. If something like that was going to happen, I'm glad it happened when I was there to help." He looked into her deep brown eyes. "So how are you doing? How long will you have to stay here?"

"Because they got it in time, I'm feeling pretty well and the doctor doesn't anticipate any complications. But he says they want to keep me here for a few days just to make sure. It'll probably be another week before I can go back to work."

Naomi had returned with a pitcher she'd borrowed from the nurse's station. When she saw Agnes and Morris close together on the bed, she cleared her throat to let them know she was back.

"Hey, you two, this isn't a date, you know."

Morris and Agnes laughed, again. Seeing the pitcher half filled with water, Morris picked up the roses, which lay across Agnes's lap, and carried them over to Naomi. Just then a nurse bustled in.

"Getting to be a crowd in here, Agnes. You are one popular young woman."

She walked to the bed and slipped a thermometer in Agnes's mouth and held her wrist to check her pulse. Turning toward Morris and Naomi, she said, "This is just routine. Any time an appendix blows we keep a good eye on the patient to make sure no infection sets in. She's doing great. That country girl constitution of hers got her through this in pretty good shape."

She patted Agnes's hand. Satisfied that things were in order, the nurse made notations on the chart at the foot of Agnes's bed and strode briskly out of the room. Naomi pulled a chair close to one side of the bed, Morris did the same on the other side, and the three young people chatted about nothing in particular for three-quarters of an hour. Agnes felt herself growing drowsy; Morris and Naomi saw her eyelids drooping. Naomi retrieved her coat from the rack in the corner.

"Okay, you two, I can see that Agnes needs to get some more rest." She walked over to the bed and kissed Agnes on the forehead. "You just concentrate on getting well, Sis. I'll be back tomorrow." With a big smile and a wave of her hand, she was gone.

Morris didn't want to leave, but he knew Naomi was probably right. He lifted Agnes's hand from the bed and raised it to his lips.

"I should go, too, so you can rest." His lips brushed her hand so softly she almost didn't feel it. "Good night, sweet Agnes. Keep on feeling better. I'll be back tomorrow."

When he was gone, Agnes looked at the dark, red roses in the pitcher on the windowsill. She smiled at the thought that Morris had brought them just for her. She slid her hand across the blanket to the area where the doctors had left stitches in her abdomen. She couldn't actually feel the needlework through the bedclothes, but when she pressed, it hurt. She wasn't surprised by that, but it told her she did need to sleep so her body could repair things and she could get back on her feet. She closed her eyes and tried to thank God for getting her through this latest traumatic experience, but she drifted off before she finished her prayer.

She remained in the hospital for the rest of the week. Morris showed up every day, a fresh batch of flowers in hand, and Naomi appeared punctually at the start of visiting hours, with orders from Neil and Irene to keep them updated on Agnes's progress. The girls from the boarding house came by and entertained Agnes with tales of their latest adventures, along with Mrs. Sisko, who wanted to be sure her charge was being properly cared for. Agnes mended quickly; by Monday she was up walking around. The doctors were so pleased they released her exactly a week after she arrived, with orders to rest another few days at home before heading back to work. Other than brief trips to deliver her two sons, Agnes would not enter a hospital as a patient for thirty-five years.

She returned to the office in time for the Christmas party Mrs. O'Leary had convinced General Groves to let her organize for their dedicated crew. He had agreed to it on the condition that, for security reasons, only staff members would be in attendance, no guests. And he didn't want it too festive. They were engaged in a deadly serious task; he wanted the atmosphere in the office to reflect that. O'Leary understood. Nonetheless, she invited the general's wife, Grace, to help her get things ready. The day of the party, Mrs. Groves and their teenaged daughter, Gwen, both joined in the merriment.

Agnes had already met them, when they'd stopped in the office to see the general. Gwen sometimes came to the office after school, and did her homework at the desks in the outer room while she waited for her father to finish work. Agnes knew Gwen sometimes used her desk because the rubber stamps would occasionally be out of order when she came in the next day. Not that Gwen or her mother knew what Agnes's "Top Secret" stamp or any of the other stamps were for. Abiding by Groves's edict of days long gone by, they did not ask. They would be as surprised as everyone else when the project was finally made public nearly two years later.

Near the end of the party, someone suggested they all pose for a picture. Groves pulled on his uniform jacket and joined Grace, who was wearing a holiday appropriate red, plaid suit, in the center of the room. The rest of the staff and officers spread out in two rows behind them. Agnes, always a little shy about photographs, gravitated to the left side of the back row. Even though she was feeling much better, she couldn't bring herself to reveal her bright, white smile when the photographer encouraged everyone to say "Cheese!"

Part of the reason for that was that she was simply tired. Because she was the only person, other than Groves and O'Leary, authorized to process all of the documents, they had backed up during her absence. Mrs. O'Leary had dropped a large stack of papers on her desk the day she returned to the office, and Agnes had been putting in longer than normal days to catch up.

A week after the party, Neil and Irene met their daughters at the Uniontown station as they arrived home for the holidays. They were extremely proud of the work their daughters were doing, even though they didn't really know what their work was. Irene hugged and kissed them as they stepped off the train. In an uncharacteristically emotional moment, Neil's eyes grew moist as he reached out to hug his little girls, now confident young women. Irene and the girls, caught up in animated conversation, headed for the Packard, with Neil following behind, a loaded suitcase in each hand.

At home, as they all shed their coats, Irene thought Agnes looked unusually thin. After dinner, she followed Agnes into the parlor and sat down next to her.

"My darling daughter, what a time you've been having in the big city. You know we think about you often while you're down there, don't you?"

Agnes smiled and nodded.

"Yes, Mom, we know that. Why do you think I write those letters so regularly? I don't want you to worry about us. You did a good job raising us. We can take care of ourselves."

"I know that, dear. But just the same, in hardly a year, you've witnessed a murder and now this near-miss with your appendix. I can't stop feeling like a mother and worrying a bit, even if you are old enough to manage your own affairs."

Irene turned toward Agnes.

"Now stand up for a minute."

Agnes looked at her mother, curious to know what she was up to. But she stood, as Irene had requested, and faced Irene.

"Why am I standing up?"

Irene scrutinized her from head to toe.

"You've lost weight, haven't you?"

"Oh, a little, maybe."

"Is it from the appendicitis or from all the pressure you're under in your job or just the strain of living in a city where awful things happen?"

Agnes smiled again.

"I don't know, Mom. I missed a few regular meals with the appendix. I may have lost a couple of pounds there. Why are you so worried about this?"

Irene stared at her for a moment.

"Well, for one thing, your face is too thin. Your face has never been that thin in your whole life. And the rest of you looks too thin, too. Is there something else wrong with you that you haven't told us about?"

Agnes laughed.

"No, Mom! There's nothing wrong with me. And if I've shed a few pounds and look a little slimmer, good. I've never liked being so big anyway. And if I'm this size, I can buy nicer looking dresses and just look better all over, which is something I'd really like to be able to do at this point in my life."

Irene's eyes lit up. She raised her hand.

"Oh, yes. That's it! There's this man in your life. Are you dieting to impress him? Is that what's going on?"

"No, Mom. I am not dieting for Morris. But I want to look nice for him. I really like him."

Irene leaned closer, her voice almost a whisper.

"Your father isn't happy to hear that you've gotten involved with someone. As far as he's concerned you won't be old enough for that till you're about thirty." She looked toward the doorway to make sure Neil wasn't listening in. "I'm not terribly excited about the fact that both of my daughters have gone off to the big city and immediately gotten involved with men. You're both still quite young, you know. But I also remember how old I was when I started to notice the fellas." She grinned at Agnes, and sat back on her side of the sofa. "So tell me about this young man, this Morris Racklin."

Agnes had always felt comfortable talking to Irene about the events of her life, but until now she'd never had any romantic details to share. She blushed as she told the story of meeting Morris, this handsome, well-educated young man she had grown so close to. She described the places they had gone together, and she told Irene the things they had talked about. Irene listened quietly, remembering the days when her own heart had first beat faster at the thought of a young man, his eyes, his voice, the touch of his hand. When Agnes finished, she took her daughter's hands in her own and looked deep into her eyes.

"Do you really love this man, Agnes?"

Agnes sighed and smiled.

"Yes, Mom, I do. I really think he's the one."

"Well, you have always been a sensible person, Agnes," Irene told her. "I trust your judgment probably more than anyone else in this household, except me. If you really care for him, and you know he cares for you, then God bless you both. My only advice is to take your time, don't rush into something in the heat of passion that might turn out wrong down the road."

Irene's words made Agnes think of the turbulent times in this house, when Neil and Irene seemed to have hit some very large bumps in the road they had taken together. She wondered if that's what her mother had in mind as she offered this counsel. But she couldn't see any rough patches like that in the future she envisioned for herself and Morris. He wasn't like Neil. He was refined and gentle and always treated her with the utmost respect. She looked into her mother's eyes and saw concern laced with pain.

"Mom, I'm not going to rush into anything. I know I fell pretty quick and pretty hard for Morris. But we're still just very good friends. And we enjoy spending time together. I hope it will lead to something wonderful, but we'll just have to wait and see. Does that make you feel better?"

Looking at her daughter, Irene thought, as she had many times with this child, that Agnes was indeed special, that she had a sixth sense, a way of knowing and understanding life, a maturity beyond her years. She was a sensible young woman.

"Yes, Agnes, that does make me feel better. I've always trusted you to do the right thing. I'm sure you will this time, too." Just then she heard Neil and Naomi talking as they came toward the parlor. She dropped her voice and offered her last bit of advice in a whisper.

"Love him if you must, Agnes. But don't bring him home to meet your dad until you're really sure."

She pinched Agnes's cheek and winked at her as Neil and Naomi came in.

CHAPTER EIGHT

As Agnes began her second year with the Manhattan Project, she felt its already urgent pace accelerating. Her first day back in the office after the holidays, Mrs. O'Leary brought her another large stack of documents to process. While most of the staff enjoyed a little R-and-R with family and friends, Groves and O'Leary had worked through Christmas and New Year's, churning out reams of orders and reports.

The documents painted a picture of a rapidly expanding organization. Oak Ridge--Site X in code name and sometimes referred to by the nickname, Dog Patch--now employed thousands of civilian workers, whose central task was to purify the uranium ore brought to them from all over the world. In O'Leary's phone transcriptions, Groves instructed his aides to identify and control every known source of uranium, to ensure he had enough for the project and to short-circuit German efforts to build the bomb, which were still rumored to be underway.

The documents made clear that Groves had all the power and funding necessary to commandeer any materials he needed. One invoice requisitioned, under total secrecy, the first of an eventual total of nearly fifteen thousand tons of silver from Treasury Department vaults. Treasury Secretary Henry Morgenthau was not consulted. Agnes was impressed by the unrestricted access Groves enjoyed as leader of the project. The general himself reinforced her impression, not that it needed reinforcing, the day he called Agnes and her desk mate, Eleanor, into his office. There on a table sat a gigantic stack of cash, all in thousand dollar bills. Groves pointed to the table and looked at the two, wide-eyed young women, a tight smile on his face.

"Ladies, can you guess how much money that is?"

Speechless in the presence of so much currency, Agnes and Eleanor looked at each other, then back to Groves and slowly shook their heads.

"Well, I'll tell you. It's one million dollars. It's just a small portion of the cash I have access to in several secret accounts set up for the project. Have either of you ever seen that much money before?"

Eleanor recovered her voice first.

"No, General Groves, I think I can safely say neither of us has ever been anywhere near that much money in our lives," she said breathlessly, adding, with the usual twinkle in her eye, "except when we're standing in the lobby of a bank."

Groves's smile grew a little broader. He enjoyed Eleanor's spirited personality. He also enjoyed grandstanding once in a while, flexing his immense importance.

"Well, you may have this experience several more times before our work here is done. For now, I'd like both of you to pack this cash in those canvas bags over there and take it to this bank." He picked up a paper from his desk with the hand-written name and address of a Washington bank, and gave it to Agnes. "Mrs. O'Leary will provide you with the appropriate deposit slips and arrange a guard to drive you. Any questions about this?"

Agnes and Eleanor replied at the same time.

"No, sir."

"Good, then get this table cleared off. I have a meeting in ten minutes."

The young women grabbed the bags and began stuffing wads of cash into them. As they worked, Groves added one more instruction.

"Oh, yes. I probably don't need to mention this, but you will, of course, not mention this to anyone else here in the office or to any of your acquaintances elsewhere. Is that understood?"

Again, Eleanor and Agnes answered in unison.

"Yes, sir."

Seeing the vast resources Groves had access to helped Agnes understand how the hugely expensive project was able to grow so rapidly. The rising number of workers at Site X was more than matched by the work force already in place at Site W--the Hanford branch where they were producing enriched U-235; some documents referred to the end product as plutonium. The sprawling Hanford site now had more than five hundred buildings, over six hundred miles of roads, a hundred and fifty miles of railroad tracks, and upwards of one hundred thousand employees. Groves documented all of his frequent visits and phone contacts with DuPont officials, who had taken on the task of building and operating the nuclear reactors at Hanford that produced U-235. According to the paperwork, Hanford was running more than a hundred hours a week, all day and all night.

Work proceeded apace at Site Y-Los Alamos-where Oppenheimer and company had taken over the Ranch School site. They were already a year into construction of laboratories, technical facilities and machine shops. Oppenheimer reported on his efforts to recruit the very best theoretical and practical physicists to help build what he now and then referred to as "The Gadget." Agnes assumed that was what they were calling the bomb. It didn't sound particularly sinister by that name, almost comical. In early 1944, Site Y already housed and fed and tried to entertain thirty-five hundred scientists, soldiers and technicians. It would eventually mushroom to a population of ten thousand. It was a town with a single purpose, intentionally located far from other towns, in the inhospitable, remote reaches of New Mexico, its residents united in the task of creating the most devastating device in the history of humankind.

Agnes was stunned by Groves's ability to push forward relentlessly on all fronts, including counter intelligence, which he had assigned to Colonel Lansdale, his Chief Security Officer, after being surprised by the English raid on the German nuclear facility in Norway. He pushed Lansdale and his Chief of Foreign Intelligence, Robert Furman, to track down all traces of German bomb efforts, and to find Werner Heisenberg, who was thought to be their leader. That had triggered the Alsos project which, Agnes read in the reports, had already scoured Italy for clues by late 1943 and come up empty-handed.

Agnes found these report especially interesting; unlike many of the more technical documents, she understood most of what she read. She had always enjoyed reading mysteries, and Alsos was a real-life, cloak-and-dagger story. She never had time to read all the way through any of the documents, but she'd seen enough to know that the Office of Strategic Services, whatever that was, had loaned Groves a Princeton-educated, former professional baseball player, Morris Berg, who was fluent in French, Italian, German and several other languages, to snoop around Italy on his own to see if the Italians knew anything about the German bomb project. None of the documents included a picture of Berg, but Agnes wondered if he might be the handsome young man she remembered seeing Robert Furman usher into General Groves's conference room shortly before Christmas.

All of the intelligence coming in from Europe kept pointing to a scientist named Werner Heisenberg as the king pin of the German project. In one of O'Leary's phone transcriptions, Groves proposed kidnapping, even killing Heisenberg as a way to stop German efforts literally dead in their tracks. Berg's reports, filed through Lansdale, confirmed that Italian scientists weren't up to anything, but he had discovered something else: Heisenberg was hiding out in the Alps.

Groves's responses to the reports made it clear he was not satisfied. He wanted Heisenberg, preferably dead. The general had ordered a bombing raid on the Kaiser Wilhelm Institute in Berlin in February, but Heisenberg was not among the casualties. If he'd fled to the mountains, that would explain why they'd missed him.

Agnes felt a sense of excitement as she read of Berg's daring exploits. But exhilaration turned to dread when she read that Berg had been ordered to attend a lecture Heisenberg was scheduled to give in Zurich, and, if the German scientist so much as mentioned a bomb project, shoot him dead right there in the lecture hall. The report said Berg had concealed a pistol for dispatching Heisenberg in one pocket, and a cyanide tablet for dispatching himself in the other, in case he was caught. Heisenberg, according to the report, had not doomed himself with his own rhetoric.

Agnes shuddered as she imagined what might have been Berg's fate, had he been caught. She admired this young man she did not know for his willingness to sacrifice his life for his country, and she wondered if she'd be willing to do as much if she somehow found herself on the dangerous frontlines rather than in the safe confines of Room 5120. Had anyone been watching her face as she worked through documents like these, they would have seen her usually serious expression grow even more somber as she realized just how high the stakes were in this very dangerous game.

****

Agnes found herself looking more and more to Morris's warm affection and Naomi's always bright spirits to help her hold back the growing sense of foreboding planted in her mind by the deadly, dark details of the documents crossing her desk. Naomi was more than ready to provide that support. Even though they could not talk about what Agnes was doing at the New War Building, Naomi, Agnes's twin in intuition, sensed that her sister was carrying an increasingly heavy burden, truths of the business of war that made her even more melancholy than usual.

Naomi redoubled her efforts to make Agnes laugh and keep her entertained. She made sure Agnes joined the other girls whenever they ventured out for a night of bowling, a nice meal in a restaurant, or a day of hiking around the city to see the sights and tour the museums. And she prattled on endlessly about her latest letter from Franklin. As 1944 got underway, he was still in England, although he couldn't tell her exactly where or what he was doing. He wrote detailed accounts of his outings in the English countryside, humorous anecdotes of encounters with eccentric villagers who spoke with an accent so exotic he had trouble understanding what they were saying, and he expounded on the virtues of his new, favorite food, steak-and-kidney pie, which sounded absolutely awful to Agnes, when Naomi insisted on reading her Franklin's description of the English delicacy. She made Agnes count the Xs and Os, kisses and hugs, that covered the bottom third of the last page of every letter he wrote to his gorgeous, dark-haired beauty back home. He promised to be back in Washington, take her in his arms, and sweep her off her feet just as soon as the war was over. Naomi beamed as she shared his missives, and Agnes smiled and hugged her sister, happy to see Naomi so full of love for this young man.

Like most Americans in those turbulent years, the girls at Mrs. Sisko's boarding house made sure to scan the front page of the newspaper--the Washington Post in their case--every morning for news from the war front. Several of them, like Naomi, waited anxiously for their soldier to come marching home. Even though they weren't exactly sure where their sweethearts were at the moment, they wanted to know as much about what was going on as they could. They'd read the stories of the Nazi blitzkrieg over London which Franklin somehow never mentioned in his letters to Naomi. They read every story they could find. They coped with the uncertainties as best they could. They and the soldiers they waited for--lovers and brothers--were, after all, little more than children. They talked amongst themselves, bragged to each other of the prowess of their American boys, to keep their spirits up.

They gathered in Mrs. Sisko's parlor in the evening, pulling their chairs up close to the round-topped radio with its big, lighted dial in the center, and heard Ed Murrow and others reporting from the roof tops of London as bombs exploded around them. The broadcasts left them feeling uneasy; it didn't sound like the war was going so well for the good guys. But hearing Murrow's voice surrounded by the din of war made them feel just a little closer to the loved ones they'd offered up to fight the German and Japanese aggressors. And in the quiet of their own rooms at night they prayed that God would bring an end to the fighting soon.

Agnes was coming down to breakfast on the morning of June 6th, 1944, when she heard a cheer go up in the dining room. She rushed in to find the girls and Mrs. Sisko bent over the front page of the Post. The banner headline read: Allies Land in France, Wipe Out Big Air Bases. Beneath the headline was a sketch of the English Channel, showing the landing points where the troops had gone ashore. Agnes understood why the girls were excited. The Allies were obviously taking this war in hand, marching onto the continent to put an end to the hateful Nazi threat. The girls were so encouraged by the news and so distracted by the broad headline that few of them noticed the much smaller article beneath the sketch. In unassuming font, the headline read: Roosevelt Sees Costly Fight Ahead for Victory.

Agnes looked up to see if Naomi had seen the second article. It didn't appear that she had; she was still hugging and kissing the other girls and dancing around the room with a happy grin on her face. Agnes walked over to her.

"So what do you think, Sis? Is this going to be over soon?"

Naomi grabbed Agnes and crushed her in a bear hug.

"I sure hope so. I'm ready to get Franklin home and get hitched. We've got babies to raise." She smiled broadly and laughed. But she pulled Agnes even closer to whisper in her ear before she released her.

"I know what you're thinking. I saw the part about lots of casualties. But I don't want to weigh the other girls down with that. I just have a feeling that all of our guys will get through this just fine. So don't worry about me."

She kissed Agnes on the cheek and let go of her. Agnes looked into Naomi's eyes and smiled.

"I'll be praying for him, Naomi, as I'm sure you will, too. I believe in the power of prayer. If we put Franklin in God's hands, it's the best place he could ever be."

Coverage of the D-Day invasion dominated the front page of the Post for the next several days. As Roosevelt had predicted, the death toll on the Allied side rose steadily. Journalists who rode the landing crafts onto the beach alongside the soldiers described the violent reception that greeted them, the withering machine-gun fire from German bunkers, that mowed down row upon row of young, American boys following orders to charge across the sand and gain a foothold from which to begin the deadly task of reclaiming France and the rest of Europe.

Everyone at the boarding house waited nervously for the paper to arrive each morning with the latest word and they glued themselves to the radio when they got home from the office. They called home to see if there had been any word on their brothers, and called their sweethearts' families, hoping to hear that the one they loved had survived the attack, if they'd been ordered into it. No one heard anything for nearly a week. Then, the phone in Emily Sisko's house began to ring. One by one, families called to tell the girls they'd been notified that their son had been wounded in the invasion, but was alive, if not entirely well, and would be coming home soon.

Naomi waited by the phone each night, but it never rang for her. *No news is good news*, she thought to herself. Her hopes began to rise; Franklin must have made it through, or maybe he wasn't even part of it. Maybe he was still hanging out at that silly English pub, trying to understand what that old accordion player was singing. By the fourth day, she stopped sitting in the hall by the phone. Everyone who was going to hear had heard, she thought. Now I can start counting the days till Franklin's next letter, and we can get on with planning our lives.

She and the other girls were in the parlor after dinner, listening to Murrow's latest update, when they all heard the phone ring. As she had taken to doing in these especially stressful times, Mrs. Sisko rose and stepped into the hall. A moment later she reappeared in the doorway and looked across the room.

"Naomi, it's for you."

Naomi stood and extended her hand toward Agnes, who rose and walked over to her. The other girls had stopped talking; the only sound in the room was Ed Murrow's voice. Naomi walked toward the hallway, grasping Agnes's hand tightly. She continued to hold it as she picked up the receiver.

"Hello, this is Naomi."

She recognized the voice that greeted her on the other end; it was Franklin's mother. Naomi could hear voices in the background, but couldn't make out what they were saying. Mrs. Franklin spoke in a voice entirely devoid of emotion.

"Naomi, I have very bad news to tell you."

Naomi drew in her breath, but did not speak.

"Naomi, are you still there?"

"Yes, I'm here."

"I am so sorry to tell you we received a telegram from the war department a few minutes ago. They say Franklin was killed in the Normandy invasion."

Naomi gasped and clutched Agnes's hand more tightly.

"No, Mother Worthy, that just can't be. Everyone who was going to hear has already heard. God was watching over Franklin. He can't be..."

She couldn't bring herself to say the word.

"I'm so sorry my dear. We are all just devastated. I won't keep you tonight, but we will be in touch when Franklin comes home. I'm sure you'll want to be here for the funeral. God bless you, Naomi. I'm so sorry to be telling you this..."

She broke down and Naomi could hear her sobbing. She said good-bye through her tears.

"God bless, Naomi. Pray for us all as we will be praying for you. Good night, dear."

Agnes didn't need to ask what the phone call was about. She had put her arm around Naomi partway through it. Now she pulled her close. Naomi slowly lowered the phone into its cradle. She turned to look at Agnes--white as a sheet, her eyes wide and brimming with tears--and then dropped to the floor. Agnes uttered Naomi's name in a stricken voice that brought Mrs. Sisko and the other girls rushing into the hall. Mrs. Sisko hustled into the kitchen and soon returned with smelling salts she always kept around for the benefit of the excitable young women who inhabited her house. The pungent chemicals brought Naomi back to life quickly. Mrs. Sisko helped Agnes get Naomi on her feet and up the stairs to her room. Naomi mumbled incoherently as they undressed her and tucked her into bed. She chanted a ragged litany punctuated by racking sobs, "Franklin...(sob)...married...(sob)...the babies...(sob)." Agnes pulled a chair close to the bed and sat down. She spoke softly to her sister and gently stroked her forehead. After a while, Naomi seemed to relax. She drifted off to sleep. Agnes lay down beside her on the bed and took her hand. She stayed by Naomi's side through the night. In the morning, Agnes awoke to find Naomi sitting up in bed, watching her.

"Hey, Sis, what are you doing here?"

"Oh, I just thought you shouldn't be alone last night."

Naomi smiled.

"That was sweet of you, Agnes. But I'll be okay."

Agnes sat up and put her arm around Naomi.

"I know you will, Sis, because we're strong women and we can handle whatever life throws at us."

Naomi's smile faded, as the awfulness of last night's phone call filled her mind like a dark, menacing cloud.

"That's right, Agnes. We can do it, can't we?"

She looked at Agnes, tears rolling down her cheeks. Agnes's heart ached to see her sister suffering so. She wondered if Naomi, the beautiful, spirited Jenkins sister, would ever be able to throw off the sadness that had descended on her. Naomi would, she knew, make a valiant effort to get on with things. But, in that terrible moment, knowing how deeply and totally Naomi had loved Franklin, Agnes couldn't imagine that the old Naomi would ever return.

Naomi briefly considered fleeing Washington and all its memories of Franklin, but the thought of returning to western Pennsylvania left her feeling even emptier and more disconsolate. She stayed in the city with Agnes and the girls and, after Franklin was laid to rest, made herself join in the girls' adventures. She still flirted with the boys, and teased everyone. Most people would have said she was back to normal. But Agnes knew otherwise. This was a diminished Naomi, who laughed but not as much as before, who flirted with the boys but not with quite the same sparkle in her eye, who reached out to her friends when they seemed a bit down but not with quite the same energy she once had. She would even find love again, but not the all-consuming passion she had for Franklin. The war denied her the life she had dreamed of having. It would, ultimately, do the same thing to Agnes.

CHAPTER NINE

In September, 1944, not long after her nineteenth birthday, a report filed by Groves's foreign intelligence chief, Robert Furman, crossed Agnes's desk. It detailed his successful search, in concert with nuclear physicist Samuel Goudsmit, scientific director of the Office of Scientific Research and Development, for a huge cache of uranium ore the Nazis had been hiding in Europe for use in their nuclear program. The two men had found the ore, thirty-one tons of it in steel barrels, stashed in a warehouse in Toulouse, France.

Furman had drafted American soldiers to load the stuff into trucks and then railroad cars for shipment to England, and then on to the U.S. by sea on Navy transports. The report noted that the soldiers had asked about the yellow powder sifting out of some of the barrels, but, in accordance with Groves's stringent security policies, no one told them what it was. They'd been told to follow orders and keep their mouths shut.

That same month, shortly after lunch, General Groves stepped into Room 5120 and curtly summoned Lansdale, his security chief, into his office. A few minutes later, Lansdale emerged, his face stretched taut with concern. He grabbed his coat and headed for the door. As he passed his secretary's desk, Agnes heard him give her instructions. She couldn't make out most of it, but she thought she heard him say something about the naval yard in Philadelphia. Agnes had seen only a few documents dealing with Manhattan Project work in Philadelphia, but she knew it was some sort of experimental lab developing what the paperwork referred to as an isotope separation process for use in a larger facility under construction at Oak Ridge. Agnes wondered what could have happened at the lab to cause Lansdale to race north. But she didn't dwell on it; like most of her colleagues, minding her own knitting had become a reflex.

Three days later, in the latest batch of O'Leary's transcriptions of Groves's phone calls, she learned the story. Groves had sent Lansdale packing because he'd just been notified of an accident in the Philadelphia lab. A cylinder of uranium hexafluoride gas had exploded, breaking some nearby steam pipes. The steam reacted with the gas to form incredibly corrosive hydrofluoric acid. The radioactive cloud had drenched two civilian scientists and a soldier. The acid-steam mixture had seared their entire bodies and they had inhaled large amounts of radioactive chemicals.

A soldier outside the room had braved the caustic cloud thrown up by the explosion and dragged the three men outside, where he cut off their clothing and got them into a shower. All three, Groves had been told by officials in Philadelphia, lay dying on the building's concrete floor. A priest had been called in to administer last rites. He finished with the first two, Douglas Meigs from Maryland and Peter Bragg from Arkansas, and moved on to the third, a soldier named Arnold Kramish. Kramish lay burned and blinded, but he was alive enough to tell the priest, "I'm not going to die. I refuse to die." Corpsmen rushed him to a hospital, but there had been some delay and confusion in treating him there because Groves had classified the procedure for treating radiation burns.

Agnes felt queasy reading the vivid description of the accident and the men's injuries. She assumed she now knew why Groves had sent Lansdale rushing to Philadelphia: to help those poor, stricken people, of course. But the next transcriptions disabused her of that notion. As soon as Lansdale reached the naval yard, Groves had repeated to him over the phone the orders he'd given him before he left D.C., and he expanded on them. Lansdale's primary task was to make sure word of the accident did not reach beyond the walls of the building where it happened. Even the families were not to know. Groves said his biggest concern was for other workers; he didn't want them to hear about the accident and be so frightened they'd leave the project.

Lansdale had gotten right to work. When Meigs' s wife arrived at the Philadelphia train station, hoping to lure her husband away for a weekend of R-and-R, she was met by one of Lansdale's deputies, who sadly informed her that her husband had died at work, but he couldn't give her any details. Bragg's family had received a similarly vague notification. Lansdale had met Groves's chief medical officer, Colonel Stafford Warren, who'd also been dispatched to Philadelphia, and had taken him to the bodies.

Warren collected the men's now radioactive internal organs and shipped them to Oak Ridge for testing. Technically, because they were now laced with uranium, and the Manhattan Project controlled all uranium in any form in the country, the organs had become classified material. Groves had ordered the bodies surrendered to the families with no mention of the missing parts. The last thing Agnes gleaned from the transcriptions was that the soldier, Arnold Kramish, was still alive and had regained his sight. He had been ordered to keep his mouth shut.

Groves's handling of the Philadelphia incident did not surprise Agnes. She knew the President had set up an Office of Censorship to prevent word of the project from getting out. And she had read reports of how Groves dealt with reporters who somehow managed to penetrate Groves's veil of secrecy. A Cleveland reporter had sniffed out the fact that the military was up to something in the remote reaches of New Mexico; he had even shown up at the gates to Los Alamos, where he was, of course, turned away. He didn't have the whole story--he speculated that the army was doing research on chemical weapons or some sort of explosives--but what he reported, including the fact that renowned physicist Robert Oppenheimer was leading the effort, infuriated Groves. The general proposed drafting the reporter and posting him to the South Pacific to put an end to his snooping, but backed away from that idea when his investigators informed him the reporter was over sixty.

Groves had taken a tougher approach when a Pennsylvania radio commentator told millions of people in his Mutual Broadcasting System audience that the U.S. had already built an atomic bomb and planned to use it soon. Groves had the man picked up and hauled to Washington, where investigators subjected him to a full day of questioning. The security men reported that the radio man claimed someone else wrote the script and he couldn't remember who told him about the project. Again, Groves erupted angrily, urging Lansdale to prosecute the commentator for revealing highly classified information. Lansdale dutifully documented that he had informed Groves that the government itself might have violated the law by snatching the broadcaster from Pennsylvania and driving him to Washington. Again, Groves had agreed to drop the matter, but he ordered Lansdale and his men to redouble their scrutiny of the press to prevent any further disclosures.

Agnes's emotions ranged across the spectrum as she processed the documents flowing across her desk. Some, like the accounts of General Groves's battle with reporters, made her smile. Others, the more technical ones, left her confused with their diagrams and formulas. And some, like the report on the civilian deaths from the bombing raid in Norway and the tragic deaths of two young men in Philadelphia, made her sad. But, in every instance, she told herself that her feelings were not important in Room 5120. All of the documents, letters, transcriptions, reports, were part of what had to be done to get the war over with. None of the documents, not even the ones that left her feeling uneasy and a little fearful, had made her feel personally threatened. The next document she picked up changed all of that.

It was a letter from project physicist Arthur Compton to Secretary of War Stimson. Stimson had sent it on to Groves with a hand-written note attached that read: *Is this on the level? Do we know one way or the other whether what he's talking about is actually a possibility? I await your reassurance that it is not. HLS*

Agnes lifted Stimson's note and read the letter. Compton told Stimson he needed to make the secretary aware of what some scientists at Los Alamos were talking about. He said Oppenheimer had recently told him that Edward Teller was speculating that the bomb they were creating might generate so much heat that it would ignite the earth's atmosphere and destroy the planet. Teller was already theorizing about an even more powerful bomb, built on a fusion reaction rather than the fission model at the heart of the gadget. Compton said Teller wondered if the fission bomb might cause a fusion reaction between the nitrogen atoms in the atmosphere that would instantly vaporize the entire globe in a massive nuclear blast. Compton said Oppenheimer had sent the theoretical physicists back to the drawing board to recrunch the numbers to see if Teller's speculation was valid. Compton concluded by saying he didn't mean to speak out of turn by writing the letter, but he thought if Stimson hadn't already been informed about the speculation, he would certainly want to know. At the bottom, Groves had scribbled: *Meddling scientists! If they'd just do their jobs, things would be just fine.*

Beneath the letter, Agnes found the transcription of a phone call, dated the same day Groves had received the letter from Stimson, in which Groves had ordered Oppenheimer to Washington, post haste, to explain what was going on in New Mexico. He told Oppenheimer he was incensed that the scientists were engaging in such loose talk, and ordered him to shut them up before such ideas found their way to other parts of the project. He said he did not want the project impeded by fear.

Agnes realized, as she laid the letter on her desk, that her hands were shaking. At that moment, her desk mate, Eleanor, had glanced up from her work and looked fondly at her good friend. She saw Agnes blanch, and noticed that the paper she was laying down was rattling slightly. She reached her hand toward Agnes.

"Agnes, are you all right? You look like you've seen a ghost."

Agnes's head jerked up, her face pale, a startled look in her eyes. She forced a weak smile.

"Oh no, Eleanor, I'm fine. Probably just a little tired. We've been working so hard lately."

Eleanor wished she could ask Agnes what was really going on, but she knew, no matter how close their friendship had brought them, their involvement in this secret project made that impossible. In lieu of a confiding ear, she flashed Agnes what she hoped was an encouraging smile.

"I know you can't tell me what it is, but if there's anything I can do to help you feel better, I'm right here."

Eleanor's sensitivity touched Agnes.

"Thank you, Eleanor. It does make me feel better, just hearing you say that."

She smiled and returned to her work, but what she really longed to do was rush into Morris's arms and tell him about it, and hear his gentle voice telling her not to worry, it would be all right. That, of course, was not possible. Across the desk, Eleanor heard her dear friend sigh. Before Agnes had even finished her thought of Morris, she told herself that this horrifying speculation about the bomb was simply another boulder she must pile onto the growing mountain of disturbing details to lock away. She also knew, in her youthful wisdom, that this secret—that the bomb might bring an end to the world—would exact a higher price on her peace of mind than anything she had learned so far.

****

In December, Robert Furman sent a cable, followed by a report, documenting an even bigger success than the discovery of Germany's uranium cache. He and Goudsmit had apprehended a German nuclear scientist holed up in Strasbourg. Letters in the scientist's office confirmed that the Nazi bomb program had been decentralized from Berlin to small towns in the Black Forest. That intelligence led to other scientists and a nuclear reactor project in a mountain cave. Furman and Goudsmit had interrogated the Germans for two straight days. The report included Goudsmit's conclusions: "The evidence at hand proves definitely that Germany has no real atom bomb program and is not likely to have one in any reasonable time."

At the end of the report, Furman included a verbatim recounting of his conversation with Goudsmit after the mission was completed. In the margin, knowing that Groves was perpetually aggravated by the way the scientists tended to think, he had penciled: *Thought you'd want to hear this. Scientists!* Goudsmit: Isn't it wonderful that the Germans have no atom bomb. Now we won't have to use ours. Furman: Of course you understand, Sam, if we have such a weapon, we are going to use it."

Agnes had felt a sense of relief akin to Goudsmit's as she read Furman's report. In the past weeks, Teller's speculation about the gadget had, as she'd predicted to herself, begun to haunt her. And even though she would never have allowed herself to question what Groves was building, the idea that it might never have to be used crept into her mind. Goudsmit's conclusion was perfectly logical. But, on the other hand, what choice did General Groves have? The order for the atom bomb came directly from the President, and Groves was relentless in driving himself and everyone connected to the project to get it done. As O'Leary had said, it would win the war. Then again, if the Germans had nothing to compare with it and the Allies were already gaining the upper hand, the President might not need it. Agnes couldn't work it all out. She shook her head to clear her mind, picked up the stack of documents, and walked to the filing cabinets.

Agnes succeeded, for the most part, in putting the concerns of the project aside when she returned to Mrs. Sisko's each evening. But even there, the trials and tribulations of a nation at war intruded more and more into the carefree atmosphere she and Naomi and the other girls had once enjoyed. Naomi made a valiant effort to play her usual part, the teasing, laughing life of the party. But losing Franklin had plunged her into a grief so deep she continued to struggle to put on a happy face for her friends. Agnes, more than any of the others, knew how she felt and made a special effort to stay close to steady her. Many nights, after everyone had gone to bed, the sisters sat in Naomi's room, Agnes with her arm around Naomi's shoulders and

Naomi leaning against Agnes, her slender frame racked by heaving sighs and a flood of tears.

Mid-April, 1945, would inflict even more pain on these young women, as it would on people across the nation. On April 12th, after dinner, the girls and Mrs. Sisko gathered as usual around the parlor radio to enjoy the evening programming. They switched on the set, but instead of the comedy show they were expecting, they heard a news announcer telling them that President Roosevelt was dead. According to the reporter, the President had been resting at his retreat in Warm Springs, Georgia, when he succumbed to what appeared to be a massive cerebral hemorrhage. The announcer said plans were already underway for bringing the President's body back to Washington and then on to his Hyde Park estate in New York for burial.

For a long moment, everyone in the room sat in stunned silence. Then, Naomi, already numbed by the loss of Franklin, began to weep. Agnes moved to comfort her, her eyes moist with tears. Mrs. Sisko looked around the room and felt a deep compassion for these girls, so young in years and in life experience, who had come to Washington to serve their country in a time of crisis, only to have this heavy burden added to the already considerable weight of war. She reached out to each of them with tears rolling down her cheeks, embracing them, patting them on the back and encouraging them to have faith and be strong in the face of such tragic news.

Agnes began reciting the Twenty Third Psalm in her mind. *The Lord is my shepherd, I shall not want.* As it always did in times like this, each word of the psalm helped to soothe her troubled mind. *He maketh me to lie down in green pastures.* As she thought her way through the psalm, she looked at the distraught faces of her young friends around the room. The girls generally followed the wisdom Agnes had learned from Irene: Two topics to avoid in friendly conversation are politics and religion. But in this moment, as they all struggled to know what the President's death would mean to the nation, the war, themselves, Agnes decided to ignore the sage advice. She stood and addressed the emotional group.

"I think it might help all of us if we recited the Twenty Third Psalm together."

The girls, even those not prone to expressions of spirituality, nodded. Naomi found her voice to say, "Yes, Agnes, that would be a good thing to do."

With her eyes closed, Agnes led them through a somewhat ragged but entirely fervent recitation of the beloved psalm.

The Lord is my shepherd, I shall not want, He maketh me to lie down in green pastures, He leadeth me beside still waters. He restoreth my soul. He leadeth me in the paths of righteousness, for His name's sake. Yea, though I walk through the valley of the shadow of death--some of the girls' voices quavered at this point--*I will fear no evil, for Thou art with me; Thy rod and Thy staff, they comfort me. Thou preparest a table before me, in the presence of mine enemies; Thou annointest my head with oil; my cup runneth over. Surely goodness and mercy shall follow me all the days of my life, and I will dwell in the house of the Lord forever.*

When they'd finished, Agnes intoned a heart-felt "Amen," which all of the girls repeated after her. The girls thanked Agnes for leading them and told her it did make them feel a little better, less alone in facing this terrible development. Most of them gave Agnes a hug and headed off to bed. Once again, the youngest member of the group had provided the greatest sense of strength, maturity and stability. Naomi was the last to leave the parlor. She squeezed Agnes's hand and kissed her on the cheek.

"Good night, Sis. Thank you for being you."

Agnes smiled and sat down, her mind whirling with thoughts about what FDR's death would mean. She pictured countless families back home who had been rescued from the abyss of the Great Depression by the President's New Deal. Young as she had been when he put it in place, she had seen men getting back to work, and families again able to buy enough food to feed their children. She remembered the chain-smoking artist who had come to Southwestern Pennsylvania under the WPA to record in oils the rural countryside of Pennsylvania and West Virginia. He had given one of his paintings to her brother's buddy, Allen Flaherty. Neil, Jr. and Allen had spent many hours talking to the artist and watching him paint. Would those programs continue under a new president? Back in Smithfield, Irene had tacked a picture of FDR on the kitchen wall, and had called the children into the living room to hear his fireside chats on the radio. The whole family had become very fond of Franklin Roosevelt, a man of privilege who had devoted much of his life to helping the disadvantaged. Agnes and Irene especially liked the First Lady, Eleanor, who had shown the nation through her writing and public speaking that it was high time women had a voice in the real issues facing the nation. Like most Americans, the Jenkins family had no idea how sick the President really was. That made his sudden passing even more shocking.

Agnes thought about what this would mean for the Manhattan Project. It was, after all, FDR who had assigned it directly to the army and to General Groves. She'd never seen any documents indicating that Vice President Truman even knew about it. They'd have to tell him about it now. What if he, as President, decided to stop it? Would he understand, as President Roosevelt had understood, that this was the project that would end the war? Or would he realize, after reading Goudsmit's comments, that they didn't need to use the bomb at all? She sat in the parlor for some time, thinking and praying. She may have been the only nineteen year old in America having such thoughts at nine o'clock in the evening on April 12, 1945.

The girls at Mrs. Sisko's house, along with the rest of the nation, followed the next dark days through radio reports and the newspaper. They heard descriptions of the crowds that lined the tracks as FDR's funeral train made its way from Georgia to Washington. They heard children in Greenville, South Carolina leading a crowd of ten thousand trackside mourners in "Onward Christian Soldiers."

The reporters were there when the train pulled into Washington's Union Station. The President's copper and mahogany casket, wrapped in the flag, was placed on a black-draped military caisson pulled by six mounted white horses, with a seventh riderless horse beside them in honor of the fallen Commander-in-Chief. The announcers informed the nation that those in attendance at the station included President Truman, White House war advisor James Byrnes, Commerce Secretary Henry Wallace, and Secretary of War Stimson.

Agnes wondered what Stimson was thinking as the funeral procession moved slowly away from the station for the mile long march to the White House.

Everyone in her office, except General Groves and Mrs. O'Leary, joined the throngs of weeping people that lined Constitution Avenue and the rest of the route to the White House. It broke Agnes's heart to see her fellow Americans, young, old, black, white, men, women, is such a terrible state of grief. The tap-tap of the drums in the honor guard rang out in the reverent atmosphere along Washington's streets.

After the procession had gone by, Agnes rushed back to the office to hear the radio reports of the funeral service at the White House. She heard a military band playing the national anthem as the President's casket was carried up the front steps and then wheeled down a long, red carpet to the East Room, the same room, the announcer said, where President Lincoln had lain after he fell to an assassin's bullet. Banks of lilies lined the East Room walls as officials crowded in for the Episcopal funeral service. The announcer said there were so many in attendance that the crowd overflowed into the Blue Room.

At exactly four o'clock that afternoon, the telegraph and the radio signals went dead and Americans everywhere stopped their work in a moment of silence to honor the nation's fallen leader. Then bells rang and ship whistles blew in respectful observance of the nation's great loss. At the White House, Bishop Angus Dun eulogized the President, quoting FDR's own words from a Fireside Chat to reassure a worried nation: The only thing we have to fear is fear itself. Then the funeral procession retraced its measured steps to Union Station and the President's casket was loaded onto the funeral train for the final leg of the journey to his estate in Hyde Park, where he was buried.

CHAPTER TEN

One of Mrs. O'Leary's phone transcriptions and a report filed by Groves's top assistant, Brigadier General Thomas F. Farrell, soon answered Agnes's questions about President Truman and his knowledge of the project. Farrell's report confirmed that Roosevelt had died without informing the Vice President of the a-bomb project.

Farrell said Truman's staff had contacted Groves some time ago; Truman had heard rumors of a secret weapons project and wanted to know what was going on. Groves referred the inquiries to Stimson, who had convinced the Vice President not to look into them. Truman's staff had been told the project--a central element in winning the war-- was classified "Top Secret" to prevent our enemies from catching wind of it. Stimson urged Truman's staff to understand that no one outside the project and only a handful of people inside were privy to its essential details. The Secretary said a Washington state congressman had tried to force his way into one of the project work sites--Stimson did not give the location-- but had instead been taken to an interrogation room where he was questioned about what he knew rather than being briefed on what the army was doing.

Mrs. O'Leary had transcribed a phone call Groves received from the White House, shortly after FDR's funeral, ordering the general to meet the President in the Oval Office to give him a full explanation of the project. Farrell's report ended with a summary of the Oval Office conversation, in which Groves had explained what he was doing, under direct orders from FDR. Farrell reported that Truman immediately embraced the new weapon, and told Groves to keep him posted on its timely completion.

As she made her way home that night, Agnes realized that the war and this dangerous weapon had permeated virtually every corner of her life. Every day in the office new documents crossed her desk detailing the progress toward the bomb. At Mrs. Sisko's, Naomi still struggled with losing the man she loved so much, and the other girls fretted about whether the war would end before their brothers and sweethearts were killed. She and Naomi shared that same concern; Neil, Jr. and his buddy, Allen Flaherty, had signed up the minute they finished high school, and were in training right this minute; Neil, Jr. to man a tailgun on a B-29; Allen, his flyboy dreams dashed, was becoming a radioman. And the trusted President who had led the nation into war had been taken away. Agnes's only escape was her time with Morris. She found herself cherishing each and every moment with him.

Three weeks after FDR's funeral, they were dining in a restaurant not far from the Capitol, avoiding talk of war, chatting instead about childhood memories, places they had visited with their families, how long Morris thought Agnes should let her hair grow, and whether or not Agnes thought Morris should grow a mustache. They had just tucked into their peach pie a la mode when a waiter burst through the swinging doors from the kitchen. He rushed into the midst of the diners, solicited their attention, and then addressed them in a voice quavering with excitement.

"Ladies and gentlemen, the Nazis have just surrendered, unconditionally, to the Allied forces! The war in Europe is over!"

The room erupted. Everyone jumped to their feet and began hugging whoever they had come with, and then anyone, friend or stranger, they could get hold of. Agnes and Morris embraced and kissed. The pie was forgotten. They pulled on their coats and ran outside to catch a cab back to the boarding house. The girls were still jumping up and down when they arrived. Even Naomi had been buoyed by the news, which they'd all heard on the radio in the parlor. Morris stayed with Agnes and the others for another hour or so, then invited all of them to go bowling with him and his friends the next night to celebrate V-E Day, which the radio announcer told them the President had declared for the next day, May 8th. The girls took turns using Mrs. Sisko's phone to call home and share their excitement with family. Morris headed for the apartment he shared with his friends to do the same.

When Agnes finally reached her room that night she opened her Bible to Mark chapter 14 and read several verses aloud to herself: *And going a little farther, he threw himself on the ground and prayed that, if it were possible, the hour might pass from him. He said, "Abba, Father, for you all things are possible; remove this cup from me; yet, not what I want but what you want."*

She gently closed the book and knelt down by her bed to pray. "Lord, thank you for the end of the fighting in Europe. May your will be done to bring an end to the war with Japan as well, before Neil and Allen Flaherty and so many others are called upon to give their lives for their country. And, Lord, may this wonderful news tonight mean that the Manhattan Project need not be finished. I know General Groves and President Truman are your servants and only doing your will in creating this terrible weapon, but if the need for it might pass, it would make all of our lives less frightening. I pray for peace in my heart, Lord. But as Jesus taught us, thy will be done in all things. Comfort Naomi and keep everyone at home safe. Amen."

As fervent as her prayer might have been, Agnes soon learned that not all of it would be answered as she had wished. General Groves made more frequent visits to Oak Ridge, Hanford and Los Alamos. He took with him copies of reports documenting the quickening pace of the project. A growing supply of enriched plutonium, U-235, was arriving at Los Alamos. According to the reports, it was shipped from Hanford in converted army ambulances, guarded by soldiers with submachine guns. The documents noted that the plutonium was delivered in a nitrate solution, a bluish slurry, eighty grams worth in each metal container, each container packed inside a sixteen-by-sixteen inch wooden box.

At Los Alamos, technicians mixed the slurry with gallium, a rare type of metal that Agnes had never heard of, that allowed them to shape it into what they called cores, the size of a tennis ball. Diagrams, accompanied by technical notation Agnes couldn't decipher, showed the cores being pressed into hemispheres and coated with nickel, to prevent oxidation and to contain the radioactivity.

A phone transcription detailed Groves's recent conversation with Oppenheimer, who had convinced the general some time ago that they needed to test the gadget to make sure the physicists and engineers had it right. Groves repeated his concern that a test gone bad would simply deplete the supply of enriched plutonium available for the weapon the army would ultimately use. In the phone call, Groves and Oppenheimer agreed to change the date for the test-- which Oppenheimer had dubbed Trinity--from July 1st to July 16th.

Agnes was startled by Oppenheimer's name for the test of an atomic bomb; for her, the Trinity was the Father, Son, and Holy Ghost. She couldn't imagine why Oppenheimer would attach such a sacred name to this beastly weapon.   Groves had promised to have the weapon in working order by the time Truman sat down with Churchill and Stalin at Yalta to work out the reorganization of Europe. The President was eager to have the ultimate weapon in hand as he negotiated with Stalin, a man the U.S. had already grown leery of. Groves pushed Oppenheimer on his ability to deliver the bomb on schedule.

Oppenheimer had confirmed that the gadget was coming together nicely, since they'd solved the trigger problem. Agnes had seen diagrams of the trigger, and had processed reports on the engineering work underway to design and build it, but she didn't even try to figure out why a bomb needed a trigger. Oppenheimer also told Groves work was proceeding at the test site, the Alamogordo Bombing Range, four hundred twenty three square miles of deserted land in central New Mexico's Jornada del Muerto (the documents had translated that *Journey of Death)* Valley, chosen because it was close enough to Los Alamos but far enough away from civilians to prevent them from claiming exposure to radiation from the blast and filing lawsuits. Groves had been emphatic about that. His concern was to get the test over with without attracting attention that would tip off the enemy.

The reports now were from Kenneth T. Bainbridge, who had located the test site and was responsible for preparing it for the gadget. His assistant was Oppenheimer's brother, Frank. Together, they had overseen construction of a one hundred foot steel tower, called the shot tower, from which the bomb would be suspended and detonated, a base camp located ten miles south-southwest, and three observation shelters to the south, west and north of the tower (designated Ground Zero), each ten thousand yards from where the bomb would go off, if it worked. The shelters were built of wood reinforced with concrete and covered with earth. The work crew, including soldiers and scientists from Los Alamos and local construction workers, totaled more than two hundred.

It was at this point, around the middle of June, 1945, that those closest to Agnes--Morris, Naomi, Eleanor, Mrs. Sisko and the girls at the boarding house-- noticed a gradual change in her. She was still her usual, serious self most of the time, but her sober demeanor was punctuated less often by her bright smile; she seldom laughed. The circles that had long darkened the spaces beneath her eyes grew even grayer. She looked as if she were not sleeping well.

Naomi noticed the change first. She followed Agnes to her room one night and asked her about it.

"Are you feeling okay, Sis? You don't have your usual glow of health these days."

Agnes sat down on the bed and sighed. She longed to be able to share with Naomi, her closest, dearest friend in the world, the fear and anguish that had come to haunt her day and night. But her sense of duty told her she could not. She tried to deflect her sister's concern.

"Oh, Naomi, I'm all right. I know I look a little tired lately. It's probably because we're working so hard at the office. You wouldn't believe how much paperwork this project creates. Report after report after report. I think I'm just a little worn down."

Naomi sensed there was much more to it than that. She didn't doubt that Agnes was tired, but she suspected something more taxing than typing and filing was responsible. Her thoughts jumped to a more dangerous possibility.

"Agnes, are you sick? You've been through a lot since you got here, what with the burst appendix and all. If you were sick, you'd tell me, wouldn't you?"

She sat down beside Agnes and put her arm around her.

"You would, wouldn't you?"

Agnes turned toward her and smiled.

"Of course, I would. I can't keep anything from you. We're like two halves of one soul. The intuition we inherited from Mom works both ways. Yes, if I were sick, you'd be the first to know."

Naomi was determined to get to the bottom of this.

"Okay, so are you having problems with Morris? He hasn't said or done something he shouldn't has he?"

This time Agnes burst out laughing.

"Oh, Sis, you slay me. I'd tell you if I were having problems with Morris even quicker than if I had some dread disease. Who else would I turn to for romantic advice, if not my vivacious older sister?"

Naomi had run out of ideas, but her concern was unabated.

"Honey, I don't want anything to get in the way of you having a long, beautiful life. But if you tell me there's really nothing wrong, I guess I'll have to accept it. Maybe you should get more rest, if the work is so tiring." She got a twinkle in her eye. "Of course, that would mean seeing less of Morris." She snickered at her own joke.

Agnes chuckled, too, and leaned toward Naomi to kiss her lightly on the cheek.

"I don't know if I can see less of Morris. But I will try to get more sleep. Don't worry about me. I'm just younger than you are; I don't have the stamina that keeps you going."

Both girls laughed. Agnes had always been sturdier than Naomi. She never missed a day of high school in four years. Naomi had been out for a variety of illnesses, most seriously scarlet fever when she was a junior. She'd missed so much school she almost wasn't able to graduate with her class.

Naomi sighed. She stood up and turned to look at Agnes.

"Well, sweetie, if sleep is all you need, I'm going to let you get some." She walked to the door and turned back toward Agnes. "Good night, Sis. Sleep tight, don't let the bed bugs bite." She smiled as she walked out of the room and pulled the door closed behind her.

Agnes sat on the bed, her hands in her lap. Then she stood and walked to her dressing table and gazed into the broad mirror attached to it. She switched on the table lamp on the edge of the table and looked at herself. She had never liked the circles under her eyes. She envied Naomi, who never seemed to have them, but then Naomi used a lot more makeup than Agnes did, so it was a little hard to know whether she got them or not. She picked up her tooth brush and toothpaste and walked down the carpeted hall toward the bathroom. She wished so much that she could tell Naomi the truth. She tried never to lie, not even little, white ones, but she was trapped by her conscience and her obligations. She had given General Groves her word, and she must keep it, no matter how hard it was to bottle up the torrent of frightening information swirling around her at work.

Mrs. Sisko realized something was happening to Agnes shortly after Naomi did. The first sign was that Agnes was packing hardly any lunch to take to the office. When she'd first arrived, she'd taken a whole sandwich, an apple, and a cookie or two. Some days now she skipped the sandwich and tossed only an apple into her brown paper bag. In the evening, Mrs. Sisko noticed that Agnes took smaller and smaller helpings as the bowls were passed around the dinner table. She thought it strange that this sturdy, young country girl, who had always eaten so well, seemed to have lost her appetite. Then she thought of Agnes's friend, Morris. Maybe this lovely young woman was trying to look even lovelier by losing weight for her beau. She considered asking Agnes about it, but she decided not to. She always tried to respect the girls' privacy; she was reluctant to approach any of them about such personal things.

Morris saw it, too. He observed the darkening shadows beneath Agnes's eyes, but assumed she was just tired, as everyone often was during these difficult war years. What set off alarms for him was the night he and Agnes embraced on Mrs. Sisko's front porch after a night out. He loved her figure and the fullness he felt when he hugged her. But this night it seemed as if she had shrunk overnight. Her sweater hung loose on her shoulders; she felt almost fragile. He kissed her and then stepped back to look at her. There was no doubt she had lost weight.

"Agnes, what's happening to you? You're disappearing before my eyes. Where's that shapely girl I fell in love with?"

Agnes's eyes welled up and her lip quivered.

"Oh, Morris, I really, really wish I could tell you. But it's just not possible. I'm not sick, though, if that makes you feel any better."

"What do you mean you can't tell me? If you can't tell me, who can you tell? What's wrong, Agnes?"

She threw herself in his arms; he pulled her close, and stroked her hair.

"Agnes, What is it?"

She looked up at him pleadingly.

"I can't tell you or anyone, my love. It's just the war and stuff I can't talk about. And one way or the other, it will soon be over, and I'm sure I'll be all right then."

She put her arms around him and pulled him even closer.

"Just hold me, Morris. That's all I need."

They stood on the porch together, silently, for several minutes. Morris could smell her cologne, and felt her body trembling slightly in his arms. Agnes luxuriated in the brief moment of security she found in his embrace. Then she pulled free and stepped toward the front door.

"Good night, sweet prince, parting is such sweet sorrow. Good night."

She blew him a kiss which he caught and applied softly to his lips.

"Good night, Agnes. Sleep well."

Just as their tender farewells ended, the front door opened and Mrs. Sisko appeared in the doorway, framed by the light in the hallway behind her.

"Good evening, Morris. Thank you for seeing Agnes home safely. Come in, Agnes. It's getting late."

She took Agnes's arm and guided her into the house. Mrs. Sisko smiled at Morris, closed the door and turned off the porch light.

****

Eleanor had seen the shadows lengthening below Agnes's eyes, as well. She also noticed that Agnes's face seemed thinner, her high cheekbones more prominent. She'd observed similar changes in several of the girls in the office, as the project ground toward its goal. But as she looked across the gray, steel desks at this young woman she'd become so attached to, she thought Agnes's face was more drawn than most. She hoped Agnes was all right. She thought about asking her if she was okay. But she, too, knew that Agnes was not one to dwell on the downside of things, nor did she tend to share her most private thoughts and feelings.

Eleanor was fairly certain that their friendship was deep enough that Agnes would voluntarily tell her if something was really wrong. She was sure her own face showed a similar anxiety, a nervousness they were all feeling as July 16th approached. Even though they observed General Groves's edict not to discuss the specifics of their work, everyone in the room was hoping the test would go well, and the bomb would work. Eleanor told herself that was probably all that was wrong with Agnes. She just took everything a little more seriously than anyone else, with the exception of the general and Mrs. O'Leary, of course.

It was a logical conclusion for her to reach. But Eleanor and the other girls had not seen Stimson's letter to Groves, the letter that told of Teller's speculation that detonating an atomic bomb might trigger a nuclear conflagration large enough to annihilate the human race. She also had not seen the transcriptions of the angry phone calls from Bainbridge, who was furious that the scientists at Los Alamos kept talking about the Trinity test destroying every living thing on earth. Only Groves and O'Leary and nineteen year old Agnes Jenkins had seen those. And of that trio, only Groves and O'Leary knew that physicist Hans Bethe had recomputed the possibility of such a holocaust and concluded that it simply couldn't happen. Oppenheimer had told Groves that Bethe estimated the safety of the test at a factor of sixty.

So strong was Agnes's will power that not even the terror growing in her mind prevented her from focusing on the tasks at hand, processing and filing documents brought to her desk by Mrs. O'Leary. On July 10th, she opened a folder containing a photograph of the gadget. It didn't look like the bombs she'd seen pictures of before, with a point on one end and fins on the other. The gadget was a metal sphere with wires and sockets jutting out like pins in a pin cushion. Cables attached to the fixtures drooped loosely over its surface. At first glance, Agnes thought it looked almost comical, a Rube Goldberg device. But when she thought about what this odd-looking metal ball was meant to do, might do, she shuddered and quickly closed the folder.

Under that folder she found a report on the third target committee meeting that had been held in Oppenheimer's office at Los Alamos. With Germany out of the way, the committee had focused on where to use the bomb in Japan. Five original sites-- Kyoto, Hiroshima, Yokohama, the Kokura Arsenal, and Niigata--had been reduced to three--Kyoto, Hiroshima, and Niigata. An addendum to the report indicated that Secretary Stimson had scratched Kyoto, over Groves's objection, telling the committee Kyoto was an ancient Japanese city with significant cultural value and, in the aftermath of the war, he wanted to be able to tell the world that America had spared it out of humanitarian concern. In its place, the committee had added Nagasaki. Agnes was surprised the committee was moving forward so determinedly, considering that the future--*God help us all, she thought*-- might end on July 16th.

The last report Agnes processed before she went home that night detailed the security measures in place at the Trinity test site. It mentioned the three reinforced observation shelters positioned about six miles from Ground Zero where the gadget would be suspended from the one hundred foot high steel tower. A control site was set up about ten miles from Zero. The report listed the instruments installed to measure radiation from the blast (which it said would be used to calculate the destructive force of the explosion), and pointed out that vehicles would be standing by to evacuate soldiers and scientists if radiation levels rose unexpectedly high.

Pretests at Alamogordo had convinced Bainbridge to station one hundred sixty men off-site to evacuate local residents--ranchers, farmers, townspeople--if fallout from the blast moved in unexpected directions. Agnes wasn't sure what fallout was, but it sounded hazardous. The report concluded by noting that Groves had met with New Mexico Governor John J. Dempsey to alert him to the fact that, depending on what happened in the Jornada del Muerto Valley on July 16th, he should be prepared to declare martial law.

Agnes knew from the other reports that Groves, Oppenheimer, and Bainbridge had chosen Alamogordo because few people lived in the immediate area. Interior Secretary Harold Ickes had demanded that they protect any Native American people living within range of the blast. She also knew no civilians in New Mexico had any idea what was about to happen. She wondered what they would be thinking right now if they had been told. She thought they'd probably be frightened, as she was. And if they had known, she guessed that reading the security measures General Groves had put in place would have been small reassurance against a dangerous future.

The next day, July 11th, Groves and Vannevar Bush, the science advisor who had lobbied FDR to build the bomb, left Washington on a circuitous journey that would end at Los Alamos five days later. Agnes had already deposited the itinerary for the trip in the files.

Groves and Bush would be ten thousand feet from Ground Zero at four o'clock, Mountain War Time, on the sixteenth.

Agnes still joined the other girls for breakfast each morning, but her already shrunken appetite had all but disappeared by this time. She tried not to make it too obvious to her friends and Mrs. Sisko, but they all observed that she refused the oatmeal and eggs with hash browns she usually enjoyed in the morning, opting instead for a cup of coffee, a small glass of orange juice and a half-slice of toast. Mrs. Sisko couldn't bear to see this young woman wasting away. She pulled Agnes aside the morning of July 14th, as she readied herself to go out the door.

"Agnes, I don't mean to pry, but what is wrong? You look terrible, and it's obvious to everyone that you're not eating. Is there anything I can do?"

Agnes put her hand on Mrs. Sisko's arm and smiled at her.

"No, Mrs. S, there's really nothing you can do. I don't mean to cause anyone concern. There's just something on my mind that I can't talk about, and it has me pretty worried. It's nothing personal, if that's what you're thinking. I just have to deal with it."

Mrs. Sisko touched Agnes's cheek gently.

"Well, honey, I am worried about you, and so are all the rest of the girls. I just want you to know that we're here if you need us. Okay?"

She looked imploringly into Agnes's eyes. She saw them start to well up with tears, but then Agnes took a deep breath and cleared her throat to hold them back.

"Thank you, Mrs. Sisko, I know you all care and I'm sorry if I'm parading around with my problems on my sleeve. If I can ever tell you about it, I will. I wish I could now. But, in the meantime, I'm praying a lot and I'm sure the Lord will bear me up."

She kissed Mrs. Sisko on the cheek and patted her arm.

"I'd better go before I miss my bus. Mrs. O'Leary doesn't like us to be late."

She turned and walked out the front door. On her way down the front sidewalk she glanced back toward the house. Mrs. Sisko was standing in the doorway, a somber expression on her face. Agnes waved goodbye and smiled. Mrs. Sisko returned the wave, backed into the hallway, and closed the door.

Agnes spent most of that day and the next hoping against hope that a phone transcription would settle on her desk saying the test had been postponed or even called off completely. Instead, she processed endless reports and updates on preparations for Trinity. Every thump of the "Top Secret" stamp, every word she read, every file drawer she pulled open to deposit the papers enlarged her fear. She had always refrained from too much casual conversation during business hours, now she withdrew from her coworkers even more. Not even her beloved friend Eleanor could get through. Eleanor stole a glance at Agnes periodically throughout the day, and each time she felt pain in her heart to see this lovely girl, with the dazzling smile and bright eyes, so despondent.

By this time, Mrs. O'Leary had noticed Agnes's transformation, but as long as whatever was bothering Agnes didn't affect her work, there didn't seem to be any need to say anything. O'Leary knew Agnes was one of the youngest people in the office. She also knew the burden of secrecy they had asked this teenager to bear; she and Groves had been very pleased with Agnes's performance. They wanted no-nonsense workers, who carried out their duties and kept their mouths shut, and Agnes had been exactly that since her first day.

At five o'clock on the evening of July 15th, Agnes finished her filing for the day, cleared her desk of any sensitive documents, turned off her desk lamp, pushed her chair neatly against the desk, said good night to the girls who worked near her, and walked to the elevator. Eleanor hurried to catch up with her.

"Agnes, what are you doing tonight? Want to go bowling or something?"

As Agnes turned to look at her, the elevator bell rang and the doors slid open. They stepped to the back of the car and turned to face the front. As the elevator descended, Agnes leaned close to Eleanor.

"Bowling would be fun, but I'm not up to it tonight. I'm still feeling a little tired. I think I'll just go home and have an early night, and catch up on my rest."

She felt a little guilty responding to her dear friend that way. The truth was she hadn't been sleeping much at all for the past two weeks, and she doubted she could fall asleep this night, the night before the Trinity test. Eleanor took her at her word.

"All right, my dear. But promise me you'll go to bed early. I want you to get your beauty rest, you know?"

Agnes bumped Eleanor's shoulder and smiled.

"You are just too good to me, Eleanor. You worry more about my health than I do. I promise to take better care of myself."

When the elevator doors opened in the lobby, Agnes and Eleanor went their separate ways. Agnes stopped for a moment in front of McCleary's mural. She stepped closer to reread the plaque at the bottom. She looked at the title, "Defense of Human Freedom." She remembered being inspired by the mural and its title the first day she walked into the New War Building. She had believed then and still believed that good, Christian people sometimes had to step up and protect their freedoms. But she had never imagined that protecting freedom would ever call for creation of a weapon as devastating as the one about to be tested in New Mexico. She glanced at her watch and realized she needed to hurry or she'd miss the bus.

As soon as she walked in the front door of the boarding house, the phone rang. It was Morris calling, as he had every night since he noticed the changes in her, asking if he could come over or if she wanted to go out for dinner or a movie. As she had for the past week or so, Agnes thanked Morris for calling but told him she just wasn't up to a visit or a movie tonight. Morris kept the conversation going as long as he could, so he could listen to her voice and try to gauge how she was doing. Agnes worked hard to sound like her usual, sensible self, but Morris thought he heard a note of despondency, almost despair, under her calm responses. Finally, he wished her a restful night and told her he loved her. Agnes felt tears coming on. She told Morris she loved him, too, and then said a hasty goodnight and hung up.

Agnes took a deep breath, dabbed away her tears with a handkerchief, and joined the other girls and Mrs. Sisko in the dining room. Morris's phone call had made her the last to arrive. Everyone turned to look at her as she entered the room, her pale face blotchy with the emotion that gripped her, her eyes still moist from her tears. They all pushed back their chairs and rushed to comfort her. Naomi reached her first.

"Hey, Sis, what happened? Did Morris say something on the phone?"

Agnes struggled to regain her composure, but lost the battle. The tears rolled down her cheeks as Naomi pulled her close and the other girls gathered around them. Agnes couldn't think of anything to say. She clung to Naomi and sobbed. Mrs. Sisko pushed her way through the girls.

"Agnes, do you need a doctor? What is wrong?"

Agnes took another deep breath, and managed to speak to all of them. She was embarrassed and abjectly unhappy.

"I'm sorry to be doing this in front of all of you. There really isn't anything wrong with me. It's just...it's just..."

She wanted terribly to spill it all, get it out where these good friends could help share the burden. More than any time since she joined the Manhattan Project, she wanted to share her secrets, tell them everything. She knew it would make her feel better. But breaking her oath to General Groves was something Agnes Jenkins could not do. No matter the cost to her personally, she was in this thing for the duration, every bit as much as Neil, Jr. or Allen Flaherty or any of the other boys from Smithfield and the rest of the country who had signed on to protect our freedoms and win the war. Agnes pulled away from Naomi and looked around the room at the concerned faces of these young women she had come to love almost as much as she loved her family.

"You are all such wonderful people. I thank God for you every night. And I will tonight, too. But this is a struggle I can't share with any of you. Thank you for caring so much. I hope I am half as good at that when each of you faces trials and tribulations. I'm sorry to be such a mess. I think I'll just turn in early and let this thing run its course."

Her face clouded up and more tears rolled down her cheeks.

"I'm okay, though, I really am. This is just a rough patch I need to get through. I'm sure I'll feel better in the morning. Good night."

As she turned to leave, Naomi grabbed her wrist.

"Do you want me to come up with you and keep you company?"

"No, Sis, it's okay. I'll be all right by myself."

They all wished her good night as she left the room and walked toward the stairs. In her room, Agnes sat down on the bed and reached for her Bible. For a long moment, she held it in her hands with her eyes closed, trying to settle her mind. Then she opened the book and turned to the Psalms. She read several of David's pleas for the Lord to give him strength and peace. Finally, she came to her favorite, the Twenty-Third. She read it slowly, trying to extract the feeling of peace and security it had given her so many times before. But this night, it remained words on the page. She did not feel God's hand reaching toward her to stem the rising tide of fear. She laid the Bible on her night stand and knelt beside the bed to pray. She remained on her knees, hands clasped in front of her, eyes tight shut, for more than an hour.

Around eight o'clock she heard a gentle tap at her door. Naomi opened it and leaned her head in.

"Sis, I saw your light was still on. Are you going to sleep soon? It's already eight o'clock. If you're going to get some extra rest, you'd better get started."

Agnes looked up from the bedside, her hands still clasped tightly in front of her.

"You're right, I should get to bed. I will soon, I promise."

Naomi blew her a kiss and closed the door. Agnes stood up and undressed. Then she pulled her nightgown over her head and walked down the hall to wash her face and brush her teeth. When she returned, she pulled down the covers and climbed into bed. She did not turn the light off and she kept her watch on. She lay in bed half-thinking and half-praying. She closed her eyes now and then, hoping the dark curtain of sleep would descend on her and allow her to escape her fear for even a few moments. But it did not come. She watched the hours tick slowly by on her watch.

At six o'clock she rose and started dressing for work. She felt as if she were moving through molasses, her mind totally preoccupied with what was about to happen. She knew from the reports that Trinity was supposed to happen at four a-m, Mountain War Time, that was seven a-m Washington time--just one hour from now. She had no idea what a person should be thinking, alone in a room, during the last sixty minutes of her life. She had already prayed for her family and her friends and Morris and all of the good people of the world. And for herself. She had been so happy, so deliriously happy, to have met Morris and to have him love her as much as she loved him. She'd been excited to be in Washington during wartime, doing her part to help bring peace.

She looked at her watch--6:45. She sat down at her dressing table and stared into the mirror. Agnes Jenkins, nineteen years old going on twenty, in love, in Washington for the first real job of her life, about to be vaporized with the rest of the human race, the good incinerated with the bad. She suddenly realized that a sense of calm had come over her. God had answered her prayer. She was going to her great reward in her right mind, happy with her life, and sorry it hadn't lasted longer, so she could marry Morris and know the wonder of giving birth, the joy of raising children.

She turned away from the mirror and gazed at her picture of Morris. She thought him the handsomest guy she'd ever seen. He was certainly the nicest, most considerate man she'd ever known. And he was the only man she'd ever loved, would ever love. She thanked God for the moments she and Morris had shared together. Then she looked at her watch--6:55. She stared at the second hand as it swept around the dial. She pictured the gadget suspended from the platform atop the steel tower. She saw General Groves and Oppenheimer and the others peering through the slit in the front of the observation posts, waiting for the end.

6:58--then 6:59. Agnes imagined she could hear the final countdown. She knew everyone at the test site was hearing it over the P-A system Bainbridge had installed. She could think of nothing but that voice, the countdown to eternity: sixty seconds--fifty-nine seconds--fifty-eight seconds--fifty-seven seconds. Agnes reached for her Bible and then sat absolutely still at the dressing table. Ten-nine-eight-seven-six-five-four-three-two-one-now!   Agnes strained to hear the roar and feel the heat of the fire that would incinerate the world.

Ten seconds passed, then thirty, then a full minute. Nothing. No sound, no fury, nothing but sunlight shining through her bedroom window and the sound of cars passing by on the street out front. Agnes opened her bedroom door. She saw the girls rushing around, getting ready for another day of work in Washington. Her spirits soared. It hadn't happened. The bomb didn't ignite the world, everyone was still alive. Agnes was absolutely jubilant as she bounced down the stairs and into the kitchen. Her appetite had come racing back. She ate a bowl of oatmeal, two eggs with toast, and packed a whole sandwich for lunch. The other girls were stunned to see the radical transformation from the night before, but they didn't question it. They hugged her and told her the beauty rest really worked.

Agnes was still euphoric when she walked into Room 5120 at eight o' clock on the dot. Mrs. O'Leary was pacing around the office with a scowl on her face. She called Agnes over to her.

"Agnes, I want you to be on stand-by this morning, in case I need you to do some quick typing."

"Certainly, Mrs. O'Leary. Was General Groves pleased with the test?"

O'Leary gave her an annoyed look.

"What test? They've had bad weather out there all night. The test hasn't even happened yet. They postponed it till 5:30 MWT, that's

8:30 our time. We won't know if Trinity worked for another half hour or longer."

Agnes suddenly felt light-headed. The scene in Room 5120 began to whirl. She clutched at the edge of a nearby desk. O'Leary grabbed her arm.

"What is it, Agnes? Are you feeling ill?"

Agnes steadied herself and took a deep breath.

"No, I've just been a bit tired lately."

"Yes, I've noticed that. Well, things are going to start hopping around here in a few minutes. Why don't you go sit down at your desk and wait till I need your help?"

Agnes made her way through the maze of office furniture, pulled out her desk chair and sat down heavily. She couldn't think, she couldn't pray, her mind was spinning. She sat erect in her chair and stared at the clock on the wall, waiting for it to reach 8:30, the new time for the test. As the hour approached, she no longer imagined hearing the countdown. Now she sat straining to hear the first sound of the approaching maelstrom. Her eyes followed the clock's sweep second hand around from 8:29 to 8:30. Agnes braced at her desk, waiting for the blast, the heat, the ultimate destruction. Nothing happened. Mrs. O'Leary had gone into her office and was sitting by the phone. Everyone else got to work, but they were obviously waiting for some word from New Mexico. There was little of the usual banter among the officers or laughter as the officers teased the girls.

At 9:45, O'Leary's phone rang. The girls in the outer office saw her grab a stenographer's pad and start writing. Three minutes later, she hung up the phone and motioned to Agnes to join her in the office. Her eyes were flashing with excitement. She motioned to her own desk and told Agnes to use her typewriter. Then she started dictating:

"Operated on this morning. Diagnosis not yet complete but results seem satisfactory and already exceed expectations. Local press release necessary as interest extends a great distance. Dr. Groves pleased. He returns tomorrow. I will keep you posted."

When O'Leary finished, Agnes looked up at her.

"I know I don't know all the codes, Mrs. O'Leary. But does this mean what I think it does?"

O'Leary shed her usual reserve just long enough to exalt, "You bet it does, young lady, you bet it does. The gadget worked!" Then she resumed her strictly-business demeanor. "Now, retype that and put a copy in the file."

Agnes's fingers blazed on the typewriter keys. In less than a minute, she handed O'Leary the new copy.

"Thank you, Agnes. I need to deliver this personally to the Pentagon so it can be cabled to Secretary Stimson in Potsdam. File that copy and you can get back to your regular work."

"Yes, ma'am."

She started for the door, then stopped and turned toward O'Leary.

"I hope this isn't out of line, Mrs. O'Leary, but thank you for letting me know this so soon."

"Of course, Agnes, you're part of this team. But don't forget, you can't tell a soul, no matter how excited you are about it."

Agnes beamed, absolutely regenerated by this development.

"Don't worry about me, Mrs. O'Leary. I know how to keep a secret."

"I know you do, Agnes, otherwise you wouldn't be here. Now get back to work."

Agnes took the message to her desk, classified it "Top Secret" and slipped it into the proper file. Then she sat down at her desk and looked across at Eleanor, who could see the dramatic change in Agnes's appearance. Agnes spoke first.

"Did you hear? The gadget worked."

Eleanor broke into a broad smile.

"Oh, that's wonderful. Of course, I was pretty sure it would all along. How about you?"

Agnes didn't see any reason to revisit her long days of doubt and fear.

"I guess I may have wondered a little, but I'm thrilled it all worked out so well. That has to be a big load off everyone's mind."

Eleanor looked into her friend's eyes.

"Yes, a big load." She winked at Agnes. "And some more than others, right?"

Agnes smiled and nodded.

"Agreed. Some more than others. Now we'd better get to work before Mrs. O'Leary comes over here and cracks the whip."

Shortly after two, Washington time, Groves called O'Leary to tell her he was boarding a plane at 1500 hours MWT, and would be back in the office by early afternoon on the 17th. An hour later, a cable arrived from New Mexico. It contained the text of a statement released by General William O. Eareckson, commanding officer of the Alamogordo Army Air Base, in response to inquiries from local reporters about the huge explosion and brilliant flash of light on the base early in the morning:

"Several inquiries have been received concerning a heavy explosion which occurred on the Alamogordo Air Base reservation this morning. A remotely located ammunition magazine containing a considerable amount of high explosive and pyrotechnics exploded. There was no loss of life or injury to anyone, and the property damage outside of the explosives magazine itself was negligible. Weather conditions affecting the content of gas shells exploded by the blast may make it desirable for the Army to evacuate temporarily a few civilians from their homes."

Agnes smiled when she read the statement. The heavy blanket of security that had lain over the project from the beginning remained intact, even after the test. General Groves was determined to use the bomb to end the war before anyone--inside or outside of the United States--knew it existed. The pieces of the puzzle continued to fall into place.

CHAPTER ELEVEN

When Agnes arrived home that night, the girls and Mrs. Sisko were all happy to see that her dramatic turnaround had lasted through the day. Morris was thrilled when he called to check on her and was immediately invited to dinner. Agnes met him at the door with a bear hug and a long, passionate kiss. He started to ask her about the dark period preceding this moment, but Agnes headed him off, putting a finger to his lips and shushing him. They went for a long walk after dinner, and then sat together on the front porch until it was time for Morris to leave. When the time came, Morris stood up and helped Agnes to her feet. He put his hands around her waist and pulled her close.

"I know you probably can't ever tell me what was wrong all those weeks, but I hope whatever it was is gone and never comes back. I'm so happy to have my beautiful Agnes back."

He bent his head and kissed her lightly on the lips. She buried her face in his jacket and sighed. Then she pulled back slightly and gazed deep into his eyes.

"I know what you mean. I hate to make promises I can't keep, but I think it's safe to say I won't be turning into a worry wart again any time soon, probably never. I don't even want to think about it or talk about it. I just want to think about being with you and talk about what our life might be like after the war is over."

Morris held her close for several minutes. Then he kissed her on the forehead.

"Welcome back, sweet Agnes," he said, in a soft voice. Agnes's reply was little more than a whisper.

"I'm happy to be back, Morris. Good night."

"Good night, Agnes."

Morris reluctantly let her go and strode down the front sidewalk toward the bus stop. Agnes watched him move in and out of the glow from the street lights until he disappeared into the darkness. She sighed and thought, *It really is good to be back. Thank you, Lord, for putting things right.* She stepped inside a darkened house. Mrs. Sisko and the other girls had already gone up to their rooms for the night.

****

At two o'clock the next afternoon, General Groves strode into Room 5120, wearing one of his infrequent smiles. He nodded to everyone in the room, then walked into his office, where Mrs. O'Leary was waiting, and closed the door. A short time later, O'Leary came out and called three of the secretaries, Eleanor, Agnes, and Jeannie Emmett, General Farrell's assistant, into the office and closed the door behind them. Groves did not acknowledge them; he was sitting at his desk poring over a stack of documents. O'Leary gave the orders.

"Ladies, I hope you got a good night's rest last night, because you'll need to stay late tonight. General Groves needs to compile a report on the Trinity test for Secretary Stimson, and it must be in the hands of a courier by the wee hours of tomorrow morning at the very latest. You three will be typing the report, and it must be neat and accurate and you have to do it quickly. Anyone have a reason why you can't do this?"

O'Leary's tone of voice made the answer obvious. The three young women all shook their heads to indicate they had no schedule conflicts.

"Very well, then. You may return to your other work and General Groves and I will call you in when it's time to get started."

The three young women kept themselves occupied at their desks until O'Leary called them back into Groves's office, just after everyone else had packed up and left for the day. O'Leary instructed Jeannie to take a seat at her typewriter and hammer out the first draft. Agnes and Eleanor sat at Groves's small conference table and waited their turn. Agnes was eager to hear the details. Eleanor caught her eye and raised her eyebrows. Agnes cleared her throat to discourage her vivacious friend from making light of this assignment in any way.

Groves sat behind his desk, his face impassive. He picked up a sheaf of papers. Before he started dictating, he gave them all one instruction.

"Be sure that the final copies of this are on War Department letterhead, please."

Then he began dictating from his notes.

"18 July 1945, Memorandum for the Secretary of War, Subject: The Test."

"Point one: This is not a concise, formal military report but an attempt to recite what I would have told you if you had been here on my return from New Mexico."

"Point two. At 0530, 16 July 1945, in a remote section of the Alamogordo Air Base, New Mexico, the first full scale test was made of the implosion type atomic fission bomb. For the first time in history there was a nuclear explosion. And what an explosion."

As Groves went on, Agnes was impressed, as she had been many times before reading his reports, by how articulate and clear he was in his writing. She thought it equally impressive that he could sit here, barely twenty four hours after this momentous experiment took place, and talk about it in his amazingly calm tone of voice. As she looked at him, his blue eyes, wavy gray hair, and neatly trimmed mustache, she thought again how handsome he was, but with his rounded face and full cheeks, she had always seen a certain softness in his appearance. Sitting in his office that night, she saw that his physical beauty masked a hardness, the adamantine heart of a warrior. Groves paused only briefly, then returned to his notes.

"Point three. The test was successful beyond the most optimistic expectations of anyone. Based on the data, which it has been possible to work up to date, I estimate the energy generated to be in excess of the equivalent of 15,000 to 20,000 tons of TNT; and this is a conservative estimate."

Agnes remembered what it sounded and felt like when they blasted loose the coal in the mines back home. She was sure they never used more than a stick or two at a time, and a mile underground, at that, and yet you could hear the low rumble and feel the earth shake several miles away. She couldn't even imagine what kind of explosion twenty thousand tons of TNT had created. She was about to learn as Groves informed Stimson.

"There were tremendous blast effects. For a brief period there was a lighting effect within a radius of 20 miles equal to several suns in midday; a huge ball of fire was formed which lasted for several seconds. This ball mushroomed and rose to a height of over ten thousand feet before it dimmed. The light from the explosion was seen clearly at Albuquerque, Santa Fe, Silver City, El Paso and other points generally to about 180 miles away. The sound was heard to the same distance in a few instances but generally to about 100 miles."

No wonder they'd put out the press release yesterday, Agnes thought. It would be hard to deny that anything happened if that many people saw and heard it. Mrs. O'Leary had transcribed a phone call from Los Alamos earlier in the day in which Bainbridge had reported that the local newspapers had published the account of the "munitions accident" verbatim, and no one seemed to suspect there might be another explanation.

Groves described the massive cloud that had billowed upward from the blast with tremendous power, until it towered six or seven miles high. He said the scientists theorized that two additional explosions were ignited when iron-laden dust sucked up by the blast mixed with oxygen in the air. Groves said huge concentrations of highly radioactive materials resulted from the fission and were contained in the giant cloud. He moved on to describe conditions on the ground after the bomb went off.

"A crater from which all vegetation had vanished, with a diameter of 1200 feet and a slight slope toward the center, was formed. In the center was a shallow bowl 130 feet in diameter and 6 feet in depth. The material within the crater was deeply pulverized dirt. The material within the outer circle is greenish and can be distinctly seen from as much as 5 miles away. The steel tower was evaporated."

In Point Six, Groves talked about the great, mushroom cloud that rose out of the blast. He told Stimson medical doctors and scientists had tracked it as it rained dust and radioactive material over a wide area. Fortunately, he said, the radiation levels never rose high enough to require evacuation of the local population, but the scientists had found traces of radiation 120 miles away. Groves confessed that the spreading radiation made him uncomfortable for a few hours. Point Seven dealt with blast effects, property damage, radioactivity and the reaction of people living between one and two hundred miles from Ground Zero. As far as he knew at this point, Groves said, no one in that outer circle had been hurt and there was no property damage.

Groves explained the ninety minute delay in the test in Point Eight. He described the violent thunderstorms and lightning that had raked the area in the early hours of the sixteenth. The scientists, he told Stimson, had wanted to postpone the test, but he had instead ordered the test moved to 0530, fearing that putting it off might lead to mechanical problems with the test set-up. They had fired the gadget thirty minutes before sunrise, when the storms had abated.

By this time, Jeannie had been pounding away at the typewriter for more than two hours. When Groves paused to collect Point Nine, she looked up at Mrs. O'Leary.

"I'm sorry, Mrs. O'Leary. But my arms are really beginning to ache. Could we take a break for a few minutes?"

O'Leary glanced at Groves, who said nothing but gave her an impatient look.

"No, Miss Emmett, we can't stop. General Groves needs to get this finished."

She pointed to Eleanor.

"Eleanor, why don't you take the next turn? And Jeannie can rest her arms."

Jeannie stood up and offered her chair to Eleanor. Eleanor took her place and waited for the general to continue. In Point Nine, Groves explained that the B-29 that was supposed to conduct mid-air observation of the blast had been kept away from the immediate area by heavy clouds and the thunder storms. Despite the fact that the plane had not been as close to Ground Zero as planned, he saw no reason to think a plane would be lost when it dropped an a-bomb on a real, military target. He cautioned that what they had learned about the effects of this weapon wasn't enough to guarantee the safety of a bomber crew. Groves referenced the phony press statement about the blast in Point Ten. He said FDR's Office of Censorship had helped contain the reporting to the content of the release and a few eyewitness accounts. One of the eyewitnesses who saw the light, Groves said, was a blind woman.

Agnes realized she was sitting ramrod straight in her chair, totally immersed in the scenes General Groves was describing. Having survived the debilitating fear over the uncertainty of the bomb's impact, she now felt exhilarated to be in this room with Groves and O'Leary, to be one of the first people on earth to know what a real atomic explosion looked like. She watched the general as he wove together his account of this important test. She could see the hand-written notes he was working from, notes he had probably set down as he rode in the car and in the airplane on his way back to Washington. *It's happening again,* she told herself, *I am present at one of the most important moments in history.* She waited eagerly for Point Eleven.

"Point eleven. Brigadier General Thomas F. Farrell was at the control shelter located 10,000 yards south of the point of explosion. His impressions are given below."

Agnes knew how highly Groves regarded Farrell, his number two man on the Manhattan Project and a fellow Corps of Engineers officer he'd worked with way back on the Panama Canal. She wasn't surprised that Groves would yield space in this dramatic report for Farrell's reactions. Groves read Farrell's written comments. Agnes noticed immediately that they went beyond Groves's cut-and-dried description of events.

"The scene inside the shelter was dramatic beyond words. In and around the shelter were some twenty-odd people concerned with last minute arrangements prior to firing the shot. Included were: Dr. Oppenheimer, the Director who had borne the great scientific burden of developing the weapon from the raw materials made in Tennessee and Washington and a dozen of his key assistants."

Agnes recognized Tennessee as the site where the uranium ore was purified; Washington was the reactors at Hanford, where the uranium was enriched to produce the critical U-235 isotope needed for the bomb. Farrell listed the others in the control shelter: Dr. Kistiakowsky, the scientist who solved the trigger problem; Dr. Hubbard, the meteorologist; and several others, including a handful of soldiers, two or three Army officers, and one Naval officer. The men were surrounded, Farrell said, by an array of instruments and radios. Then Farrell revealed Oppenheimer's state of mind as the test approached.

"For some hectic two hours preceding the blast, General Groves stayed with the Director, walking with him and steadying his tense excitement. Every time the Director would be about to explode because of some untoward happening, General Groves would take him off and walk with him in the rain, counseling with him and reassuring him that everything would be all right."

Agnes had never actually talked with Oppenheimer when he came to Groves's office, but from a distance he had seemed very intense. She wasn't surprised that the general needed to calm him down in the unbelievably anxious moments before they pressed the button. Farrell said Groves had gone back to base camp twenty minutes before the blast so he could observe the test better, but also because the rules prohibited Farrell and Groves from being in the same location when there was, as he put it, "an element of danger." Farrell described the countdown as it rang in the P-A system. He said the level of tension among the men in the control shelter rose "by leaps and bounds."

"Everyone in that room knew the awful potentialities of the thing that they thought was about to happen. The scientists felt that their figuring must be right and that the bomb would go off but there was in everyone's mind a strong measure of doubt. The feeling of many could be expressed by 'Lord, I believe; help Thou mine unbelief."

The religious allusion did not startle Agnes; she knew Farrell was a devout Catholic, and even though her Free Methodist training had left her with little regard for the Holy Catholic Church, she had come to respect General Farrell, as a good and decent man. In these comments, Agnes thought, he's showing the depth of his faith. Farrell went on in that vein for a little longer.

" We were reaching into the unknown and we did not know what might come of it. It can safely be said that most of those present--Christian, Jew and Atheist--were praying and praying harder than they had ever prayed before." Farrell said he realized in that moment that a successful shot would justify the immense efforts of tens of thousands of people over the past several years.

"In that brief instant in the remote New Mexico desert the tremendous effort of the brains and brawn of all these people came suddenly and startlingly to the fullest fruition."

Agnes felt herself drawn into the cadence of Farrell's words; they seemed almost like poetry, but poetry on a most unlikely subject.

"Dr. Oppenheimer, on whom rested a very heavy burden, grew tenser as the last seconds ticked off. He scarcely breathed. He held on to a post to steady himself. For the last few seconds, he stared directly ahead and then when the announcer shouted 'Now!' and there came this tremendous burst of light followed shortly thereafter by the deep growling roar of the explosion, his face relaxed into an expression of tremendous relief. "

Agnes felt as if she were standing in the shelter with Farrell and Oppenheimer. She could see Oppenheimer's knuckles whiten as he gripped the post and see the grim expression on his face. Farrell told Stimson the tension in the room dissipated and there were congratulations all around.

"Atomic fission would no longer be hidden in the cloisters of the theoretical physicists' dream. It was almost full grown at birth. It was a great new force to be used for good or for evil. There was a feeling in that shelter that those concerned with its nativity should dedicate their lives to the mission that it would always be used for good and never for evil. As to the present war, there was a feeling that no matter what else might happen, we now had the means to insure its speedy conclusion and save thousands of American lives."

When she heard those words, Agnes closed her eyes and prayed that General Farrell's words would be true. When she opened her eyes, Groves had reached Farrell's description of the blast.

"The affects could well be called unprecedented, magnificent, beautiful, stupendous and terrifying. No man-made phenomenon of such tremendous power had ever occurred before. The lighting effects beggared description. The whole country was lighted by a searing light with the intensity many times that of the midday sun. It was golden, purple, violet, gray and blue. It lighted every peak, every crevasse and ridge of the nearby mountain range with a clarity and beauty that cannot be described but must be seen to be imagined."

Again, Farrell waxed poetic in his description. Agnes listened with rapt attention.

"It was that beauty the great poets dream about but describe most poorly and inadequately. Thirty seconds after the explosion came first the air blast pressing hard against the people and things, to be followed almost immediately by the strong, sustained, awesome roar which warned of doomsday and made us feel that we puny things were blasphemous to dare tamper with the forces heretofore reserved for The Almighty. Words are inadequate tools for the job of acquainting those not present with the physical, mental and psychological effects. It had to be witnessed to be realized."

Beside her, Agnes heard Jeannie whisper, "Oh, my." Then Groves moved on to Point Twelve, his impressions of the high points of the test. He mentioned the time he'd spent tending to Oppenheimer before the blast. He described the position everyone in the shelters had assumed, prone with their feet toward Ground Zero, before the gadget exploded. He had lain on the ground between Conant and Bush, he said, and shook hands with both of them, in turn, when the bomb had been successfully detonated. His conclusion to Point Twelve was the closest he came to revealing his own feelings about what had happened.

"Drs. Conant and Bush and myself were struck by an even stronger feeling that the faith of those who had been responsible for the initiation and the carrying on of this Herculean project had been justified. I personally thought of Blondin crossing Niagara Falls on his tight rope, only to me this tight rope had lasted for almost three years and of my repeated confident appearing assurances that such a thing was possible and that we would do it."

Agnes sensed Groves's great pride in everyone, including herself, who had helped to bring the project to this successful conclusion. She thought the reference to Blondin was interesting, as was Groves's use of the word "Herculean." Groves obviously did not indulge in the sort of humility Farrell had shown in the face of this tremendous weapon. Instead, he'd compared himself to the famous high wire artist, the first man ever to cross Niagara Falls. She thought the general probably wouldn't mind if people compared him to Hercules, too. But thinking that did not diminish her tremendous respect for the general. He had done it, again. First the Pentagon, in record time, now the a-bomb, just in time. Only a truly great man, she thought, could accomplish all of that.

Groves was nearing the end. He told Eleanor there were seven more points but they were all fairly brief. Point Thirteen promised an attachment from Dr. E. O. Lawrence, one of the scientists who'd observed the test with a large group of Los Alamos workers on a hilltop twenty-seven miles to the north. In Point Fourteen, he recounted a conversation General Farrell overheard at the

Albuquerque airport as he waited for a flight back to Washington. Two airport workers had been outside when the bomb went off.

"One said that he was out on the parking apron; it was quite dark; then the whole southern sky was lighted as though by a bright sun; the light lasted several seconds. Another remarked that if a few exploding bombs could have such an effect, it must be terrible to have them drop on a city."

In Point Fifteen, Groves included the report on the blast given to him by the liaison officer at Alamogordo Air Base, sixty miles from Ground Zero. It was similar to Farrell's description, but not as literary. A brief Point Sixteen informed Stimson that Groves had not written a separate report for General Marshall, assuming Stimson would show him this one. Point Seventeen made clear Groves's intention to carry out his entire mission.

"We are all fully conscious that our real goal is still before us. The battle test is what counts in the war with Japan."

Groves used Point Eighteen to thank Stimson for the congratulatory cable he'd wired after receiving the message Groves had sent through O'Leary and the Pentagon shortly after the test. In Point Nineteen, he confirmed the plan to hand the memo to Stimson's aide, Colonel William Kyle, who would be entrusted with carrying it safely to Stimson in Potsdam.

With that, Groves stopped dictating. Eleanor had been concentrating so hard on her typing that she didn't realize they'd reached the end until O'Leary patted her on the shoulder.

"That's it, Eleanor." She turned to Agnes.

"You're the lightning typist around here, Agnes. As soon as General Groves makes any necessary corrections on this copy, I'd like you to retype the whole thing. You can do it at your desk, if you like."

She looked at Eleanor and Jeannie. You two will just have to wait for a while, until Agnes is finished, because then General Groves will review it again, and if there are additional revisions, you'll have to make them. And we'll just keep going until we have

143

three finished copies. That shouldn't take so long; you're all quite fast."

She looked at Groves.

"Should I call Colonel Kyle now and tell him to start this direction? Then we can just hand him Secretary Stimson's copy as soon as it's ready and he can be on his way."

Groves nodded.

"That's good. I'll be busy with some other things while Agnes is seeing to the clean copy."

He looked at the three young women and smiled.

"Thank you for doing this extra duty. I think you can tell from what you've heard that this is very important stuff we're working on tonight. You are all present at a historic moment."

The girls all smiled but didn't offer any replies. All three of them stood up and walked back into Room 5120, to wait for Groves to finish marking up the memo. They all glanced up at the clock on the wall. It was already a little past eight. It had taken three hours to finish the first draft. They sat down and chatted about ordinary things, things that had nothing to do with the dramatic story they'd just heard. Thirty minutes later, Mrs. O'Leary gave Agnes the first revision. She tapped out a clean copy in forty-five minutes. Then Groves revised it again. Jeannie finished retyping it in fifty minutes. Again Groves made changes, and Eleanor produced a third copy in forty seven minutes. Groves was satisfied with that one.

O'Leary instructed Agnes to type another copy. As Agnes finished a page, O'Leary handed the original to Jeannie and then on to Eleanor. By midnight, they had produced three finished copies of the memorandum. A few minutes past midnight, Colonel Kyle entered the room, accompanied by two armed guards. O'Leary showed him into Groves's office, then handed the three memos to Agnes.

"These are all 'Top Secret,' obviously."

Agnes pulled the "Top Secret" stamp from the rack on her desk, and applied it to the top and bottom of each page. As she did so,

O'Leary retrieved two heavy gauge manila envelopes and brought them to Agnes's desk.

"Put one copy in each of these," she instructed her. "Give me the third one, that goes in the safe." Agnes slipped two of the memos in envelopes and handed O'Leary the third. O'Leary took them in her arms and waved her hand toward the door.

"Thank you, ladies. You may go home now." She wagged her finger at them, as if to scold them. "And make sure you take a cab. This is not a good time for decent, young women to be strolling around downtown Washington, D.C." She paused for a moment. "And, I guess it would be all right if you came in an hour later tomorrow. This was a pretty late night for you. Good night. I'll call a cab for you."

O'Leary did an about-face and marched into Groves's office. As the girls crossed the room, they saw her hand the envelopes to Groves, who handed one of them to Colonel Kyle and put the other down on his desk. The guards stood on either side of the doorway, facing Room 5120. As the trio reached the hallway, they heard Groves's door close. They were silent as the elevator slid down to the lobby, each of them lost in thoughts about what they'd just experienced. They stepped out into the humid heat of Washington in July as the cab pulled along the curb.

Four days later, Agnes processed a cable from Stimson to Groves. He said Kyle and the memorandum had arrived July 21st. He thanked Groves for producing such an excellent summary of the test in such a short period of time. He confirmed Groves's assumption; he had shown it to General Marshall, the military chief of staff, the moment he finished reading it, and had taken it to Truman at the little White House, his residence in Potsdam, after that.

"The President was tremendously pepped up by it and spoke to me of it again and again when I saw him," Stimson wrote. He had shown the memo to Byrnes, the White House war advisor, and then to Churchill, whose British a-bomb staff had not yet informed him of the results of the test.

Groves was already pushing on. Reports began flooding in on preparations to build and drop the first atomic bomb in wartime. The documents referred to the bomb intended for Hiroshima as Little Boy. The bombing run was set for August 6th, less than three weeks after Trinity. Parts for Little Boy were already arriving at the U.S. installation on Tinian Island. Groves, perpetually worried about security, dispatched Furman, the intelligence officer who'd discovered the impotent Nazi a-bomb program, to personally escort the plutonium for Little Boy from Los Alamos to the island for assembly. And while Little Boy was still on the assembly line, parts for Fat Man, the a-bomb for Nagasaki, the second Japanese target, were already arriving.

Agnes smiled when she read in a report that the airmen had named the plane carrying the parts the "Laggin' Dragon," and that the other cargo was a ten foot statue of Jesus, ordered by the Tinian base chaplain. And while the first bombs had not yet been dropped, the reports indicated that Groves planned to build at least twenty more by the end of the year. If the target committee had discussed where to drop those bombs, Agnes did not see it in the reports.

CHAPTER TWELVE

In the days following the Trinity test, Agnes's spirits revived quickly. The spring was back in her step as she hiked to and from the bus stop with her long, country-girl strides. She slept soundly and rose refreshed, as ready to take on the new day as she'd ever been. The brilliance returned to her smile, and her eyes sparkled again, especially when Morris was around. She found herself looking forward to evenings out with the girls or hikes around the city with Morris. She regretted, slightly, that she was gaining back some of the weight she'd lost during the dark weeks before the test, but she told herself she much preferred being a little overweight to being worried half to death. She thanked God every day that the scientists who predicted doomsday had been wrong.

But all of that is not to say she was exactly the same as she'd been before. She knew the experience had changed her. Staring death in the face, death caused by this colossal weapon, had aged her in a way the poisonous threat from her burst appendix had not. In very quiet moments, when she was alone, she sensed a shadow of danger; a premonition of pending tragic events had taken up residence somewhere in her mind. She tried not to dwell on it, she made herself stick to her mantra--*If you can't think of something nice*

147

to say, don't say anything--but her intuition told her the veil was probably here to stay.

She focused as hard as she could on the present and all the nice things with which she could occupy her mind, first and foremost Morris. He was a never-ending source of happiness for her. He brought flowers and escorted her into cabs for the ride to lovely restaurants, and planned outings around the city to places she'd never seen. And sometimes, as he had that day on the mall when he led her to the cherry blossoms, he surprised her. He arrived with one such surprise a week after the Trinity test.

Agnes had invited him to join her and the others for dinner at Mrs. Sisko's boarding house. His knock resounded at the front door at the precise minute she expected him. She threw open the door and grabbed his hand.

"Good evening, Mr. Racklin. You are right on time. Please come in."

Morris was smiling from ear-to-ear, as usual, but Agnes thought she detected an extra measure of happiness in his eyes this night. He quickly guided her into the parlor and had her sit down in Mrs. Sisko's Queen Anne's chair. Then he stood in front of her and took her hand.

"Agnes, I have something special to tell you."

Agnes's intuition had told her that much, but she couldn't begin to guess what the surprise might be. She waited for him to reveal it. He fumbled a bit, as though searching for the exact, right words. A thought flitted through her mind as he hesitated, her heart raced, but she didn't dare give the thought concrete form. And Morris showed no sign of getting on one knee as he finally found his voice.

"Guess who's coming to D.C. to visit."

Her hopes of a marriage proposal evaporated, for the moment.

"Who's coming to D.C.? I couldn't possibly guess."

"Of course, you can. Who would I most want you to meet of all the people in the world?"

Agnes had a feeling she knew who he was talking about, but she loved to tease him, so she feigned ignorance.

"Oh, I know. Mahatma Gandhi."

Morris laughed.

"Okay, silly. If you're not going to play fair, I'll just tell you. My parents are driving down in a couple of weeks and they can't wait to meet you. I've told them so much about you and when I said we've even talked about our life after the war, my mother immediately said, 'We'll be down in a couple of weeks to meet this magnificent young woman.' Isn't that great?"

Agnes smiled at Morris.

"Why, yes, that will be wonderful. How nice of them to come all that way, just to meet the girl you love. I hope I make a good impression."

Morris pulled her to her feet.

"How could you not? You are the most wonderful person I've ever known. And if I feel that way, I'm sure they will, too."

He pulled her close and kissed her on the cheek. Just then, Mrs. Sisko called everyone to dinner. As they walked hand-in-hand down the hallway, Agnes had already begun to ponder how the visit with Morris's parents would go.

****

Three weeks after Trinity and a week before the nuclear attack on Hiroshima, Agnes arrived for work to find a square wooden box on the table by her desk. Perched on the corner of the table was Lieutenant Fred Blair, a Groves aide who had just returned from Los Alamos. Blair was one of the young scientists the Army had drafted to work with the project. Compared to Groves he was a fairly flamboyant soldier with no intention of making the army a career, who always splashed on too much cologne and wore sunglasses, inside and out. When Agnes reached her desk, he smiled at her and drummed his fingers on the top of the wooden box. She greeted him and then looked at the box.

"Why is that box on my table, Lieutenant?"

Blair lifted himself off the table and rapped the top of the box with his knuckles.

"Inside this box, Miss Jenkins, are gifts for everyone here, courtesy of your friends at Los Alamos. Wanna' see what it is?"

Eleanor had reached her desk opposite Agnes in time to hear Blair's explanation and invitation. She enjoyed flirting with him, but had always turned down his offers to take her to dinner. She moved around the desk to stand beside Agnes.

"Oh, Lieutenant," she said, in a mock-Southern drawl, "Why, I'd just love to see what you've brought us."

Agnes laughed; she was always amused by Eleanor's spirited conversations with the single officers in the office. She joined Eleanor in encouraging the lieutenant to get on with it. She knew she could never sound as cute and flirtatious as Eleanor, but she tried to sound interested and encouraging. She was curious to know what was in the box.

"Yes, please, Lieutenant, won't you show us our gifts? I'm sure we'd all like to see what you've brought."

She gestured around the room. Blair always spoke a little louder than necessary, and everyone was looking toward him and the table to see what he was up to. As Agnes waved her hand, they all gravitated to her side of the office. Blair was eager to display the contents of the box. He pulled a pocket knife from his trouser pocket and pried up the lid.

"Your wish is my command, ladies."

He pulled the wooden top away and tipped the box toward the small crowd. He swept his hand across the top of the box like a magician's assistant adding dramatic flair to the end of a trick. By now, the officers had joined the audience.

" Ladies and gentlemen, I give you Trinitite."

The assembled staff stood silently, gazing at a boxful of small, irregularly-shaped, shiny, blue-green rocks. None of the women and few of the officers had ever seen anything quite like it. They stared into the box and then looked up at Blair. Eleanor asked the question on most of their minds.

"Lieutenant, what is it?"

Blair enjoyed being the center of attention. He reached into the box and picked up a chunk of rock. He beamed as he explained.

"This," he said, holding it out toward the crowd, "is the newest mineral on the charts. It's what you get when you set off an atomic bomb close enough to the ground to melt the sand under it. Some of the scientists are calling it atomsite, but most of the officers are calling it Trinitite. It's the first mineral ever created by a nuclear explosion." He did not say radioactive mineral, but it was radioactive, highly radioactive. The young women in the group probably wouldn't have noticed if he had. Groves and the other ranking officers had little real understanding of radiation themselves. "The boys who rode the lead-lined tanks into Ground Zero collected it, while they were checking radiation levels right after the blast." No one asked why the tanks used to pick up the melted sand were lined with lead.

Agnes and Eleanor gave each other knowing glances. They both remembered General Groves talking about the crater opened in the ground by the force of the explosion, and his observation that the edge of the crater had been coated with a glassy, green substance. These beautiful blue-green rocks were from that lining, which Groves had said was so brilliant in color you could see it from miles away. Blair was still explaining how it came to exist.

"You see, when the bomb went off, and the heat of the blast rose up, it sucked up sand from the hole it made in the ground, and the heat was so intense that it melted the sand and it ended up raining back to earth to form a crust around the edge of the crater."

He tossed the piece of Trinitite he was holding back into the box, set the box down on the table top, and pointed to the entire contents.

"If nothing else, it's a great memento of the success of this long project we've all been working on. The guys at Los Alamos thought you'd like to have it. Out there some folks are having it set in jewelry as a keepsake. They thought you might want to do that, too. Or whatever else you can think of. Isn't it beautiful? Come on over and take a look at it. The first atomic rocks ever."

Everyone surged forward to get a closer look. Soon they were all handling the Trinitite and running their fingers over its glossy surfaces. Agnes and Eleanor each took a piece. Eleanor held hers against the red dress she was wearing that day.

"What do you think, Agnes? Does it make a good brooch? I think I'll have it mounted right away. "

"It looks lovely, Eleanor. And it goes well with your dark hair."

She smiled and thought about what she might do with it. She didn't wear a lot of jewelry, and had never had a pin or brooch custom-made. She thought of another way to make use of it.

"You know who would be really interested to see this stuff? My younger brother, Carl. He's a very sharp little guy, and he's very interested in science and geology. I think I'll send him some of this to play with."

Eleanor reached for another piece of Trinitite.

"That's a wonderful idea, Agnes. And it makes me think I shouldn't be so selfish. I'll have a couple of brooches made, and send them home to my mother and my sister. They'll wonder where it came from, but I know they'll think it's pretty. And we can tell everyone after the war what it really is. It's an amazing souvenir, if you think about it."

Agnes held the piece of Trinitite in her hand and gazed at it.

"Yes, Eleanor, it certainly is an incredible souvenir."

As the crowd began to disperse, most of them bearing several chunks of green rock on the palm of their hand like a sacrificial offering, Mrs. O'Leary strolled out of her office.

"All right people, that's enough fun for now. This project isn't over just yet. You all have work to do. You can enjoy Lieutenant Blair's gift later."

She did an about-face and strode back into her office, and the girls hustled to their desks and got busy. Lieutenant Blair tamped the lid back on the box, walked across the room, sat down at his desk, put his feet up, and leaned back, a satisfied smile on his face. The next morning, Agnes arrived with a shoebox, which she nearly filled with Trinitite. At home that night, she showed the Trinitite to Naomi, who immediately grabbed several pieces of it to have mounted on a belt. Agnes put a letter to her mother in the box, explaining that the rocks were from New Mexico and she thought Carl might enjoy them.

A few nights later, on August 6th, Agnes noticed that General Groves and Mrs. O'Leary were still hard at work as everyone else wrapped things up for the day. She didn't give it much thought; Groves stayed late many nights. But this was not just any night. When Agnes arrived the next morning, the first document she was given to process was a message Groves had received from Captain Deak Parsons, a Navy man Groves had appointed to head the ordinance division at Los Alamos. By the time Agnes read it, it had been decoded and delivered its information in crystal clear language.

"Results clear cut, successful in all respects. Visible effects greater than New Mexico tests. Conditions normal in airplane following delivery. Target at Hiroshima attacked visually. One-tenth cloud at 052315Z(11:30 pm, EWT). No fighters and no flak." Parsons was in a position to know exactly how it was done. He had actually sighted in the target and dropped "Little Boy" on Hiroshima.

Even from such a brief report, Agnes realized the momentous importance of what had taken place. The United States had become the first nation in the history of the world to drop an atomic bomb on an enemy city. The name of the plane--the Enola Gay, named for the pilot's mother-- would be emblazoned on the minds of American school children from that day forward. Fewer would recall the name of the B-29 pilot--Lieutenant Colonel Paul W. Tibbets, Jr., a 29-year old officer who had not made a particularly positive impression on Groves when they were assembling the crew, but was nonetheless assigned the important task of delivering the weapon Groves had poured so much time and energy into creating. Word of the bombing spread quickly around the office. Everyone was immensely pleased, Groves more than anyone. They all agreed that that ought to show those Jap bastards who's in charge. Groves had been up more than twenty-four hours, but as his staff arrived for work, he stepped into Room 5120, looking amazingly fresh and rested, and shook hands with everyone there. Then he rushed back into his office to confer with the White House about the document the President was about to release. It was time to shatter the shell of secrecy they'd worked in for so many months.

At eleven o'clock, President Truman handed reporters a lengthy press release, briefly explaining the work of the Manhattan Project and announcing to the world that the U.S. had built an atomic bomb with an explosive force equivalent to 20,000 tons of TNT, and had dropped such a bomb on Hiroshima, Japan sixteen hours ago. Truman made it clear that the attack was payback for the Japanese assault on Pearl Harbor that had brought the U.S. into the war. The President praised the team of scientists and engineers that had brought the Manhattan Project to fruition, but he saved his strongest language for the Japanese leaders and included an appeal to the Japanese people.

"It was to spare the Japanese people from utter destruction that the ultimatum of July 26 was issued at Potsdam. Their leaders promptly rejected that ultimatum. If they do not now accept our terms they may expect a rain of ruin from the air, the like of which has never been seen on this earth. Behind this air attack will follow sea and land forces in such number and power as they have not yet seen and with the fighting skills of which they are already well aware."

Immediately after the bombing in Hiroshima, American planes fanned out across Japan, dropping leaflets about the attack on seventy-three cities, urging people to call on their leaders to give up. The leaflets told the Japanese people "we are in possession of the most destructive explosive device ever devised by man...this awful fact is one for you to ponder and we solemnly assure you it is grimly accurate...we ask that you now petition the Emperor to end the war."

If they didn't, the pamphlets warned, "we shall resolutely employ this bomb and all our other superior weapons to promptly and forcefully end the war."

On August 9th, with no Japanese surrender forthcoming, another B-29, this one piloted by Major Charles W. Sweeney, roared into the sky high over the Kokura Arsenal, number two on the target list, intending to drop a second bomb. But smoke from a conventional American attack on nearby Yawata obscured the target. Sweeney was diverted to Nagasaki, where Commander Frederick L. Ashworth lined up the target and dropped a bomb that destroyed the city. Groves was out of the office when the bomb fell on Nagasaki; O'Leary took the message from the Pacific and relayed it to the general. Agnes first learned of the second bombing when O'Leary handed her a copy of the notification she had sent to Groves.

A few days later, Groves ordered Farrell to lead a team of officers, scientists and soldiers into Hiroshima and Nagasaki, to assess the effects of the blasts. As they had in New Mexico, they planned to measure the levels of residual radiation, to compute the actual power of the explosion. Colonel Stafford Warren, the MED medical officer who had set radiation exposure limits for the soldiers who made the first forays to Ground Zero of the Trinity test, accompanied Farrell, with instructions to monitor the radiation and set limits for exposure at the new bomb sites. Agnes read the orders as she filed them, but paid little attention to the mention of radiation.

Before Farrell's contingent reached Hiroshima, the Japanese surrendered unconditionally. The girls at Mrs. Sisko's boarding house learned the news when they came down to breakfast the morning of August 14th and saw the banner headline in the newspaper spread across the kitchen table. Everyone, including Mrs. Sisko, engaged in a delirious hug-fest, many with tears in their eyes, some laughing joyously as the strain of many months of wartime suddenly dissolved.

They stood in line to call home and celebrate with their families. Agnes called Neil and Irene, but could only talk with her mother; Neil was already a mile underground, supervising his crew of coal miners. As they talked, she heard Carl in the background, cheering and singing the Star Spangled Banner, in a high-pitched, slightly-off-key voice. Just before Irene hung up, Carl urged her to thank Agnes for the beautiful rocks she had sent. Agnes told Irene to tell Carl he was most welcome to them; she asked her mother to give Carl a big kiss from her, which Irene did immediately, loud enough for Agnes to hear over the phone. Irene told Agnes Carl had fled the room at that point. Before she hung up, Irene told Agnes to stay safe and keep Naomi safe, too, and assured her that the family loved them both very much and was so proud of what they were doing. A few days later they would be even prouder, when General Groves's press office forwarded an article about Agnes's work with the Manhattan Project to the Uniontown newspaper. The article included a large photograph of Agnes with a serious look in her large, brown eyes, and mentioned that her sister, Naomi, was a supervisor at the Pentagon, and her brother, Neil, Jr., a B-29 tail gunner, was stationed in Texas. Many of Neil and Irene's neighbors made a point of stopping them on the street or dropping by the house to congratulate them on the fine work their children had done in helping to win the war.

A week later, Farrell's first reports from Hiroshima landed on Agnes's desk. He addressed the most important question first: His team had found no significant amounts of radioactivity in the area hit hardest by the bomb, certainly much less than technicians had found at the Trinity site. He offered no explanation for that. Others would speculate, much later, that it had to do with the altitude at which the bomb was detonated. Little Boy went off nearly two thousand feet in the air, Fat Man about seventeen hundred feet up. The gadget at the Trinity test was suspended from a steel tower just one hundred feet above the ground; its quarter-mile wide fireball actually slammed into the ground below, sucking up soil and sand and melting it into a shower of molten Trinitite, heavily laden with radioactive isotopes. That, the scientists would suggest, was why Farrell found little radioactivity in the devastation left by the second bombs. Agnes had long since ceased questioning anything in the reports, and she still knew too little about nuclear physics to realize anything was missing. She was just happy the bomb had worked and that the war had ended.

The rest of Farrell's report was sobering, nonetheless. He said there was evidence that the heat from the blast had scorched the earth and anything on it for two miles in every direction from Ground Zero. He included casualty figures provided by Japanese officials. They put the death toll at 75,000 to 120,000, with another 75,000 to 200,000 wounded. Ninety percent of the city of Hiroshima, he estimated, 68,000 buildings, had been destroyed or damaged. Agnes laid the report on her desk and applied the appropriate security stamp. Before she took it to the filing cabinet, she closed her eyes and prayed silently for the souls of those dead Japanese people. *"War truly is hell,"* she thought. *"Lord, be with those people, and with those who survived. They may be our enemies, and deserve what happened to them, but they are your children, too. And thank you for sparing Neil, Junior from such a fate."*

When she opened her eyes, she realized Eleanor was watching her, her eyes shining more brightly than ever.

"Agnes, I don't mean to disturb you, but I have some great news to tell you."

Agnes clipped the rubber stamp back into the rack and smiled at her friend.

"And what might that be?"

Eleanor held up her left hand and pointed to her ring finger, where she was now sporting a large, sparkling diamond.

"Oh, Eleanor, when did this happen? And why didn't you say anything before?"

Eleanor giggled.

"I didn't have time to say anything because it all happened so fast." She leaned across the desk and spoke in a conspiratorial tone.

"You know I met a young man last weekend, the soldier from Kansas?"

Agnes nodded. She remembered Eleanor bouncing into the office on Monday morning, brimming with excitement over the fellow she'd spent much of the weekend with.

"Yes, you said his name was Rodger, right?"

"Yes, Roger Macomber. He's an army guy, stationed here in D.C. right now." She waved her hand to clear the little details from the air, so she could get to the really good part.

"Do you remember I told you I just knew he was the one and if he asked me to marry him I'd say 'yes'?"

Agnes nodded, her smile growing wider as the story progressed.

"Well, we went out for dinner last night at that nice Italian place on Connecticut Avenue and after dessert, he slid off his chair and onto his knee and popped the question. And then he gave me this." She pointed to the ring again.

"Oh, Eleanor, I'm so happy for you. Congratulations. When are you going to tie the knot?"

Eleanor giggled again.

"Well, I'm not giving him any time to get cold feet. We're going to be married by a justice of the peace Saturday afternoon and I'd like you to be my bridesmaid. Will you do it?"

"Of course, I will. I would be honored. Where are you getting married?"

"We're going to do it at the top of the Washington Monument, where we met. Isn't that romantic?"

"Eleanor, it is, it is. This is such good news."

She pushed back her chair and walked around to Eleanor's side of the desks, pulled Eleanor to her feet, and gave her a huge hug. Eleanor returned the embrace, pleased that this wonderful young woman she had grown so close to would be part of the ceremony. The two girls were so wrapped up in their celebration they failed to notice Mrs. O'Leary approaching from her office.

"Well, Miss Dewitt and Miss Jenkins, I hate to interrupt your little reunion or whatever it is you're so excited about, but there's still work to be done today, so kindly return to your desks and get to it, if you don't mind."

Agnes released Eleanor and started back around the desks. But Eleanor's irrepressible nature emboldened her in the presence of O'Leary. She turned around and held up her hand.

"Oh, Mrs. O'Leary, we weren't fooling around. I just showed Agnes this." She pointed to the glittering ring. "I'm getting married on Saturday."

O'Leary, as businesslike as she appeared in the office, hadn't lost touch with the happiness she'd felt when her late husband first proposed. Her expression softened considerably.

"Well, well. Congratulations, Eleanor. Let's have a look at that rock." She gently took hold of Eleanor's wrist and pulled the ring closer to her face. "It is lovely, my dear. I have only one question: Does he deserve a fine, young woman like you?"

Eleanor smiled and laughed lightly, her cheeks grew rosy.

"Oh, yes, Mrs. O'Leary. He does. I only just met him a few days ago, but it truly is a case of love at first sight. He's a fine young man from Kansas. I know in my heart he's the only one for me."

"Well, that's wonderful, Eleanor. I hope Saturday is a perfect day for you. And now, if you don't mind, I have things I need to tend to, as I assume you do, as well."

She spun on her heel and marched back to her office. Eleanor returned to her desk and winked at Agnes. Agnes flashed her wide, bright smile and whispered, "Can't wait till Saturday."

Eleanor returned the smile and the whisper. "Me, either."

Agnes and Morris met Eleanor and Roger, and the justice of the peace, on the observation deck of the Washington Monument promptly at one o'clock Saturday afternoon, and fifteen minutes later, Eleanor was Mrs. Roger Macomber. As she hugged Eleanor after the ceremony, Agnes thought about how wonderful it would be when she and Morris made the same commitment to each other. She was just waiting for him to pop the question. As they waved Eleanor and Roger off on a brief honeymoon in Virginia, her intuition told her it might be very soon. Morris had mentioned that he would have a big surprise for her when they went out for dinner that night. Her hopes began rising as he dropped her off at the boarding house and promised to be back to pick her up at 7:30. She spent the rest of the afternoon getting ready; she even asked Naomi to give her a hand with some extra make-up touches, so she could be at her very best for whatever Morris's surprise turned out to be.

Exactly on time, as usual, Morris appeared at the door with a bouquet of red roses. Agnes took a minute to slip them into a vase with some water and parked them on the hall table by the phone. Morris helped her pull on a light sweater; the weather had turned unseasonably cool for August in Washington. Then Morris ushered her out the door and down the front sidewalk. As they approached the end of the walk, Agnes noticed a large, black Cadillac nosed in along the curb. A distinguished looking man sat behind the wheel, with an equally distinguished looking woman at his side. They were both staring at Morris and Agnes. Morris waved to them. Agnes looked up at him.

"Morris, do you know those people?"

"Why, yes, silly. They're my parents. They drove all the way down here just to meet you. They're my surprise!"

For a split second, Agnes lost her composure. Morris's parents! And in a sleek, expensive-looking Cadillac. Suddenly she wished she'd spent more time getting ready, maybe she should have bought a really nice, new dress. She liked the blue one she'd chosen for the evening, but was it exactly the right one for meeting Morris's parents? There wasn't time for any more second-guessing. Morris had opened the back door for her to get in, which she did and slid over so he could join her. As soon as he closed the door, he began the introductions.

"Agnes Jenkins, I'd like you to meet my mother and father, Maynard and Sally Racklin." He gestured toward the front seat as his parents turned to greet Agnes. His father spoke first, in a deep, cultured voice.

"Why, Agnes, it's nice to finally meet you. Morris has told us so much about you."

Mrs. Racklin joined in.

"Yes, we've been anxious to meet the girl who swept our Morris off his feet. It's a pleasure to meet you, Agnes."

Agnes extended her hand toward the front seat, but neither Racklin reached out to take it.

"It's a pleasure to meet you, Mr. Racklin, and you, Mrs. Racklin."

When it became clear the Racklins were not interested in shaking her hand, Agnes pulled it down to her lap and clasped her hands together. She looked at Morris to see what to do next. He put his arm around her and grinned at his parents.

"Isn't she swell, you guys? Beautiful and brainy. Everything I could ever want in a girl."

Mrs. Racklin responded as Mr. Racklin pulled the car into gear and eased away from the curb.

"Well, we're anxious to get to know her, Morris. But it's a bit awkward conversing in the car. Why don't we wait until we get to the restaurant?"

She turned around and faced front, again. They traveled the five miles to a downtown hotel in silence. Mr. Racklin surrendered the car to a valet and the four of them walked silently into the hotel, found the restaurant, and were soon seated at a corner table. It was one of Washington's finer establishments, lots of silverware, linen napkins, and two wine glasses upside down in front of the very large plates, in addition to a water goblet. A string quartet played soft, delicate music on the far side of the room. Glittering chandeliers hung from the ceiling. It was the most luxurious restaurant Agnes had ever seen.

As soon as the maitre'd seated them, a waiter glided up to the table and filled their water glasses. Behind him came the wine steward, who offered a leather-bound wine list to Morris's father. He looked around the table before ordering anything.

"Young people, what's your pleasure this evening? Mrs. Racklin and I usually enjoy a cocktail before dinner and then select a nice wine to go with whatever meal we've chosen. Agnes, what's your preference?"

Morris jumped in before Agnes could respond.

"I think she'd be fine with water, Dad. She's not much of a drinker."

Mr. Racklin raised his eyebrows, Mrs. Racklin frowned. Agnes spoke for herself.

"I took a pledge at church not to indulge in alcoholic beverages. Morris is right, I'd prefer just water, thank you."

It was obvious the Racklins had never encountered such a pledge. Mrs. Racklin picked up on Agnes's reference to church.

"You took a pledge at church? What church would that be, if I may ask?"

"The Free Methodist Church, in my home town."

"Do you think it's wrong to drink alcoholic beverages?"

Agnes felt strong in her convictions, but she didn't want to offend Morris's parents.

"It's not my place to judge what others do, Mrs. Racklin. I just know it's wrong for me to drink."

"What kind of church is the Free Methodist Church, Agnes?"

"It's a wonderful church, Mrs. Racklin, with wonderful, supportive people who work together to help each other live a good, Christian life." Her mother's warning not to talk about religion and politics rang in her mind. She felt increasingly uncomfortable as the Racklins continued to grill her.

"Well, that's a new one for me," Mrs. Racklin concluded. Mr. Racklin agreed.

"We're Christians, too, Agnes, and no one in our church ever questioned the idea of drinking. We're Episcopalian, you see. In fact, far from opposing it, I remember our priest moaning all through prohibition that what he'd really like to have on a hot, summer day was a nice, cold beer. I don't think there's anything unchristian about it." He looked at his wife. "Do you, dear?"

Mrs. Racklin's face was screwed up in a look of disdain.

"I certainly do not," she said, a bit brusquely. "I hope our indulgence doesn't make you think less of us, Agnes."

"Oh, no, Mrs. Racklin. I'm not suggesting anything of the sort. I just can't, in good conscience, use alcohol."

Morris tried to steer the conversation to another topic.

"Agnes works with the Manhattan Project here in D.C. I've only just learned that, since they dropped the bombs. Isn't that pretty impressive?"

His parents were not to be deterred from their investigation. Mr. Racklin summoned the waiter and ordered a martini for himself and a brandy Alexander for his wife. He turned to Morris.

"What will you have, my boy? Still partial to that whiskey sour?"

Morris squirmed. He had never ordered a drink when he was with Agnes, especially after he realized how important her principles were to her.

"No, Dad, I don't think I care for anything, right now. I haven't been doing much drinking lately."

His father cleared his throat and looked at Mrs. Racklin, who raised her eyebrows, but said nothing. When the waiter had gone to fetch the drinks, Mrs. Racklin resumed the questioning.

"So tell us about your family, Agnes. Where'd they go to school, what do they do for a living, how many siblings do you have, where did you go to school?"

That seemed like safer ground. Agnes took a deep breath and waded in.

"I haven't been to school, other than high school."

Mrs. Racklin cut her off.

"High school? I assumed you were a scientist or engineer with the Manhattan Project. You'd need a college degree for that, wouldn't you?"

"I'm sure you would, Mrs. Racklin. But I'm not an engineer or a scientist. I was hired to do clerical work for General Groves."

The arched eyebrows, again.

"I see."

Agnes sensed that Mrs. Racklin was losing interest in her. She feared her answers to the other questions wouldn't improve the situation.

"My parents haven't been to college, either. My mother graduated at the top of her high school class; she's very smart. My father ran away from home when he was quite young; he barely finished grade school."

"Hmmm."

"My mother runs a small general store in my hometown, and my father is a supervisor in the coal mine there."

The mention of work brought Mr. Racklin back into the cross-examination.

"A coal miner, you say? Is your father involved with the union? Some of my business associates have considerable holdings in the steel mills and mining industries. They tell me the unions are trying to put them out of business."

"Oh, I don't know much about that, Mr. Racklin. My father was in the union, but he studied to become a supervisor, and that put him over on the management side. I think he has mixed feelings about the unions. He says they served a purpose when they first got started, but now he's not so sure."

Mr. Racklin seemed satisfied with that response. As he sat back in his chair, the waiter brought the drinks and waited to take their orders for dinner. Agnes looked for something familiar, and settled on a seafood dish. Morris ordered the same thing. His parents each ordered filet mignon. While they waited for their meals to arrive, the Racklins shifted the focus to their son.

"Agnes, has Morris told you the plans we have for him when he leaves Washington?"

"I didn't know he was planning to leave Washington."

She looked inquiringly at Morris, who grinned but said nothing.

"Oh, yes. You see, I run a bank back home. And, now that Morris has completed his education and had a chance to spread his wings a bit down here during the war, I'm putting him in charge of all of the accounting work at the bank. Father and son, together at last, eh, boy?" He looked proudly across the table at Morris. Morris was fidgeting with his napkin. He cleared his throat and looked up at his father.

"Well, that's right, Dad, but I've been meaning to talk to you about that. I really like it here in Washington, and Agnes does, too. We've been talking about finding a life here when the war stuff is all wrapped up. We like the idea of living in a southern city." He grinned at his parents and patted Agnes's hand. Both parents stiffened in their chairs. Mrs. Racklin spoke, in a stern tone.

"Well, if you've been thinking such things, you should have mentioned them to us." She glanced at Agnes. "Now may not be the optimum moment to pursue that conversation, it's more of a private matter for family to discuss. But I will say your father and I would be extremely disappointed if you chose to go another direction."

Before she could add anything else, the waiter swept up to the table with a large silver tray. He removed the plates already on the table and replaced them with equally large china bearing the most beautifully presented entrees Agnes had ever seen. Everything smelled delicious, but as she picked up her knife and fork, she realized her appetite had diminished significantly. The Racklins, including Morris, dug into their dinners, while Agnes picked at hers. She hated the idea of wasting any food, especially after seeing the hungry faces of her classmates during the Depression, but the conversation had triggered a churning in her stomach.

The Racklins ate with gusto, and the conversation was put on hold until they had finished. When the waiter inquired about dessert, the Racklins each ordered a piece of the chef's special triple-chocolate cake and coffee. Agnes ordered a small serving of pineapple sherbet.

Between dinner and dessert, and while they were eating dessert, Morris tried to keep the conversation going with questions about hometown reaction to the end of the war and his parents' plans for

Thanksgiving. They obliged with short, simple responses, and directed no more questions to Agnes. She was fairly certain they had heard what they came to hear. What she wasn't sure about was where Morris really stood in all of it. Mr. Racklin made a show of picking up the check for dinner; Agnes made a point of thanking him very politely for providing such an elegant meal. They drove back to the boarding house in the same silence that had enveloped their trip downtown. Morris walked Agnes to the door and kissed her goodnight.

"Thank you for being such a good sport tonight, Agnes. I'll call you as soon as they leave."

They embraced and Agnes slipped into the house as Morris strode back down the walk to the waiting Cadillac. In her room, she sat down heavily on the bed. The night had not gone well, she knew. Instead of hearing Morris's parents express their excitement over the match he was about to make, she had been grilled about her background and given the impression she fell far short of the Racklins' expectations. She didn't understand how someone as gentle and decent as Morris could be related to such a family. Not that their reaction was totally alien to her. Her mother had told her, more than once, how her family had reacted to the idea of Irene marrying Neil.

As she replayed the night's conversation, she felt like crying, but the tears did not come then. They came when Morris called her Sunday night. Mrs. Sisko summoned her to the phone in the hallway shortly after eight. By this time, everyone in the house recognized Morris's voice on the phone; Mrs. Sisko winked at Agnes as she handed her the receiver. Agnes took a deep breath and exhaled slowly before she put the phone to her ear.

"Hello, this is Agnes."

"Agnes, it's Morris. How are you tonight?"

He spoke to her in a formal tone she had never heard from him before. She hesitated before she answered.

"Agnes, are you still there? It's Morris."

"Yes, hello, Morris. I'm fine. Did you want to come over and listen to the radio with us?"

Morris cleared his throat and launched into the reason for his call.

"No, I don't think I should come over tonight, Agnes. I just need to talk to you for a couple of minutes. Do you have time right now?"

"Morris, I always have time for you."

"Thank you, Agnes," he said, still in that stiff, business-like tone. It struck Agnes that he sounded a bit like his mother on the phone.

"Agnes, I want to apologize for the way my parents worked you over last night. They had no right to do that. And it was partly my fault. I apologize for that, too."

Agnes felt a twinge in her heart as he spoke the words. Dear Morris, always trying to be sensitive and caring.

"It's all right, Morris. It was a little brusque, but I suppose they were just doing what any parents would do, making sure their child didn't get mixed up with the wrong kind of people."

"Well that's just it, Agnes. I'm not a child anymore and they don't need to protect me anymore. I'm obviously old enough to look out for myself."

Morris was sounding more like himself every moment. Her love for him welled up and her eyes grew moist as she listened.

"Oh, Morris. You are such a good person. I'm sorry your parents haven't learned that yet. But let's not worry about it. We've got our own lives to think about."

For a long moment Agnes heard only Morris's breathing; it almost sounded as if he were crying, too.

"Agnes, you are such a wonderful person. I don't deserve you. And I never will."

Morris's last comment jolted her.

"Morris, what do you mean you never will?"

"Agnes, I won't drag this out on you. Even though I don't agree with my parents on everything, I am their son and even though I'm a grown man, they still have ways of controlling me."

"Morris, what are you talking about?"

Agnes heard him take a very long, deep breath.

"I had a long and difficult talk with my parents after we dropped you off last night. It lasted well into the early morning hours." He paused, searching for words. "Oh, Agnes, how can I say this without hurting you? The upshot of their comments was that while they're sure you are bright and you're attractive, you are not in my family's class."

Agnes gasped at what she was hearing. She tried to steel herself for what she knew was coming.

"Agnes, they won't let me marry you. That's all there is to it. I tried to stand up to them and say it's my life and I'll live it as I see fit, but they played the trump card. They said if I tried to marry you or anyone of your station--that's the word they use for people who aren't rich--they will disinherit me and even force me to pay back the cost of my college degree. Oh, Agnes, I can't expect you to ever understand this, but we have to break it off."

Agnes stood in the hallway with the phone to her ear, unable to make a sound.

"Agnes? Agnes, are you still there?"

She forced herself to reply. It came out in a lifeless tone.

"Yes, Morris, I'm here."

"Agnes, I am so sorry. Some part of me will always love you. But I must say goodbye. I wish you a happy life. The man you marry will be the luckiest guy in the world. It just won't be me. Goodbye, Agnes."

Again the flat, lifeless tone.

"Goodbye, Morris."

She heard Morris hang up and did the same. Then she walked back into the parlor and sank into a chair. She covered her face with her hands and began to cry. Naomi and the other girls surrounded her to find out what was wrong. When she told them, they were united in condemning Morris as the most unworthy, wretched man ever. Agnes thanked them for caring, excused herself and walked slowly up the stairs to her bedroom.

CHAPTER THIRTEEN

Naomi was so worried about how Agnes would manage last night's devastating news that, despite Agnes's protestations that she was fine, she got off at Agnes's downtown bus stop Monday morning and walked her all the way to the New War Building. She had her arm around Agnes during the entire bus ride, and kept a firm grip on her arm as they covered the several blocks to Agnes's office. As they walked, Naomi tried her best to raise Agnes's spirits.

"Look, Sis, I know how much this hurts. Remember how many guys have dumped me over the years? Morris Racklin is just another guy, too stupid to know what's best for him. If you ask me, you're lucky to find out what kind of person he really is before you got permanently mixed up with such a family."

Agnes had prayed long and hard before she fell asleep Sunday night, and had risen in somewhat better spirits, but she hadn't found a way to simply switch off her love for Morris.

"Naomi, I just can't agree with you, at least not yet. I've never felt this way about any man before. I wonder if I'll ever have this same feeling again. I love him, Naomi." Her eyes filled with tears. "That's all there is to it. And it's going to take some time for me to get over him. Why, you're only just now getting back to your normal self, all this time after Franklin died. I know you care for me, and would do anything and everything to make me happy. And I love you for that. But you're just going to have to let me deal with this in my own way."

She leaned her head on Naomi's shoulder as they walked, and sighed. Naomi's heart ached to see her younger sister so hurt.

"I understand, Sis. I won't keep pushing on you to get over him. I'd just like to be able to reach into your heart and jerk Cupid's Morris Racklin arrow out right now. He never deserved you in the first place. He makes me so mad I could scream."

The vehemence with which she denounced Morris brought a hint of a smile to Agnes's pale face.

"You have such spirit, Naomi. You're such a fighter. I'm so glad you're my sister."

She put her arm around Naomi's waist and the two young women covered the last block to Agnes's building in silence. When they arrived, Naomi turned to face Agnes and gripped her shoulders firmly.

"Well, just know this, Agnes. We're in this whole thing together, and anyone who hurts one of us, should have to answer to all of us. I hope Mr. Morris Racklin, Mr. Moneypants I should call him, never crosses my path again, or he's gonna' get a real piece of my mind."

That brought out Agnes's full, dazzling smile.

"Thank you, Naomi. Even if we can't change what happened, it makes me feel better knowing you would if you could. I love you, Sis."

They embraced briefly; Naomi kissed Agnes lightly on the cheek and wiped away the tear in her eye, and started back toward the bus stop. Agnes watched her go, wondering how long it really would take to mend her badly-broken heart. Then she joined the crowd of people streaming into the building.

She pinched her cheeks and took a couple of deep breaths as she got off the elevator, so she could enter Room 5120 looking like her normal self. But she need not have worried about anyone noticing her expression. General Groves was standing in the doorway to Room 5121, waving a sheaf of papers, and barking orders for the men in the press office nearby to get into his office immediately. The general had set up the press office shortly before the Trinity test to manage the flow of information to the public once the bombs had been dropped on Japan. Agnes heard him muttering something about reporters being as bad as the Japs, and vowing to get things under control. She heard him say to Mrs. O'Leary, who was standing just behind him in the office, "This is exactly the kind of thing we didn't want to happen." He stepped back into his office and slammed the door.

Agnes soon learned the reason for the general's fit of pique. Mrs. O'Leary had already dropped a cable bearing the full text of a newspaper article on her desk for filing. The article had apparently been published September 5th, yesterday, in the London Daily Express. The byline identified the reporter as Wilfred Burchett. Agnes didn't recognize the name, but she soon learned that Burchett was an Australian journalist who had evaded General MacArthur's control to become the first reporter to reach Hiroshima. His article bore the title, "The Atomic Plague."

After reading the first line of the story, Agnes realized that Burchett's account of conditions in Hiroshima was squarely at odds with Farrell's version of things, the version that had been released to the public. Farrell had reported finding little residual radiation amidst the devastation left by the bomb. He attributed the deaths and injuries to the force and heat of the blast. Burchett told a very different story.

"In Hiroshima, 30 days after the first atomic bomb destroyed the city and shook the world, people are still dying, mysteriously and horribly--people who were uninjured in the cataclysm--from an unknown something which I can only describe as the atomic plague."

Burchett confirmed Farrell's report that ninety percent of the Japanese city had been destroyed. "In this first testing ground of the atomic bomb I have seen the most terrible and frightening desolation in four years of war. It makes a blitzed Pacific island seem like

Eden. The damage is far greater than photographs can show." Burchett estimated that hardly a building or even a fragment of a building could be seen in a twenty-five to thirty square mile area. What was left, he wrote was "reddish rubble. That is all the atomic bomb left of dozens of blocks of city streets, of buildings, homes, factories and human beings." Then Burchett described what Japanese doctors had shown him in the hospitals, victims of the blast who had inspired the title of the article.

"In these hospitals I found people who when the bomb fell suffered absolutely no injuries, but now are dying from the uncanny after-effects. For no apparent reason their health began to fail. They lost appetite. Their hair fell out. Bluish spots appeared on their bodies. And then bleeding began from the ears, nose and mouth."

Agnes felt queasy, as Burchett's words created gruesome images in her mind.

"At first, the doctors told me, they thought these were the symptoms of general debility. They gave their patients Vitamin A injections. The results were horrible. The flesh started rotting away from the hole caused by the injection of the needle. In every case the victim died."

Even with her paucity of knowledge about nuclear physics, Agnes could see why General Groves was so exercised over Burchett's reporting. The reporter was identifying yet another devastating effect of the bomb--radiation sickness--Burchett called it the atomic plague. Agnes felt sad for these new victims of the bomb, but she told herself it was part of the price Japan had to pay for attacking the United States. She briefly thought about what an education working with the Manhattan Project had been, but she felt no personal threat, even from this tragic news. She now understood why General Groves wanted to get this kind of reporting under control. Even if it had been necessary to drop the bombs, it might be problematic for the project and the country if the world reacted negatively to the U.S. unleashing such a monstrous weapon.

A few minutes later, the door to Groves's office opened and the press officers rushed out, grim expressions on their young faces. An hour or so later, Groves strode through Room 5120, a bulging briefcase at his side and O'Leary in tow. O'Leary returned an hour later, without the general. She walked into her office and closed the door, without informing anyone of the general's plans.

Agnes learned what Groves was up to, along with the rest of the country, from the Washington Post, the morning of September 10th. There on the front page was a photograph of Groves, with Oppenheimer beside him, standing in the crater left by the Trinity test at Alamogordo. The general has returned to New Mexico, the article said, to counter Japanese propaganda that radiation generated by the blasts in Hiroshima and Nagasaki was still killing people.

Groves had invited twenty reporters to accompany him to Ground Zero to prove that no lingering radioactive danger existed. The girls at the house were puzzled by the story. It hadn't occurred to them that there might be anything out of the ordinary about the a-bomb. They had not seen Burchett's story from Hiroshima. Agnes read the Post's account of Groves's visit silently; she did not offer to explain his actions.

Two days later, she found the New York Times account of Groves's visit on her desk, along with a marked up set of stories by well-known Chicago Daily News reporter George Weller. The Times story was written by William L. Laurence, a name Agnes recognized. She knew Groves had invited Laurence to be present for the major events of the project, including the Trinity test and the bombing of Nagasaki, so he could write an official account of it. She knew, from documents she'd filed earlier, that Groves trusted Laurence to write the stories from the official point of view.

Laurence's report on the return to Trinity delivered the official line in spades. Like all the other journalists present, he affirmed that Groves's special dispensation to visit Ground Zero "gave the most effective answer today to Japanese propaganda that radiations were responsible for deaths even after the day of the explosion, Aug. 6, and that persons entering Hiroshima had contracted mysterious maladies due to persistent radioactivity."

Laurence described the tremendous damage left by detonation of the relatively small, Trinity blast. He mentioned the "green, glass-like coating resembling fine jade" that lined the crater hollowed out by the force of the explosion. Agnes knew he was referring to the Trinitite Lieutenant Blair had brought back to D.C. two weeks ago. She glanced at the wooden box beside her, which was still half-full of smooth, green rocks. Laurence wrote that the press corps had been told that "the radioactive material on the fused surface constituted only about one-eighth of an inch. It would therefore be relatively easy to remove this surface material and make the ground safe for immediate habitation. At the rate the radiations have diminished during the past two months," he reported, "the entire area will be free of them within a relatively short time."

The story included Groves's explanation of the difference in ground radiation levels between Trinity and Hiroshima and Nagasaki. Groves explained to the reporters that the amount of lingering radiation was directly related to the altitude of the explosion. Laurence faithfully repeated Groves's contention that because the Japanese bombs had been detonated much higher in the air than the gadget--which was a mere one hundred feet above the ground--it had "greatly reduced the absorption of the gamma rays in the ground, so that there were fewer of these radiations in Japan than New Mexico." Therefore, Laurence invited his readers to conclude, if Trinity's Ground Zero was already nearly back to normal, the less exposed Japanese sites would soon be fine, as well.

Groves had pointed to Farrell's reports as supporting evidence. Laurence wrote, "...the studies of the American scientists are still in the preliminary stage, General Groves stated. But he added that, according to General Farrell, Japanese sources now admitted that eleven days after the bomb had pulverized Hiroshima the radiation there was much less than the tolerance dose, which means, he added, that 'you could live there forever'." The rest of the article recounted Groves's point-by-point refutation of radiation-related claims made by Japanese officials since the bombings.

Agnes finished the Times article and sat back in her chair, breathing a sigh of relief. *That,* she thought, *ought to shut those people up for a while.* She stamped the article and laid it aside, then picked up the Weller stories. They looked more like drafts of stories, and across the top of each one someone had written, "Kill." A brief note at the top indicated that Weller had submitted all of his copy to

General MacArthur's censors in Tokyo, and they had decided to bury them. Agnes was curious why the army would do that to the work of such a highly-respected journalist. When she read them, she understood.

The first piece detailed Weller's arrival in Nagasaki. In it, he praised the a-bomb as a very effective military weapon. "The atomic bomb may be classified as a weapon capable of being used indiscriminately," he wrote," but its use in Nagasaki was selective and proper and as merciful as such a gigantic force could be expected to be." Even though she knew Weller must have faked his way into the city, against MacArthur's restrictions, Agnes couldn't imagine why anyone would object to that report.

But the focus of Weller's reporting shifted in the second story. In it, he described his visit to two hospitals during his first day in Nagasaki. He wrote about people who had survived the initial blast unharmed, but who were now dying of what he termed "Disease X." He admitted he was upset to see these people, with "neither a burn or a broken limb...blackish mouths and red spots...and small children who have lost some hair" dying a month after the bomb had destroyed the city.

In part three, Weller was still writing about the "peculiar disease" caused by the bomb. He reported it was "still snatching away lives here. Men, women and children with no outward marks of injury are dying daily in hospitals, some after having walked around three or four weeks thinking they have escaped." He recounted his conversation with a local X-ray specialist who told him he was certain the victims were dying from some unidentified radiation effect produced by the bomb. He reported, "The doctors...candidly confessed...that the answer to the malady is beyond them." At one hospital, he wrote, 343 such people had been admitted, and two hundred were already dead. "They are dead--dead of atomic bomb--and nobody knows why." Weller ended his third dispatch with "Twenty-five Americans are due to arrive Sept. 11 to study the Nagasaki bomb site, Japanese hope they will bring a solution for Disease X."

Agnes assumed Weller was referring to Farrell and his group, ordered into the devastated cities by Groves, to assess the power and impact of the blasts. She hadn't seen any orders instructing them to get involved in solving medical mysteries. Agnes filed the documents in the appropriate drawers and returned to her desk. She understood why General MacArthur had killed Weller's reporting. She understood why General Groves had arranged the press visit to Ground Zero at Alamogordo. This talk of radiation sickness from a nuclear weapon might not reflect well on the United States.

It was becoming a sensitive issue, and obviously needed to be handled carefully. She knew General Groves was the right man to do that, as he'd been the right man to lead the Manhattan Project. And, before she got any deeper into thinking about it, she told herself it was not her job to deal with it. Her job was to "stick to her knitting," and keep her mouth shut. *A strange sickness in Japan has nothing to do with me*, she told herself. But even as those words ran through her mind, she had a vague premonition that that might not be completely true. The next day premonition turned to fear.

Soon after Agnes arrived at the office, General Groves swept in the door, still clutching his heavy brief case, a look of satisfaction on his face. He nodded to several of the officers as he crossed the room and entered his office, where Mrs. O'Leary was already busy at her desk. A few minutes later, a radiant looking Eleanor walked in, fresh from her three-day honeymoon in Virginia with Roger. When she reached her desk, Agnes looked up and smiled.

"Welcome back, Mrs. Macomber. Did you have a nice time in Virginia?"

"Oh, Agnes, it was wonderful. Roger is wonderful. Life is wonderful. I have never been so happy."

Eleanor's joy was contagious. For a moment or two, Agnes relaxed her usually serious demeanor and allowed herself to be overcome with happiness to see her dear friend so excited.

"I'm so glad, Eleanor. I don't know anyone who deserves to be happy more than you do."

Eleanor looked deep into her friend's eyes and saw the warm, sincerity that undergirded Agnes's comments. But she thought she detected something else, a sadness she had not noticed before.

"Thank you, Agnes, for being such a good friend and being willing to share my joy. But something tells me you aren't as happy as I am. Did something happen while I was away?"

Agnes tried to keep her happy face going, but Eleanor's gentle probing had found the crease in her heart. Her smile remained in place, but her eyes grew moist. Eleanor lowered her voice.

"Oh, Agnes. What is it? Something awful? Not your family, I hope."

Agnes shook her head and dabbed her eyes with the lacy handkerchief she sometimes kept in her sleeve.

"No, it's not my family. Everyone's okay there."

"Then what is it? Not Morris."

As soon as she uttered the name, Eleanor knew she'd hit the spot. Agnes's shoulders slumped, her smile dissolved, and her lips began to quiver. Eleanor reached across the desks to touch Agnes's hand.

"Oh, Agnes, not Morris. Did something happen to him, is he all right?"

Agnes shook her head, and blotted away a few more tears.

"No, Morris is fine, I'm sure, but I'm not."

Beyond Eleanor's shoulder, she saw Mrs. O'Leary coming out of her office. She pulled herself up straight in her chair and took a deep breath.

"Maybe we should talk about this later, during our coffee break. I don't want Mrs. O'Leary to think we're goofing off over here."

Eleanor withdrew her hand and looked around. O'Leary was moving toward an officer on the far side of the room.

"All right, Agnes. I'll let you keep it secret until then, but not a minute longer."

They both applied themselves to the paperwork in front of them. Promptly at nine, they excused themselves and walked arm-in-arm to the ladies room. When the heavy door had closed behind them, Eleanor took Agnes's hand again.

"So what is it, Agnes? What happened?"

She was totally unprepared for what Agnes proceeded to tell her. Agnes gave her every detail, starting with her hope that Morris might propose on the same day Eleanor and Roger had become one. She described her apprehension when Morris's surprise turned out to be his parents, seated in a very expensive, black car. She told Eleanor how uncomfortable she had been when the Racklins chose to ride to dinner in silence and how embarrassed she had been when they declined to take her hand in the car.

Then she recounted the conversation over dinner. Eleanor's eyes grew wide with astonishment as she heard how the Racklins, especially Mrs. Racklin, had raked Agnes over the coals and gradually implied that she wasn't a good enough match for their son. At this point, Eleanor interrupted indignantly.

"Who do those people think they are? You are one of the most dignified, proper, intelligent and attractive girls I've ever had the privilege to call my friend. They're just awful people."

Agnes felt her friend's loving support wrap around her like a warm blanket, and she welcomed it.

"That's nice of you to say, Eleanor. But we must not judge lest we be judged, you know?"

Eleanor muted her condemnation, just a bit.

"Oh, yes, I know that's true, Agnes. But, really, who do these people think they are?"

Agnes smiled and continued on with her story.

"When we got back to Mrs. Sisko's, Morris kissed me goodnight and promised to call as soon as his parents left town, which he did, Sunday night. I invited him to come over to the house, but he said no. And the way he said it made me think something bad was coming. And a minute later it did. He told me his parents refused to let him marry me, they said I wasn't of his class." The tears came full force now. "They said I wasn't good enough to become part of their family."

Eleanor was furious.

"Oh, Agnes, what wretched, horrible people. Don't they know money can't buy character? You are twice the person any of them will ever be, including Morris."

Agnes went on, tears rolling down her flushed cheeks.

"Well, maybe Morris isn't quite as bad. He apologized for his parents' comments, but then he told me we had to break up. He said they threatened to disinherit him, even make him pay back the money they spent on his college degree, if he married me."

"And he let them get away with that? He is a cad, no doubt about it. A spoiled little rich kid who doesn't have the moxy to stand up for himself. How did he end it?"

Agnes looked at her, heart-stricken anguish in her eyes.

"He said the man who married me would be the luckiest guy in the world, it just wouldn't be he. And then he said good bye. That was it."

Eleanor grabbed her friend's shoulders and pulled her into a long embrace. Then she pulled back, still gripping Agnes's arms.

"Agnes, I am so sorry. And I'm sorry I wasn't here to support you when it happened. I feel a little guilty knowing I was off having such a wonderful time while you were going through hell."

Agnes smiled through her tears.

"Please don't feel that way, Eleanor. You're here now, and you're doing everything a dear friend can do. As I told Naomi, I'll get through this, I just need some time."

"And you shall have it, my friend, along with all the love we can shower on you until you mend."

She glanced at her wrist watch.

"Oh, time's flying. We should be getting back to the office. But I wanted to get your opinion on something while we're here."

She motioned to the pin she was wearing on her blouse. It was a silver setting with a roughly oval-shaped green stone, about two inches long with a glossy surface, embedded in it. Agnes immediately recognized it as Trinitite. It was the first piece of

Trinitite jewelry she'd seen since Lieutenant Blair brought the boxful back from Los Alamos.

"Oh, Eleanor, it is lovely. The green color goes so well with your dark hair and fair complexion. How long have you been wearing it?"

"Oh, it was ready just before Roger and I got married. I've had it on every day since then. I think it's very pretty. But I wanted to show you something."

She undid the top button of her blouse and pulled back the material on the side where the pin was attached.

"What do you make of this?"

On Eleanor's chest was a raw, red welt, with some sort of fluid seeping out of it. Agnes looked closer and then pulled the material back in place to scrutinize the pin. When she reexamined the welt, it seemed to be almost the exact shape of the Trinitite in the pin. That seemed odd.

"Eleanor, do you have any idea what's causing that red patch?"

"I'm not sure, but the fact that it's right where the pin lies against my skin makes me wonder if maybe I'm allergic to the Trinitite or something. It bothers me that the welt is oozing like that."

"Yes, it would bother me, too. You wear lots of pins. Have you ever seen anything like this before?"

"Never."

"Then I just have to think there's some connection between the Trinitite and that sore spot. I think we should talk to Mrs. O'Leary about this."

Eleanor agreed. She rebuttoned her blouse and they walked arm-in-arm back to the office. Instead of returning to their desks, they walked to Room 5121 and knocked on the door. Mrs. O'Leary opened it. She noted the very serious expression on their faces.

"Yes, girls, what is it?"

Agnes responded first.

"I'm sorry to bother you, Mrs. O'Leary, but there's something we'd like you to take a look at."

"If it's paperwork, you know you should consult the officers before bringing your problem in here, girls."

"It isn't a clerical issue, Mrs. O'Leary. It has to do with this."

Agnes pointed to Eleanor's pin.

"Why that's a lovely setting, Eleanor. What stone is that you have in there?"

"It's a piece of Trinitite, Mrs. O'Leary. From the box Lieutenant Blair brought back from New Mexico."

O'Leary was growing a little impatient, thinking the girls had interrupted her simply to show off a new piece of jewelry.

"Well, that's very nice. It suits you, Eleanor. Now, if there's nothing else, I think we should all get back to work."

The young women stood their ground. Agnes reached over and unbuttoned Eleanor's top button and pulled back the material.

"We thought you should see this."

The moist, red blotch was in full view. O'Leary leaned in close to examine it. Then she looked up at the girls.

"What is that?"

Eleanor explained.

"I've never had anything like it before. It showed up after I started wearing my new pin."

Agnes chimed in.

"And if you look at the pin and welt closely, you'll see that the red patch is almost exactly the same shape as the Trinitite. The skin seems very irritated and it's oozing something."

General Groves had been listening to the conversation from behind his desk. He didn't particularly like what he was hearing. He spoke from across the room.

"Mrs. O'Leary, I'm sure whatever problem Miss Dewitt is having has nothing to do with the Trinitite. I've only just come back from Ground Zero, where I was assured that it poses no threat to anyone. I would advise Miss Dewitt to consult her personal physician. It's probably some sort of allergy flaring up, maybe to the metal in which the Trinitite was set."

O'Leary was still staring at the welt. She flipped the material back and forth, comparing the dimensions of the stone with the wound. Without turning her head, she responded to Groves.

"I'm not so sure, General. This looks nasty to me. I think I'll check it out."

Groves knew better than to resist O'Leary when she had her mind made up.

"Very well. But I'm sure it's nothing serious."

He returned to the documents on his desk. Mrs. O'Leary addressed the girls.

"Eleanor, go ahead and button up there. And both of you may go back to your desks. I'll make some inquiries about this and let you know what I find out. And, Eleanor, you may want to make an appointment with your physician, just in case it's some sort of allergic reaction. Thank you both for bringing this to my attention."

As Eleanor and Agnes made their way across the office, O'Leary grabbed the phone and dialed a number. While it was ringing, she pulled her stenographer's pad in front of her and picked up a pencil. Only Groves heard her conversation when the phone was answered.

"Yes, this is Mrs. O'Leary in General Groves's office. May I speak with Colonel Warren."

Groves lifted his head when he heard Warren's name, but soon lost himself in his documents again. A few seconds later, O'Leary greeted Colonel Stafford Warren, the MED's Chief Medical Officer, who was still working at Los Alamos. As she did for most of Groves's calls, she recorded every word of their conversation. An hour later, O'Leary dropped the transcript of her call on Agnes's desk along with a memorandum that she instructed Agnes to make twenty four copies of and distribute to everyone in the office.

Agnes typed up the phone call transcription first.

O'Leary: Good morning, Colonel Warren. I'm sorry to bother you, but I have a medical situation here in our offices that requires your attention."

"Warren: Of course, Mrs. O'Leary, I'm always glad to be of help, any way I can."

"O'Leary: Thank you, Doctor. It has to do with a skin irritation just shown to me by one of our clerical staff."

"Warren: Oh, I'm not a dermatologist, Mrs. O'Leary. I may not be qualified to speak to that condition, especially over the phone."

"O'Leary: Please let me explain the circumstances, Colonel Warren. I think you are exactly the man to speak to what's happening here."

"Warren: Please proceed, Mrs. O'Leary."

"O'Leary: One of my girls has just shown me a mean-looking red welt on her upper chest. It's not only quite irritated looking, but it's also oozing some sort of fluid,"

"Warren: That does sound unpleasant. How did she come to have this sore?"

"O'Leary: I'm not sure we know exactly, but it may well be connected to your work there at Los Alamos."

"Warren: In what way?"

"O'Leary: Let me back up just a bit and tell you that shortly after the Trinity test, Lieutenant Blair, of our office, returned to Washington with a boxful of Trinitite, which he proceeded to present to the staff here as a memento of the successful detonation of the gadget."

"Warren: He did what?"

"O'Leary: He gave out pieces of Trinitite as souvenirs and suggested that people here might want to have them set in jewelry or some such as a memento of their work with the project."

"Warren: Damn! How did he manage to do that? I gave no one permission to remove anything from Ground Zero."

"O'Leary: He told the staff he'd gotten it from the soldiers who made the first forays into the area after the blast in lead-lined tanks. Would that be possible?"

"Warren: Possible, I suppose. But highly irregular. The radiation levels in there were much higher than we anticipated. You've probably seen the reports indicating that our measuring equipment was obliterated by the blast, and instruments that weren't destroyed outright were overwhelmed by the levels of radiation left by the bomb."

"O'Leary: Well, that's not my concern this morning. What I need to know from you is whether the Trinitite brought into this office poses any health threat to my staff. Is it possible that the Trinitite is responsible for the injury shown to me here?"

"Warren: Not only possible, but probable."

"O'Leary: Have you seen anything like this out there?"

"Warren: I am a bit chagrined to admit that I have. Somehow, maybe through the same source, some of the locals managed to get their hands on Trinitite. A couple of gas stations were giving it away as souvenirs. And, yes, some people here had it made into jewelry and I have had several reports of similar wounds appearing on the skin where it comes into close proximity with the material."

"O'Leary: I need your best advice, Colonel Warren, and I need it fast. What are you telling people to do about this?"

"Warren: First things first, especially in light of General Groves's recent visit here discounting the danger of lingering radiation. I have retrieved any samples of Trinitite I became aware of and have sworn anyone who experienced these lesions to absolute secrecy. I've also covered any medical costs involved in treating the wounds. So that's the first thing, which should be no problem, since you've already got your staff under tight security agreements."

"O'Leary: Yes, I understand that part, Colonel. But what about our people? What should I tell them to do about this?"

"Warren: That stuff should never have fallen into their hands. Put out a directive immediately telling them to dispose of any Trinitite they may have, and to avoid any further direct contact with the material. And by all means, if there's any Trinitite still in your office, get rid of it."

"O'Leary: Should we dispose of it in any special way?"

"Warren: No, the radiation is decaying fairly rapidly. Just throw it in the garbage and see that it gets hauled to the dump. And force your people to throw away any jewelry or other keepsakes they may have created from this stuff. Have I answered your questions, Mrs. O'Leary?"

"O'Leary: Yes, Doctor, thank you very much. I will proceed accordingly. Goodbye."

"Warren: Goodbye, Mrs. O'Leary, and good luck."

Agnes's anxiety level had begun rising with the first sentence she typed. She looked across the desk at Eleanor, and then thought about Carl, sitting on the back steps at home playing with the beautiful stones she had sent him from Washington. Colonel Warren's words rang in her mind, especially the word radiation. Snatches of the newspaper articles by Burchett and Weller came back to her. They had talked about the mysterious illness cutting down otherwise uninjured Japanese people long after the roar of the atomic blast had ceased echoing across the pulverized countryside.

She looked down at her hands, the long, slender fingers with which she had lovingly packed a shoebox with glistening, green rocks that she now considered deadly. She held her hands close to her face, looking for red spots, any sign that radiation had begun working its destructive way into her flesh. She didn't see any damage, nothing like the ugly welt on Eleanor's skin, but she noticed that her hands were shaking slightly. She told herself that was just her emotions getting the better of her. She also told herself, with a feeling of relief, that she had escaped this threat.

It would be many years later before she realized how very wrong she was.

She turned her attention to O'Leary's memo. She could make only three carbons at a time, which meant she had to type the entire message six times before she had enough to distribute to every person in the office. By the time she finished, she had memorized it. O'Leary instructed anyone who had taken even one piece of Trinitite to dispose of it immediately. There would be no exceptions, she said. Even if a staffer had spent a sizable amount of money having the glistening stones embedded in an elegant setting for a pin or necklace or bracelet, it had to go. If they had given any Trinitite to an acquaintance, they should retrieve it and dispose of it or instruct that person to do so. If they had experienced any sort of injury where the Trinitite contacted their skin, it should clear up shortly after they got rid of it. If wounds persisted, they should contact their physician and seek treatment for a burn.

As Warren had done in New Mexico, O'Leary told the staff the government would cover any medical expenses they incurred in dealing with their wounds. She did not elaborate on what kind of burn it was; Agnes noticed she did not use the word radiation anywhere in the memo. Finally, she told her staff, they were not to speak of the problem to anyone outside the office. She reminded them that they had taken a vow of secrecy when they joined on, and that vow was still in force, even though the project had been revealed to the public.

When Agnes had the memos ready to distribute, she walked to O'Leary's office and asked if O'Leary wanted the staff to assemble so she could explain the situation to them all at once. Groves was still at his desk and looked up when Agnes posed the question. O'Leary responded without looking at the general.

"No, I don't think that will be necessary, Agnes. I suspect there are a few others in the office who have seen the same results as Eleanor, but General Groves prefers that we not make more out of this than necessary. Just pass out the memos and we'll leave it at that."

As she moved around the room handing the memo to her officemates, Agnes heard murmuring, and a few gasps, as people learned the explanation for the lesions several of them had recently developed. Across the room staffers pulled chunks of Trinitite from their drawers and deposited them in the box beside Agnes's desk. Eleanor pulled off her pin and tossed it in the waste basket by the wall. Several other pieces of Trinitite jewelry clanked into the can, as well. While Agnes was distributing the memo, O'Leary opened her office door and summoned Lieutenant Blair into Room 5121. A few minutes later, Blair emerged, a tight-lipped expression on his usually smiling face, and headed straight for the wooden box. He stood silently as the last staffers dropped their souvenir stones into it, then replaced the lid, tucked the box under his arm, and walked briskly from the room. He returned a few minutes later, his trademark sunglasses firmly in place, but without the box.

Agnes sat down and wrote a letter to her family, instructing them to get rid of the pretty stones she had sent for Carl. She told them she couldn't explain why she was asking them to do it. She said everyone in the office had been ordered to get rid of the stones, because the government didn't want anyone to handle them. When the letter arrived, Neil found the shoebox in Carl's room and buried it in the backyard.

CHAPTER FOURTEEN

Groves left the office early on the night of September 20th, but Agnes had not been given an itinerary to file, which meant she again had no idea where he was going. She found out two mornings later when the Washington Post ran a large, front page photo of Groves with his wife Grace and daughter Gwen standing on the steps of City Hall in New York with a smiling Mayor Fiorello H. LaGuardia. The mayor was presenting Groves with a scroll in which he lauded Groves's great service to the country. LaGuardia had then escorted the family to a gala luncheon at the Waldorf Astoria, where the assembled dignitaries rose *en masse* to applaud the General's service. It was the first of many such accolades that would be showered upon him.

While the other girls oohed-and-aahed over how handsome and dashing the general appeared in his dress uniform, with his wavy hair and firm jaw line, Agnes thought about the threat to his reputation posed by reports of a-bomb induced radiation sickness in Japan. The Post's article detailing his triumphant visit to New York convinced her that his crusade to squelch the negative publicity out of Japan had been quite effective. She had seen no more stories from the press about the "atomic plague," and that was fine with her. After dodging the bullet in the Trinitite scare, she felt weary of carrying so much frightening knowledge in her head. She wanted to move on to happier things, and she planned to start with Christmas. She'd already written to tell her mother she would definitely be home for the holidays.

But troubling details about the bomb kept finding their way to her desk. A week after O'Leary's memo about Trinitite went out, she was given a newspaper clipping to file. A note attached to it, signed by Colonel Stafford Warren read: Mrs. O'Leary, Per our recent conversation, thought you'd be interested in this. The article, from the Albuquerque Journal, included a picture of a pretty, fair-haired model, posing with some sort of jewelry. The caption beneath the picture explained: "New Mexico atomic jewelry is worn by Lovely Pat Burrage of Fort Worth, Tex., who will reign at the 'Night in Paradise' at the United Seamen's Service club in New York October. She is shown holding the palladium jewelry inset with atomsite, the substance formed on the ground at the scene of the first atomic bomb test, in New Mexico." Agnes recognized the name atomsite. Lieutenant Blair had told them that's what the scientists called the green glaze formed by the blast, before the soldiers renamed it Trinitite. Her second thought was to wonder if anyone had told Miss Burrage what Trinitite could do to you. She hoped somebody had.

Later that morning, Mrs. O'Leary delivered a stack of reports from Los Alamos. They recorded the results of the army's testing and investigation around Ground Zero in the hours and days after the first atomic blast. They were dated July and August. Either they had taken the slow road to Washington, Agnes thought, or General Groves had been perusing them before he made his recent trip to the Trinity site.

According to the first report, the lead-lined tanks had rolled up to the crater left by the blast ninety minutes after the bomb went off. It said the radioactivity in the crater was much higher than anyone had estimated. The tanks had made a total of four passes through the area that day and the next, once rumbling through the center of the crater. Radiation levels were still high the second day, the report said, "far beyond the range of our measuring instruments (even with the 50 fold shielding factor provided by the tank)."

The highest radiation levels could only be estimated, the scientists reported, somewhere between 600 and 700 roentgens per hour. Even with the protective lead barrier fitted to the tank, the report indicated that one driver had accumulated thirteen to fifteen roentgens of exposure, a second racked up nearly three-and-a-half roentgens in two trips to the crater, a scientist onboard absorbed about eight or nine roentgens, and another observer showed five roentgens of exposure in one trip to Ground Zero. The medical experts had set a limit of five roentgens as the safe limit for anyone entering the hot zone. All of the men had showered carefully when they exited the area, to remove any dust that might have seeped through their protective suits and reached their heads, hands and feet.

Several other teams entered the area the day of the blast, but none of them approached any closer than 350 yards from Ground Zero. Even there, more than a thousand feet from the crater, radiation levels were still between six and ten roentgens per hour more than seven hours after the explosion. The scientists had postponed any further forays until the radiation levels dropped to a more acceptable level. A footnote to that section of the report indicated that safety officers had originally set the safe dose at one-tenth of a roentgen per day, but had raised it to five roentgens per day so the crews could get into the site and recover test data.

Agnes wasn't sure what to make of all the numbers. But she was impressed by the safety precautions the scientists had taken to protect themselves from the radiation. And she wondered, again, about Farrell's report from Hiroshima that there was no residual radiation on the ground after the blast there, which was many times more potent than Trinity had been. General Groves had gone out of his way to convince the world that atomic bombs didn't leave any lasting effects that could kill people not visibly injured in the blast. Yet here was the army, examining an a-bomb site, taking all sorts of steps to prevent their personnel from being harmed by the same thing Burchett and Weller were talking about in their reports from Japan.

She shook her head slowly; there was so much she did not understand about the a-bomb. She couldn't know it in that moment, but she was not alone in her confusion. Groves, and most of those who worked with him, had marched the entire way through the Manhattan Project with almost as many holes in their understanding of the forces they unleashed as this country girl from western Pennsylvania.

The scientists and technicians had worked outward from Ground Zero in subsequent days, searching for evidence of the bomb's impact, finding higher than expected radiation levels as they went. The reports said the cloud column created by the explosion had risen to a height of fifty to seventy thousand feet and hung in the air over the northeast corner of the test site for several hours before moving off in the same direction. By the time it drifted offsite, the scientists reported, most of the largest particles sucked up into the fireball had fallen out, but obviously not all. The crews had found what they called "fission products" across an area one hundred miles long and thirty miles wide.

Within that area, just twenty miles northeast of Trinity, a man named William Wrye had told the investigators that "for four or five days after that [the blast], a white substance like flour settled on everything." A mile east of the highest off-site radiation readings, the team had discovered rancher M.C. Ratliff, who lived in an adobe house with his wife and grandson, several dogs, and a herd of goats. Ratliff told the scientists "the ground immediately after the shot appeared covered with light snow" and especially at dawn and dusk "the ground and fence posts had the appearance of being frosted."

The crews did not examine the Ratliffs themselves, nor did they look for any evidence that the family or its animals might have been contaminated by the blast. The report made no mention of the fact that the Ratliffs collected and drank the rainwater from their roof. It rained the night after Trinity. It is highly probable that the family and their animals drank that run-off and, in the process, ingested radioactive material. Agnes wondered why the scientists hadn't shown as much concern for the well-being of the local residents as they had for their own crews in the hours after the blast.

In general, the crews found much more fallout and radiation than expected beyond the twenty mile radius. So much so that they nicknamed part of the Chupadera Mesa "Hot Canyon." It was on the mesa, the principle grazing land for local ranchers, that the crews discovered a herd of cattle that had experienced the effects of the bomb unprotected. All of the animals had what the report referred to as "local beta burns," on some of them, the hair on their backs had already fallen out. Technicians estimated the animals had been exposed to twenty thousand roentgens of radiation as the plume drifted northeast over the mesa.

According to the report, the team had radioed in their discovery of the cattle, and been instructed to buy all seventy five head. Trucks were dispatched immediately. The most seriously burned were being kept at Los Alamos for observation; the rest had been trucked to Oak Ridge for long-term study. That was the only harm to living things included in the reports. Agnes knew from documents she'd seen before the test that the army had tried to locate anyone living within a forty mile radius of Ground Zero. She assumed that information would be used to check up on those people after the blast. Where was the report on the condition of those people who had lived through the world's first a-bomb test, totally unaware that it was going to happen? She flipped through the stack of papers, rereading the headings. There was nothing. She told herself that data would arrive later. She was wrong. There would be no full-scale study of the bombs impact on human beings for at least three years, long after she had left the Manhattan Project.

Agnes stamped the reports "Top Secret," and dropped them in the file drawers. As she sat down at her desk, a wave of fatigue washed over her. She was tired of reading these reports, and she felt bad about the thoughts she was having about the way things had been done. She vowed not to read any more of the documents; she wasn't expected to anyway.

She had just turned twenty in August, but the weight of responsibility, the burden of top secret knowledge she'd been shouldering for nearly three years, made her feel much older. It was only a couple of months until Christmas. She longed to sit at the kitchen table with her family and just relax and have fun. The holiday couldn't come soon enough to suit her.

****

Irene noticed the change in her daughter the moment Agnes stepped off the train in Uniontown. Her fair complexion had taken on a gray cast; her somber eyes reflected a sadness that had not been there before. The circles that had always appeared beneath her eyes, especially when she was tired, had grown and darkened. She rushed to embrace her brave daughter, home for the holidays, with what seemed like the weight of the world on her young shoulders. She lifted the traveling case from Agnes's hand and handed it to Neil, who brushed past her to give Agnes a quick, one-armed hug, and then hurried ahead of them to deposit her suitcase in the Packard.

Irene put her arm through Agnes's and looked up at her daughter, who towered over her by nearly a foot.

"Oh, sweetheart, it's so nice to have you home with us again. You've had quite a time down there in D.C. The article in the paper made us so very proud of you and Naomi and Neil, Junior."

Agnes leaned against her mother as they strolled through the station.

"Oh, Mom, I was ready to be home weeks ago. I'm just so glad the war is over and we can all get back to living our normal lives."

Irene knew about Agnes's breakup with Morris; her daughter had told her about it in a long, plaintive letter. Her intuition, that special sense she had passed on to both of her girls, told her that partly explained the heaviness that darkened Agnes's fresh, young face. But she elected not to raise the issue so soon after Agnes's arrival. She was determined to revive her daughter's spirits first, and maybe then talk about it. Besides, she had a plan that she hoped would make any discussion of Mr. Morris Racklin totally unnecessary. She turned the conversation to the brightest topics she could think of.

"Carl is so excited to have you home. I think he misses both of you even more than your father and I do, if that's possible. We were so looking forward to having you with us for Christmas. I haven't told him yet that Naomi won't be joining us."

"Sweet Carl, bless his heart. I'm anxious to see him, too. I'll bet he's grown a yard since I last saw him."

"Well, maybe not quite that much, but he is stretching out by the day. It is a shame Naomi didn't come. She said in her letter it had to do with a social engagement and a young man. Are you allowed to tell us what that means?"

Agnes smiled. Naomi had told her she'd take care of informing Irene and Neil of her plans for the holidays. Agnes had assumed she'd tell them the whole story, which she obviously had not. She didn't think Naomi would mind if she filled in the gaps.

"Yes, she does have a social engagement and it does involve a young man. The short version of the story is she's fallen for another soldier, this one's from Wisconsin and his name is Cliff Racine. She struck up a conversation with him one night when we all went bowling right after Thanksgiving, and they've been seeing a lot of each other ever since."

"Do you think she hesitated to tell us the whole story because she thought your father would be angry again?"

"That could be part of it. But what she told me was that Cliff couldn't afford to travel all the way to Wisconsin for the holidays, so he asked Naomi if she could stay in D.C. and celebrate Christmas with him."

Irene was torn between feeling happy that her daughter had found someone to take the place of her beloved Franklin--the man Neil had refused to entertain in their home--and wishing Naomi could have interrupted her courtship to be with her own family after so many months away.

"Well, I guess she's old enough to decide what she wants to do, isn't she? She is twenty-two."

Agnes sensed the battle in Irene's mind. She opted to pitch in on Naomi's side.

"Yes, that's what she said when we talked about it. She really seems interested in this guy. He's a decent young fellow, as far as I can tell from the couple of times I've talked to him. And you'll like this part--he's a farm boy. Ought to be a good fit for a country girl like Naomi."

"Well, you have excellent judgment, Agnes. If you think he's good enough for Naomi, I'm willing to just wait and see what happens."

Agnes smiled and squeezed her mother's arm.

"That's the spirit, Mom. And we might as well be honest about it; whether Dad ever gets used to the idea of a man falling in love with his daughters or not, it's going to happen and we're going to go off and live with that man someday. I do wish he was just a little more understanding about such things. Naomi and I almost feel guilty when we start getting involved with someone, and then we start to worry about what will happen if we ever decide to bring that someone home to meet all of you."

Irene gazed up at her daughter.

"You are wise beyond your years, Agnes. But sometimes you think too much. You just go ahead and get interested in the man you want to, and I'll help handle your father."

"Thanks for those words of encouragement, Mom. But, as you know, I'm not in a position to even worry about such things at the moment."

Her voice clouded up as she obliquely introduced Morris and the breakup into the conversation. Irene patted her arm.

"There, there, my dear. Let's not get into that now. Besides, I have a good idea how we can get you back into the fray."

Agnes stopped walking and turned to her mother, her eyes wide with curiosity.

"Mom, what on earth does that mean? You're not trying to play matchmaker for me, are you?"

Irene wagged her finger in Agnes's face.

"Now don't you pay any mind to such thoughts. I don't need to tell you everything that's on my mind. You'll just have to wait and see."

Agnes laughed.

"Oh, boy! Sounds like this is going to be a very interesting holiday."

Irene smiled up at her.

"Oh, I hope so."

They had crossed the parking lot to the car. Neil stood by the back door, holding it open for them.

"Ladies, your chariot awaits. Won't you please get in?"

Agnes let Irene climb into the spacious back seat and then slid in beside her. Neil closed the door and jumped behind the wheel. Agnes leaned her head back and felt herself relaxing as the Packard glided smoothly over the city streets and then country roads to Smithfield. Her hopes for a happy holiday seemed to be coming true. She was very glad to be back in western Pennsylvania.

When they pulled into the driveway, ten year old Carl came whooping out of the house and yanked open the car door. As Agnes stepped out, he blanketed her in the biggest bear hug he could manage.

"Hi, Sis, I was so anxious to see you."

Agnes returned the hug, then put her hands on Carl's shoulders and pushed him out to arm's length.

"Let me get a look at you, young man. I think you've grown six inches since I last saw you."

Carl grinned and answered in his still high-pitched, pre-pubescent voice.

"Well, maybe not quite six, but pretty close to it." He wriggled out of Agnes's hands and stood behind Irene as she emerged from the car. "See, in another couple of months, I'll be taller than Mom."

Agnes smiled and laughed.

"Good for you, Carl. If Dad's any measuring stick, you're going to be a tall man one of these days."

"Yeh, I know," Carl shrilled, and then grabbed Agnes's hand. "Want to see where Dad buried those green rocks you sent me?" He pointed past the house. "He dug a hole in the back yard, a very deep hole, and dumped them in and covered them up."

The mention of Trinitite threatened to crack Agnes's reviving peace of mind. She didn't want to think about any aspect of her work right now. She tugged on Carl's arm.

"Not right now, Carl. Maybe later. I just got home and I want to sit down and have some coffee and cookies and catch up with everything that's been going on around here."

Carl was disappointed, but Irene came to the rescue before he could plead any further.

"Carl, why don't you go get those book reports you did so well on last week to show Agnes? Come, Agnes, let's get you off your feet so you can rest up from your trip."

She led them all inside and put on a pot of coffee. Soon the cookies she had baked that afternoon were on the kitchen table and the family was gathered around it, chatting about all sorts of ordinary things, just the things Agnes wanted to hear. Irene sat at one end of the table, happy to have at least this much of her family in one place again.

Neil sat at the opposite end, smoking cigarettes and drinking black coffee, and watching this daughter who had gone off to the war hardly more than a child, who now sat here at the table with the poise and maturity of someone much older than twenty. He felt as pleased as Irene to have all of them together again, even if it was only for a few short days. He would feel even better when Neil, Junior and Naomi joined the family circle once more. He cherished his family; it was an experience he wanted his children to have, an experience he had never had.

On Christmas morning, after they'd all opened their presents, Agnes went upstairs to take a bath and get dressed for dinner. As she was deciding what to wear, she heard a quick knock and then Irene's cherubic face appeared around her bedroom door.

"Oh, Agnes, I wanted to tell you that you might want to take special care picking out your dress today. I neglected to say that I invited the Flahertys to join us for Christmas dinner." She paused, a special twinkle in her eye. "Oh, and did I mention that Allen will be with them? He's home on leave; he'll be mustering out as soon as he gets back to camp. Since the war's over, they apparently don't need him anymore."

Agnes turned around slowly, a confused look on her face.

"Did you say the Flahertys? Allen Flaherty? Neil, Junior's little buddy from school?"

Irene nodded, as though it were the most natural thing in the world.

"But, Mom, we don't really know the Flahertys, do we? I mean, yes, Neil is fast friends with Allen, but why would you invite the whole family for Christmas dinner?"

Irene smiled and continued her explanation.

"You don't know everything, Miss Smartypants. Since you went off to Washington, I've gotten to know Mrs. Flaherty quite well. She's a regular customer at the store, and Carl has become good friends with Allen's younger brother, Gary. They have another daughter and a fairly new baby girl, too. I thought it would be nice to have them over and it would be a welcome respite for Mrs. Flaherty, what with the new one and all."

Agnes began to see through her mother's scheme.

"Mom! You're not doing all of this because you want me to become friends with Allen Flaherty, are you? Why, he's nearly two years younger than I am. What in the world would we ever have in common?"

Irene was ready with the answer to that question.

"The war, for one thing. Allen has been training to be a radio man. And you've been working with that very technical Manhattan

Project down there in D.C. I thought you'd have a lot to discuss." She waved at Agnes and disappeared into the hallway.

Agnes sat down at her dressing table and stared at herself in the mirror. She knew her mother was only trying to be helpful, but Allen Flaherty? The last thing she knew really meant anything to him was his bicycle, which he rode endlessly alongside Neil, Junior. How could her mother do this to her? She sighed and talked to herself in the mirror.

"Well, young lady, this isn't the toughest duty you've been asked to bear lately. And there's no getting around it. You'll get through it."

She leaned closer to the dressing table.

"I do wish I'd spent a little more time on my hair, though."

At one o'clock, Agnes heard a sharp knock on the front door. Irene, busy in the kitchen, called to her.

"Agnes, that must be the Flahertys. Would you mind getting it? And be nice, my dear."

She opened the door to find the Flaherty clan bunched up on the wide front step. Mr. Flaherty was not much taller than her mother, his wife was even shorter. A pretty little girl with pigtails stood in front of them, beside a slightly taller boy. Mrs. Flaherty was holding an infant, wrapped in a pink blanket. Standing behind the family, towering over his parents much the same way Agnes exceeded Irene in height, decked out in his carefully-pressed private's uniform, stood Allen. Agnes noticed that he, like all the Flahertys, except Mrs. Flaherty, had jet black hair. Black Irish, she thought.

She also couldn't help noticing that young Allen Flaherty, the kid who always had a couple of teeth missing when he smiled, had grown into a rather handsome young man, with hazel eyes, a slender face with high cheek bones, and a warm, rakish smile. The sight of all the dark-haired Flahertys cramped into such a tight space stopped Agnes in her tracks for a moment, especially the sight of master Allen Flaherty grown into a very handsome Mr. Allen Flaherty. Agnes realized she was staring. She caught herself, smiled and invited the Flahertys to come in.

At that moment, Mr. Flaherty leaned over the front flower bed and spat a large, brown wad of spittle into the bushes. He straightened up and pointed to his mouth.

"Got a bit of snuff in there. Hope you don't mind."

Agnes smiled and motioned them all inside.

"No, of course not. I know lots of folks here in town chew one thing or another, or smoke it."

Each of the Flahertys greeted her as they passed by, the younger ones in innocent, high pitched voices, Mrs. Flaherty in a thin, soprano laced with a West Virginia accent. Mr. Flaherty nodded and said "Thank you"; Allen stopped and held out his hand in a very gentlemanly manner. He flashed a wide smile.

"Gee, it's great to see you again, Agnes."

Agnes shook his hand firmly and looked into his grey eyes.

"Yes, it's nice to see you, Allen. You've changed a lot since I last saw you."

The smile left Allen's face, but a gentle warmth radiated from his beautiful eyes.

"I guess we all have, haven't we?" Allen asked, in a serious tone. He looked at Agnes with an intensity that made her glance down.

"Yes, I guess we have. This war business has been hard, hasn't it?"

"Maybe harder on you than me. You're down there in Washington ending the war--Mom showed me the newspaper clipping--while I'm riding trains all over the country, seeing the sites and picking up a little radio ops."

Agnes realized they were getting deep into conversation and she hadn't even let Allen come in. She stepped back and opened the door wider.

"Oh, what's wrong with me? I didn't mean to keep you standing there on the doorsill. Please come in and make yourself at home. Mom should have dinner ready in a few minutes."

She showed Allen into the parlor where the rest of his family was already seated. Carl had taken their coats upstairs and thrown them on his parents' bed. Mr. Flaherty was talking to Neil; Mrs. Flaherty was sitting quietly, keeping an eye on the younger children. Agnes offered Allen a chair and then excused herself to check on dinner. She pushed open the swinging door to the kitchen and headed for her mother, who was closing the oven door on a very large, golden-brown turkey.

"Mom, have you seen Allen Flaherty lately?"

"Oh, yes, my dear. He got home a couple of days ago. I made a point of delivering my invitation to dinner personally after I knew he was here." She turned and looked at Agnes, an impish expression on her face. "So, what do you think?"

Agnes put her hand to her chin and struck a thoughtful pose.

"Why, I don't know quite what to think. What I do know is that he's come a long way from that lanky kid with hair hanging over his forehead who used to pedal his bike up and down the road out front with Neil. He's really turned into a very attractive young man."

Irene hid a grin behind her hand.

"I thought you might notice that."

"But that doesn't mean I'm interested in him. He's still just my kid brother's pal." She tilted her nose in the air. "I am in the city now, you know, where I've been keeping company with some very sophisticated gentlemen."

Irene's quick wit and sharp tongue fired before she could stop herself.

"Yes, and a swell lot of good they've done you. Broke your heart, poor girl. Maybe a nice, country boy is just the thing for you."

"Maybe, Mom, we'll just have to see."

Irene patted her cheek.

"Yes, we will, my dear. Yes, we will. Now start taking these dishes out to the table. We're almost ready to eat."

When they had all assembled in the dining room, around a table dominated by the huge, golden brown turkey surrounded by steaming bowls of dressing, cranberry salad, and mashed potatoes and gravy, Neil looked to Agnes.

"Agnes, you're the biggest Bible-thumper around here. Would you do the honors?"

"I'd be glad to. Let's bow our heads."

She prayed a brief but fervent prayer, thanking God for all His mercies and especially for bringing them safely through the war, and asked a special blessing for Neil, Junior, stranded in the hot Texas sun, training to man a machine gun in the tail of a B-29; and, of course, for the fine food before them. Everyone around the table joined in the "Amen." As they raised their heads, Allen spoke up.

"You know, we pray at mess every day. The sergeant taught us to say: Praise the Lord and pass the ammunition." He finished with a wide grin. Neil roared with laughter.

"Oh, I like that. That gets right to it."

Allen's prayer and Neil's raucous reaction broke the thin coating of ice that had chilled the gathering since the Flahertys arrived. Free to relax and enjoy themselves, the grown-ups talked about working life and the weather and the war, and the younger kids, especially Carl and Gary, talked about sports and winter and school. Young Faith Flaherty was left out for a time; there was no Jenkins girl to entertain her. Agnes noticed her slightly downcast expression partway through the meal, and asked her about her interests and school and how she felt about her big brother in his uniform. At that, Faith turned to Allen and blurted out, just as the other conversations hit a lull, "I think he looks handsome enough to marry." Again, they all shared a laugh and Agnes noticed that Allen was blushing under his Texas-training base tan.

After dinner, Irene, Agnes, Mrs. Flaherty and Faith headed to the kitchen to take care of the dishes; Neil invited the men, which included Carl and Gary, much to their satisfaction, into the parlor, where he offered Mr. Flaherty a cigar. Allen declined the one offered to him and pulled a pack of Camels from his shirt pocket. The room quickly filled with smoke, but no one seemed to notice. Gary, who was already experimenting with cigarettes, wished they'd offer him one. After a few minutes, Neil sent Carl to the kitchen to fetch some coffee for the men and homemade root beer for the boys.

The conversation in the parlor was a bit labored compared to the one in the kitchen. Neil knew Mr. Flaherty from the mines, but they worked with different crews and Neil was a supervisor, while Flaherty was just an ordinary miner; an ordinary miner, but with a serious, always dangerous job. He was a shot firer. His task was to drill holes in the surface of the ribbon of coal the crews had uncovered, insert a section of dynamite, attach a wire to it, and blast the massive slab of coal into pieces small enough to be shoveled into the small rail cars that ran up to the face on tracks laid down by yet another crew.

Flaherty had taken to drinking beer at a local tavern to take the edge off his nerve-wracking duties. He had told his son he preferred raw eggs with his beer, once boasting that he could down all the beer offered to him, as long as he had raw eggs to wash it down with it. Mrs. Flaherty, as devoutly religious as Agnes was, disliked her husband's extracurricular practices, but never complained about it. He was a hard worker and good provider, and that was good enough for her.

Neil knew little about Flaherty's working life and less about his personal life. Even though Flaherty shouldered a sobering responsibility on the job, Neil, from his exalted status as a part of management, couldn't bring himself to see Flaherty as his equal. Nonetheless, he tried to keep the conversation going. They talked about motor cars and houses and hunting, and that got them through the next couple of hours.

In the kitchen, Agnes stood by watching as Irene and Mrs. Flaherty put their heads together and buzzed about their little plan. Unlike Neil, Irene felt no distance between their families; she knew but did not care that Mrs. Flaherty had married at the age of fifteen and left behind her life in the mountains of West Virginia to share Flaherty's fortunes, which had not been great. He had managed a farm for a wealthy land owner for many years, and then headed into the mines, like so many others. Theirs had been a fairly hard life, with little left over for fun and frolic at the end of the month. But, like Neil, he had managed to keep a job all the way through the Depression, and in these parts that was saying something. Agnes listened to the mothers conspiring for a while and then broke in.

"Ladies, please! You don't need to talk about me as if I'm not here. I know what you're up to."

The two older women interrupted their chatter to look at Agnes.

"My biggest question is, how did this plan get hatched? Why would you want to get your daughter," she pointed to Irene, "and your son," she pointed to Mrs. Flaherty, "interested in each other? We're both adults. I'm sure we can do just fine on our own in the hunt for a mate."

Irene took the lead in responding.

"My dear, if you must know, we have been worried about both of you; you for some time, and Allen more recently. You are out there walking around with a broken heart after some citified cad threw you over, and Allen has taken up some unattractive habits since he went off to war, such as drinking and hanging out at taverns where he chases the skirts of floozies neither of us would ever allow under our roofs."

Mrs. Flaherty took it from there.

"So, when we were sharing our burdens down at Bertulli's recently, we thought we might be able to kill two birds with one stone by getting the two of you together. We love you both so much we want to do everything we can to protect you from the wicked world out there and point you in the direction of real happiness."

Irene wrapped it up.

"You can't blame us for wanting our children to be happy, can you, Agnes?" She held up her hands. "Heaven forbid we should make you feel like you're being forced into anything. You're both adults now and can clearly make decisions for yourself. But won't you give this a chance? You have so much in common, and your mothers are becoming such good friends. And Allen is Neil, Junior's friend and Carl and Gary enjoy palling around together. It just seems natural for this to happen."

She clasped her hands together and held them up toward Agnes.

"Will you at least give it a chance, Agnes?"

Agnes walked over and laid a hand on each woman's shoulder.

"You couple of conniving biddies. But I know the plot was hatched out of love, so I can't be too critical of it. Yes, as far as I'm concerned, I'm willing to wait and see where it goes, if it goes anywhere. Allen will have to speak for himself."

Mrs. Flaherty spoke up, again.

"Oh, Agnes, if he has any sense at all--and I admit there are times when I wonder about that--he'll give this every chance, too. Good luck, dear. I would love to welcome you as my daughter-in-law."

Irene chimed in, taking Mrs. Flaherty's hand.

"And I would be more than pleased to have Allen as part of our family. I know he's a fine man, and he's young. I predict he will do good things in the world."

The mothers looked at each other and then sealed the plan with a handshake. Agnes shook her head and tossed the dish towel she was holding over the now-empty dish drainer.

"We'll see, you two, we'll just have to see."

As she drifted off to sleep that night, she chuckled to herself, picturing the two women sitting at the kitchen table, their heads together, devising a scheme to make their children happy. Maybe it would, she thought, and then maybe it wouldn't work at all. She hoped it would be fun finding out.

CHAPTER FIFTEEN

Spending holiday time with family and friends did more to revive Agnes's flagging spirits than she had even hoped for. Being home with people who loved her made her feel secure and reminded her that as she faced the challenges of her work in Washington she was never really alone; Irene and Neil and Carl loved her, and everyone was proud of what she was doing in D.C. Her church family greeted her as if she were a triumphant warrior returning from the field of battle; they used those words in the prayers they offered up at the Sunday morning worship service she attended. And there was the added glow of Allen Flaherty.

As he and his family departed Christmas Day, he had quietly asked Agnes if he might call on her again before he headed back to duty. She had smiled and said that would be nice. One visit turned into several, and they had gotten along so well that it was Allen Flaherty, not Irene and Neil, who had driven her to the train station on New Year's Day when she returned to Washington.

She found his shy smile and gentle voice endearing, and happily let him kiss her lightly on the cheek as they said goodbye. He asked if he might write to her and if she would write to him, and she agreed to both requests. He was not Morris, the confident college man, always dressed to a "T" in his tailored suits. Allen was soft-spoken, more reserved, and came to the house in his uniform; but she thought he looked quite handsome in that. And, when she thought about it, she had to admit Allen was very attractive. Irene, who had seen a picture of Morris, told her, out of Neil's earshot, that she thought Allen won the "Best Looking" contest hands down. And, as they'd discovered in the brief days after Christmas, they really did have so much in common. It was too soon to think about such things, they'd only just struck up a relationship, but this country boy with the hazel eyes and coal black hair might be just the man for her, a young woman grown accustomed to the attractions of the city, but still very much a country girl at heart.

The only fly in the ointment was Neil. He had observed their budding friendship, noticed that Agnes took Allen's hand when they went out for a mid-winter stroll, and, true to form, he didn't like it. He endured Allen's visits stoically, retreating to the kitchen to smoke and drink black coffee when Agnes ushered Allen into the parlor, and telling Irene he didn't think this was such a good idea. Irene told him to hush and let Agnes live her life. She said she thought Allen seemed like a very nice young fellow. Neil grumped and lit another cigarette. He restrained himself until the very last moment of Agnes's visit. As Allen carried her traveling case out to his father's car, Neil gave Agnes a quick hug and then looked her in the eye.

"Agnes, I'm not trying to run your life, but I have to tell you to be careful with this young man. I don't think he's right for you, besides which, you're too young to be getting involved with anybody."

Agnes smiled up at him and patted his arm.

"Don't worry, Dad. I've only just gotten to know him. I'm your sensible daughter, remember? I promise not to lose my head."

She gave him another hug, and let Irene squeeze her tightly, then followed Allen to the car. Irene waved as they drove away; Neil stood silently in the doorway, frowning and shaking his head.

****

Agnes returned to a Manhattan Project shifting from wartime to peace time. General Groves had obviously worked straight through the holidays; stacks of documents appeared on her desk for processing. She typed up a flurry of phone call transcriptions from O'Leary. They detailed conversations Groves had with Oppenheimer about where things should go now that the bomb had won the war. Groves was pushing Oppenheimer to keep building bombs, as many as fifty of them, to undergird a post-war military strategy based on the nuclear deterrent. Oppenheimer, having seen the terrible destruction inflicted on Japan, reminded Groves that he and the scientists at Los Alamos had been arguing since they witnessed the Trinity blast that the future of this weapon should lie in the hands of the world community, something like the United Nations organization, which had been created in October at Dumbarton Oaks, in San Francisco.

Groves accused Oppenheimer of going soft on the issue and not understanding the military realities involved. He chided Oppenheimer, long after the fact, for a comment he'd made as he watched the Trinity fireball rise into the New Mexico sky. Groves said staffers had told him Oppenheimer had quoted the Bhagavad-Gita, murmuring, "I am become Death, the Destroyer of Worlds." The two men had agreed over the phone that their differences were irreconcilable. At the bottom of the pile of transcripts was a letter, dated late October, from Groves to Oppenheimer, formalizing the physicist's decision to return to civilian life. He would be replaced by a Berkeley scientist named Norris Bradbury. By the time Agnes read it, Oppenheimer had already returned to Caltech, where he was teaching when Groves tapped him to build the bomb.

Beneath the transcripts Agnes found a report from Los Alamos, with a newspaper clipping attached. Instructions at the top of the report indicated it should be classified "Top Secret." In the margin of the report's first page, someone had written: The press boys did a good job containing this one. Agnes was trying to adhere to her vow not to read the reports, but the headline on the clipping piqued her curiosity. It read, "Atomic Bomb Worker Died From Burns." It was a UPI account, datelined Los Alamos, N.M., September 20.

Agnes soon discovered that the headline was a bit misleading. Only the first paragraph of the short piece dealt with the accident. "The Government's atomic bomb laboratory disclosed today, in reply to an inquiry, that a worker died September 15 'from burns in an industrial accident' on Aug. 21. He was identified as Harry K. Daghlian, 24, New London, Conn., a Purdue University instructor prior to coming here in November, 1943." The remaining three paragraphs announced the creation of a "spare time university" at Los Alamos, that would offer military and civilian personnel courses in chemistry, mathematics, physics and metallurgy, rather than studies in "atomic bomb principles." The last paragraph identified physicist Hans Bethe as the chair of the new program and Enrico Fermi, creator of the first controlled nuclear chain reaction, as a member of the faculty.

It was clear from the "Top Secret" documents that Daghlian had experienced something far more drastic than a simple "industrial accident." The report identified Daghlian as part of the crew assigned to the final construction of the gadget's plutonium core before the Trinity test. On August 21st, it said, Daghlian was conducting experiments on the assembly of critical mass, using a sphere of plutonium and bricks made of tungsten carbide. According to the report, Daghlian had violated safety procedures by returning to the lab, alone, in the evening, to continue the experiments.

A security guard on duty that night had told investigators he was uncomfortable with Daghlian's solo efforts, but had no authority to stop him, and had instead greeted the physicist and continued reading a newspaper. The report then recounted Daghlian's explanation of what happened. He said he had begun building another critical mass, and noticed from the ever-present Geiger counters that the stack was getting hot, approaching a chain reaction. As he tried to pull the most recently added brick from the pile, he said, it slipped from his hand and fell back on top of the assembly. As the frequency of the clicks from the monitors ratcheted up, Daghlian had instinctively pushed the brick away with his right hand. As he did so, he felt a tingling in his hand and saw a blue glow around the sphere of plutonium.

The flash of light attracted the guard's attention. He told investigators he looked up to see Daghlian standing by the pile, his hands at his sides. Daghlian pulled more of the bricks away to stabilize the assembly and then admitted to the guard what had happened. A graduate student who had arrived immediately after the accident drove Daghlian to the hospital for treatment; the guard stayed behind to tell his superior about the incident.

The guard, a twenty-nine year old private from Ohio, was later admitted to the hospital for observation, but other than an increased level of white blood cells and complaints that he felt more tired than usual, doctors concluded that he had not suffered any long term injuries. They estimated that he had been exposed to thirty-one roentgens of x-rays and as little as one roentgen of gamma rays.

Daghlian, on the other hand, was a far different story, a story they had not shared with the inquiring journalists. Doctors estimated the young physicist's total body exposure at 480 roentgens of x-rays and 110 roentgens of gamma rays, far in excess of the safe exposure levels Warren had set for the crews sent to Ground Zero shortly after Trinity. The radiation had penetrated parts of his upper body, most seriously, his hands. His left hand, they reported, had absorbed five thousand to fifteen thousand rem (roentgen equivalent man); his right hand, the one he'd used to push the brick away, had soaked up twenty-thousand to forty-thousand rem.

The report said Daghlian's right hand was already swollen and numb by the time they got him to the hospital. He grew nauseous and spent much of the first day after the accident gagging and vomiting. The queasiness persisted the second day, but the vomiting stopped, replaced by persistent hiccups. By the third day, he was able to eat.

But physical symptoms continued to appear: a blister on his ring finger, bluish discoloration under his fingernails, more blisters on his palm and the back of his hand, between his fingers, and painful swelling in his fingers. The doctors lanced the blisters and removed the decaying skin, then wrapped the wounds with treated gauze. They repeated the procedures day after day, adding injections to reduce Daghlian's rising level of pain. When morphine failed to reduce the agony Daghlian was in, they packed his hands in ice to numb them. Still the symptoms of radiation sickness advanced.

Ten days after the accident, Daghlian felt nauseous after he ate. His stomach hurt. The cramping worsened and chronic diarrhea set in. On the fifteenth day, doctors administered blood transfusions and intravenous fluids, but they produced no improvement. According to the report, Daghlian grew increasingly apprehensive about what was happening; his heart began to race. His condition continued to deteriorate. On September 15th, Daghlian slipped into a coma; he died at half-past four in the afternoon. The doctors listed the cause of death as "severe burns, upper extremities and trunk." The press release issued by Los Alamos, which was appended at the back of the report, referred to chemical burns. Once again, the word radiation did not appear in the official explanation.

As Agnes stamped the documents "Top Secret," she felt a tingling in her fingers. She told herself it was just a reaction to the grim description she had just read, but the tingling was still there after she returned the stamp to the rack. She placed her hands, palms down, on top of the documents and stared at them. There was no discoloration on her long, slender fingers, no signs of swelling all these weeks after what she now knew was exposure to radiation from the shiny, green Trinitite. She had felt tired in those long weeks before Christmas, but that had gone away while she was home with her family.

She closed her eyes and prayed, *Lord, please remove this burden from me. Don't let me be sick from this dread radiation disease.* When she opened her eyes, the tingling sensation had stopped. She flexed her fingers, examined them once more for any visible signs of damage, and told herself to buck up and get her imagination under control. She took a deep breath and exhaled slowly. *I'm all right,* she thought, *this is the last time I'm going to scare myself silly over this radiation business. I'm sure it's not going to create any problems for my life.* She willed herself to put such thoughts away, and she succeeded in keeping them in abeyance for most of the next thirty years, until they forced their way back into her consciousness.

****

The new year brought with it a number of developments in addition to Agnes's budding friendship with Allen Flaherty. In early February, Eleanor announced first to Agnes and then to the other girls in the office that Roger had been discharged from the army and they were heading home to start a new life together in Kansas. Two weeks later, Eleanor and Roger stopped by Mrs. Sisko's house in the old Ford Roger had managed to find, despite the severe shortage of cars created by the country's shift to war materiel production. The Macombers joined Agnes and the others in the parlor for a last cup of coffee and a conversation laced with the laughter and high spirits of young people looking forward to the future.

When Eleanor and Roger had taken leave of everyone else, Agnes walked them to the car. The back seat was piled high with suitcases. As they reached the sidewalk, Agnes produced a bouquet of roses she had hidden behind her back. Eleanor accepted them with tears in her eyes.

"Oh, they're lovely, Agnes. You didn't need to do anything like this."

Agnes put her arms around Eleanor and held her close, then gave Roger a hug. She stepped back and wagged a finger at him.

"You have taken on a great responsibility, Mr. Macomber. This woman is as precious to me as anyone in the world. I want you to promise that you will take very good care of her."

Roger smiled sheepishly.

"Yes, ma'am. I know. And I will take care of her."

"Well, you'd better, young man." Agnes smiled at them.

"I wish for you the happiest life ever." She turned to Eleanor. "And don't forget to write to me. I want to know all about your life back on the Great Plains."

"I promise, Agnes. And you write, too. I want to be one of the first to know what happens with Allen Flaherty."

Agnes had shared her excitement over reconnecting with her brother's childhood friend.

"You know I will, Eleanor. Most of all, I'm going to miss you, and you, too, Roger. Do let's keep in touch. God bless you."

Eleanor reached out and took Agnes's hand.

"And God bless you, too, Agnes. I don't know anyone in this world who deserves it more." She turned to Roger. "Do you think we should be going, Mr. Macomber?"

"Yes, we should, Mrs. Macomber." They were both grinning.

He reached behind her and opened the passenger side door. Eleanor released Agnes's hand and got in. After Roger closed the door, she rolled down the window.

"Goodbye, Agnes. Take good care of yourself."

"You, too, Eleanor. Have a safe trip."

Roger slid in behind the wheel and pulled the Ford into gear. A few moments later, they turned the corner at the end of Mrs. Sisko's street and drove out of sight, heading in a generally westerly direction. Agnes felt sad as she watched her good friend drive off, but happy, too, that Eleanor had found such a wonderful companion. She hoped she would be as fortunate.

A week later, Naomi charged into the house with an announcement. Cliff had asked her to marry him and she had said yes. She had kept Agnes informed about her growing attachment to this young Wisconsin farm boy, admitting that she might never love him as she had Franklin, but she thought she loved him enough to find a life with him. Agnes wasn't surprised by the announcement, but neither were most of the other girls. They all knew how Naomi had grieved over Franklin's death, and they had noticed that Cliff was the first man Naomi had dated since then who really seemed to get her attention.

There was glitch in their getting hitched, she confided to Agnes later that night. She had always dreamed of a lovely church wedding, but Cliff's family was Roman Catholic, and they would not countenance the idea of their son being married in some Protestant edifice that did not fall under the Pope's watchful eye.

"So," Naomi told Agnes, "we've decided to tie the knot like Eleanor did, with a J.P., right here in D.C. Will you stand up with me, Agnes?"

Agnes was still grappling with the Catholic part. She and her Free Methodist friends took a dim view of Roman Catholics; they held even darker views of the Pope and the Vatican. But she loved her sister too much to make an issue out of it. She gave Naomi a hug and kissed her on the cheek.

"You don't even have to ask if I'll be your bridesmaid. You know darn well I'd be offended if you didn't ask me. Are you going to invite Mom and Dad down here for the ceremony or are you planning to take Cliff home to Smithfield?"

"Neither, I think. I called Mom the other night and asked her about the idea of going home to get married and she said she didn't think Dad could handle it. She said I should go ahead and get it over with and he'll just have to live with it."

"Oh, Naomi, I'm sorry. Dad can be so bullheaded, sometimes."

She looked at Naomi, who was looking at herself in Agnes's dressing table mirror. She didn't seem particularly stricken by this turn of events.

"So you're okay with this?"

Naomi turned to her, tears that she was fighting hard to hold back welling up in her eyes.

"I'm as okay with it as I can be, I guess."

"And you really do love him, Naomi?"

"I do, Agnes. He's a good, decent man. And I'm sure I'll be happy with him."

"Are you going to stay here in D.C. after you're married?"

"No, he wants to go back to the farm in Wisconsin."

"Is that such a good idea? You are a country girl, but not a typical one. And that's a long way from Mom and Dad."

"I know. But you can come visit us and I'll try to get down to Pennsylvania as often as we can. It'll be all right."

Agnes gave her another hug.

"Oh, I hope so, Naomi. I surely hope so."

The following weekend, two days after Cliff was mustered out of the army, he and Naomi stood before a justice of the peace in front of the Lincoln Memorial, with Agnes by Naomi's side, and an army buddy of Cliff's standing witness for him. Then they returned to Mrs. Sisko's to retrieve Naomi's bags, loaded them into a taxi with Cliff's duffel, and said goodbye. Agnes kissed Cliff on the cheek and squeezed Naomi's slender figure, wrapped in a stylish, knee-length, black wool coat, until her arms grew tired. Tears flowed on both sides of the hug. Naomi finally took a deep breath and pulled away.

"We'd better get going. Don't want to miss the train. I don't suppose they run that many to the wilds of Wisconsin."

Everyone laughed. Agnes pulled Naomi close to her as Cliff helped the cab driver load the bags into the trunk.

"Don't forget, Naomi. If you ever need help with anything, you just give me a call. That's what family is for, no matter what Neil Jenkins may think. And I'll bet you even he'll get over this quicker than we suspect. Take care, Sis, I love you."

"I love you, too, sweet Agnes. I know I'm lousy about writing letters, but I promise to write to you and tell you about my adventures in dairyland."

She and Agnes shared one last laugh, tears glistening in their eyes. Agnes kissed Naomi on the cheek and gave Cliff the same lecture she'd recently delivered to Roger Macomber.

"And you take good care of my big sister, Mr. Racine."

Cliff smiled and saluted.

"Yes, ma'am. I certainly will. And you come see us, okay?"

"That's a deal. And you bring Naomi down to see us when you can, too."

Cliff nodded and opened the cab door for Naomi. They hustled inside and waved as the cab headed downtown. Agnes waved as they drove away. She wished the same happiness for Naomi as she had for Eleanor, but beneath her good wishes, she felt a nagging reservation, a sense that Naomi's life in Wisconsin might not turn out to be as bright as Eleanor's would be in Kansas. She would pray fervently for both of them as they headed off to the lives they had chosen.

As the tide of young people that had flowed into Washington during the war reversed itself, more and more of them plotting a post-war course that took them away from D.C., Agnes resolved to stay in the city as long as she could. Apart from the dark responsibilities and secrecy of her current job, she loved the august beauty of the nation's capital--its buildings, its monuments, its museums, the Potomac flowing gently between its banks, and, of course, the cherry trees that brought such colorful splendor to the rim of the Tidal Basin each spring.

She assumed her work with the Manhattan Project might eventually come to an end; she had overheard chatter in the office that even Mrs. O'Leary and General Groves himself might be off to other pursuits before too long. Surely, with her skills and a good recommendation from O'Leary she could find a place in another part of the government. What she wasn't sure she would find was a partner.

The last thing she intended to be was a spinster, like the older, single women who wound up teaching Smithfield's rambunctious children at Tobin School. She respected them for their commitment to educating America's young, working to instill in each one of them a love of God and country and a desire to make something of themselves. No, she would never be critical of their lives. It just wasn't what she longed for. In her mind, she saw herself married to a good man, living in a nice house, and shepherding her children, preferably at least one boy and one girl, through the perils of childhood and adolescence into a bright future where they could seize the American dream. But would she find that right man?

The possibility that she might not, that she would end up a tired, old maid, tipped her into a melancholy not unlike the early stages of the depression that periodically gripped Irene. But she need not have worried about it. She was about to discover that her stars were indeed in alignment, and fate was descending on her, in the present time, with only the best intentions. The day after Naomi and Cliff headed toward Lake Michigan, a string of tin cans banging along the road behind them, and "Just Married" etched in soap on the back window, Allen Flaherty's first letter arrived.

He told her he had been back at camp for a couple of weeks and would soon be signing the papers to close the army chapter of his life. He would be home for good shortly before Easter. He wondered if she were planning to be home then. She hadn't really intended to go home again so soon, but his question made up her mind. She wrote him a quick note in her graceful, flowing hand, saying she would indeed be arriving home the Friday night before the holiday. "I wonder," she wrote, "if you would be able to pick me up at the train station that night?" His reply was postmarked "Smithfield, PA". He told her he was already home and would be very happy to escort her home from the station.

The visit was, to paraphrase the old saying, short but sweet. They spent most of the weekend together and Allen turned a few heads when Agnes took him to Easter Sunday services at her church. He had found a suit somewhere, a wide-lapelled, blue pinstripe, and she thought he looked as handsome in it as he had in his uniform. When the weekend had wound down, Allen drove her back to the train station and they agreed that he would come to Washington soon and let her show him around the town.

He arrived on the train two weeks later, in time to enjoy the cherry blossoms and the balmy weather of Washington as it emerged from winter. He returned in early May, by which time Agnes knew she had fallen in love again. Allen had no reservations about his feelings. He told her he thought about her all the time, at home, when he was out walking in the woods near his parents' house, even down in the mine, where his father had gotten him a job pounding in the heavy timbers that kept the roof from caving in.

As they strolled along the mall during his second visit to Washington, Allen stopped in the middle of the path and turned to Agnes. They'd been talking, lightheartedly, about what they hoped their lives would be like, and had discovered that their dreams were actually quite similar, down to the hope for a boy and a girl. As he faced Agnes, Allen took both of her hands in his and looked deep in her eyes.

"Agnes, you know I'm not a smooth talker. I mostly come right out with it, and I always mean what I say. And I need to say something to you now."

Agnes smiled and waited for Allen to continue, all the while looking deep into his hazel eyes.

"So, here it is. Agnes Jenkins, will you marry me?"

Agnes's unreserved response surprised her and Allen.

"Oh, yes, Allen Flaherty," she cried in an ecstatic voice, "I will marry you!"

Her usual sense of decorum already abandoned, she flung her arms around Allen's neck and kissed him on the lips. He wrapped his arms around her, and they kissed and held each other, in the middle of the walkway, as the crowd of sightseers, some smiling to see this public display of affection, parted around them. Agnes felt a joy beyond anything she had ever felt before. She knew it wasn't sensible to think such a thing, but she honestly thought she could feel the scar on her heart, left by Morris's rejection, disappear.

After a very long while, she and Allen released each other, intertwined their fingers and strolled on around the mall, beaming as though they'd just won a great race. Before Allen boarded the train for Pennsylvania Sunday afternoon, they had set the date: October 12, 1946. And they would try to set up housekeeping in Washington.

Neil, Junior solved that problem for them. He was due to be discharged in October, and wrote to say that a buddy of his had offered to take him and Allen on as partners in a service station he was negotiating to buy in D.C., not far from the White House. Allen leaped at the opportunity and called Agnes to tell her the good news. They decided they would still go home to be married, in Agnes's Free Methodist church. Agnes decided to break the news in a letter to her mother, rather than risk a scene with Neil over the phone.

Her assessment of the likely reaction at home was, as usual, accurate. Irene replied that she and the Flahertys were overjoyed with the news. Neil, she wrote, had erupted angrily, with the same old objections--Agnes was too young to marry anyone, and if she was going to get married, it should be someone more worthy than a laborer's son. Irene told her not to pay any attention to Neil; there probably wasn't a man yet born, she wrote, who would measure up to her father's standards for a groom. She said she was sure she could have him behaving in a more civil fashion by October. She said he had already accepted, but not necessarily given his blessing to, Naomi's marriage to Cliff, and they were both looking forward to the birth of their first grandchild, an exciting event that Naomi had recently informed them was on the way.

CHAPTER SIXTEEN

At the office, Agnes had replaced her beige desk blotter with a large, desk calendar. She put an "X" through each date as it passed, and kept count of the dwindling number of days until she became Mrs. Allen Flaherty. Most of the paperwork she handled dealt with downsizing of the project and closing of work sites. She hoped there wouldn't be any more reports of deaths caused by the bomb. She'd learned enough about all of that already to satisfy her curiosity for a lifetime. But her hope was dashed by an event at Los Alamos on May 21st.

She found the report on her desk when she returned from celebrating the Fourth of July at home with Allen and her family. Investigators detailed the death of Louis P. Slotin, a Canadian scientist who, according to the report, had worked with Harry Daghlian on final assembly of the gadget's plutonium core before the Trinity test. Slotin was demonstrating the assembly process to seven other scientists, in the same secret Omega Lab where Daghlian had earlier received his fatal dose of radiation, when a screwdriver slipped, allowing the two beryllium-coated plutonium spheres to touch, triggering an instant chain reaction.

The report said Slotin immediately reached to knock the spheres apart, but not before a blue haze of radiation flashed in the room. Investigators estimated that nearly one thousand rads of radiation had penetrated Slotin's body, more than a lethal dose.

Because Slotin had instinctively positioned himself between the assembly and the rest of the group, the others had been exposed to far lower amounts of radiation, and thus faced no life-threatening injuries.

The next section of the report documented, in detail that left Agnes nauseous and light-headed, the nine days of torment Slotin had endured as the radiation destroyed him. The progression of the excruciating disease mirrored Daghlian's last days: diarrhea, swollen hands, blisters on the skin that had borne the brunt of the deadly radiation, failure of internal organs, and gangrene. By May 30th, Slotin was dead.

The report noted that General Groves had flown Slotin's parents to Los Alamos from Winnipeg, after their son called to tell them he was too badly injured to travel and would like to see them. They arrived in time to bid him farewell, then took him home, his body sealed inside a lead-lined casket. The entire incident had been classified "Top Secret," and not even those in the lab had been given the details. The press office had issued a simple report of an assembly accident, and hailed Slotin as a hero for stopping the reaction and saving the lives of everyone else in the room. The report stated that all future core assembly work would be done using newly developed remote technology; Slotin's tragic experiment marked the end of hands-on work in the lab.

Attached to the report, Agnes found a clipping from the Winnipeg Tribune. A photograph showing the young scientist's casket being lifted out the door of a military aircraft bore the caption "Hero's Body Home." Beneath the article was a short poem, first published in the Los Alamos camp newspaper on June 14th. Associate editor Thomas Ashlock had entitled it, "Slotin-A Tribute": "May God receive you, great-souled scientist! While you were with us, even strangers knew, The breadth and lofty stature of your mind, 'Twas only in the crucible of death, We saw at last your noble heart revealed."

The last page of the document was a copy of a special citation that had been read to Slotin as he lay dying in the hospital: "Dr. Slotin's quick reaction at the immediate risk of his own life prevented a more serious development of the experiment which would certainly have resulted in the death of the seven men working with him, as well as serious injury to others in the general vicinity."

So much death, Agnes thought, from this grand project that had ended the war. She wondered how the other scientists felt, after watching their colleague die such a terrible death. Did it raise any questions in their minds about the dangerous forces they were dealing with, this invisible and devastating radiation? Her heart ached for the young Canadian's family. The newspaper story had mentioned that Slotin's father had been surprised to learn, after the war, that his son had been working on the a-bomb, and had expressed the same pride in his son's endeavors that Neil and Irene had over Agnes's work in D.C. She assumed that Slotin had gone to his death as proud of his atomic accomplishments as his family was. She prayed that God would be with them and hoped that the other scientists would not suffer any delayed effects of the accident.

All along since she joined Groves's staff, Agnes had assumed too much about how others involved in the Manhattan Project felt, and questioned too little the confident pronouncements of Groves and his colleagues, who asked the world to trust them when they vowed that they had the nuclear dragon under control. Much later, Slotin's nephew would tell a writer that his uncle "was troubled by what he was doing at Los Alamos." And follow-up studies of the accident, which she never saw, would suggest that three of the seven men in the room that day would eventually die of illness triggered by the flash of blue light and its attendant release of penetrating radiation. By the time Agnes realized her mistake, it would be far too late. It was already too late when she learned of Slotin's untimely demise.

As she had done so many times before, Agnes pushed Slotin's disturbing story into the recesses of her mind, and focused on the good things to come. When she walked into Room 5120 on her last day, she felt excited and anxious to move on with her life. At three in the afternoon, Mrs. O'Leary called her into Groves's office. The general rose from his chair, walked around the desk and extended his hand.

"Mrs. O'Leary tells me you have done yeoman duty here in these offices, Agnes. I want to thank you for that and for your service to your country in perilous times."

As he shook her hand, Mrs. O'Leary handed him a certificate which he then presented to Agnes.

"Secretary Stimson has asked me to give you this on his behalf."

Agnes took the document in her hand; she noticed that the rounded watermark embossed in the paper bore the words "Manhattan Project" along the top edge, with a large "A" inside over the word "BOMB," and the Corps of Engineers emblem at the bottom. The document was headed: United States of America, War Department, Army Service Forces-Corps of Engineers, Manhattan District. The inscription read: This is to certify that Agnes B. Jenkins has participated in work essential to the production of the Atomic Bomb, thereby contributing to the successful conclusion of World War II. This certificate is awarded in appreciation of effective service." The document was dated August 6, 1945 and signed in blue ink by Henry L. Stimson, Secretary of War.

Agnes quickly scanned the certificate, then looked up at Groves.

"Thank you, sir. It has been a privilege to work with you and Mrs. O'Leary."

O'Leary handed Groves another sheet of paper, blank side up. Groves turned it over and offered it to Agnes.

"At the risk of seeming vain, I'd like to give you this as a memento of your time with us."

Groves's gift was an eight-by-ten photo of himself seated at his desk, pen in hand, two stars on his shirt collar proudly signaling that he was now a Major General. He had signed it in the lower left corner: To Agnes B. Jenkins, With appreciation for her hard work for many months. L.R. Groves, Maj. Gen USA. Agnes felt a wave of pride and gratitude sweep over her. She looked straight into Groves's penetrating, blue eyes and reached out to shake his hand again.

"Oh, thank you, sir. This will be a wonderful keepsake. I will cherish it the rest of my life."

She started to take her leave, but Mrs. O'Leary stopped her with a hand on her shoulder.

"We're not quite finished here, Agnes."

She stepped to her desk and brought back a neatly wrapped package, with a very small note card attached. She handed it to Agnes. In a small, neat hand, O'Leary had written: To Agnes. You have done an outstanding job. Thank you. It was signed: "Major" O'Leary. Agnes looked at O'Leary and smiled.

"This is lovely, Mrs. O'Leary. Thank you."

O'Leary grew impatient.

"Yes, yes, but you don't even know what it is. Open it."

Agnes carefully pulled away the wrapping to find a small, white box. She gently lifted the lid. Inside was a cursive, capital "A," carved from wood, with a beautiful, satiny finish. Agnes lifted it from the box and discovered a pin attached to the back. She held the "A" in the palm of her hand and looked back at O'Leary.

"This is just beautiful, Mrs. O'Leary. Thank you so much."

"You are quite welcome, Agnes. You know what it stands for, don't you?"

"Atomic, I would assume."

"That's correct. I just wanted to be sure you didn't think it stood for Agnes."

She smiled, to let Agnes know she was teasing her.

Agnes smiled back.

"I may use your joke to tease people sometime when they get too snoopy about our work here."

"You are welcome to it, Agnes."

She took Agnes's hand in both of hers.

"Now we really are finished, my dear. I just want to tell you how much I've appreciated having you here. And to wish you all the best in the years to come. We'll miss you around here."

"And I you, Mrs. O'Leary."

She looked from O'Leary to Groves and back again.

"And thank you both for letting me be a part of this project. God bless you."

"And you, Agnes. Goodbye, my dear. Take care of yourself."

Agnes said, "Goodbye," softly and turned to leave the room.

By the time she reached the door, Groves was already back at his desk. Mrs. O'Leary moved to the doorway and watched Agnes as she gathered her personal items in a small box, shook hands and exchanged hugs with the girls in the outer office, gave a last spin to the collection of rubber stamps in the small, wooden rack on her desk, took a last look around the room where she'd worked so hard and learned so much over the long, grueling months, and then picked up her things and walked out of the Manhattan Project toward what O'Leary felt certain would be a bright future for a bright, young woman.

Agnes bid farewell to Mrs. Sisko and the girls still living with her, and treated herself--and her two large suitcases--to a cab ride to the train station. She leaned back in her seat as the train rolled out of the station, watching the city scenes recede, soon to be replaced by the rolling fields and small villages of rural Maryland. Other passengers in her car noticed the attractive, well-dressed young woman gazing out the window. The more curious wondered who she might be and where this train was taking her. But Agnes did not notice them. Her mind was swirling with thoughts and feelings—many pleasant, some terrifying-- generated by the experiences of the past three years.

She had indeed learned a lot over these many months and she knew she had changed; the seriousness she had already possessed when she came to Washington had been deepened by her encounter with the realities of a wartime world. The idea of being willing to die for your country, words she and her schoolmates had parroted eagerly in the classroom, had a special meaning for a country girl privy to the secrets of the atom bomb project. She thought about all the lives that had been lost in the war, American, German, Japanese. Thoughts of those who had died *for* the war, *for* the bomb, not in battle but in those dreadful laboratory accidents, vied with all the truly good things that had happened, trying to force their way into her consciousness, but she pushed them back into a dark corner. *If you can't think of something nice,* she told herself, *don't think of anything.* She let her thoughts drift toward Pennsylvania and the exciting times that awaited her there. With the power of positive thinking once again triumphant, she drifted off to sleep. She awoke to the sound of the conductor's voice calling out the stop in Uniontown.

When she stepped onto the platform, Allen was there to greet her, and there beside him stood young Neil, grinning from ear-to-ear, looking trim, fit, tanned and handsome after his long months of training in the hot, Texas sun. She dropped her bags and rushed over to them, hugging and kissing Allen first, then grabbing hold of Neil and squeezing him hard before he could say anything. He finally found his voice when she let go of him.

"Hi, Sis. Welcome home," he said, in a voice that Agnes thought sounded even warmer and deeper than it had when he went off to war.

"And welcome home to you, too," Agnes replied. "It's so good to have you back where you belong. Mom and Dad must be thrilled."

Allen had moved around her to snatch up her suitcases; Neil stepped over and took one of them in his hand.

"Here, Allen, let me help with those. If I know my sister, they're packed to bursting."

Agnes objected to his characterization good-naturedly.

"Just a minute, mister. This isn't Naomi you're talking to."

They all laughed. Agnes positioned Allen on one side of her and Neil on the other, put an arm through each of theirs, and they walked, in unison, toward the car. Neil looked down and noticed they were all stepping together.

227

"Say, look at that, Agnes knows how to march and she hasn't even been through drill instruction." He looked at Allen. "That's good news for you, Allen. Maybe you won't have to work as hard to keep her in step after you're married."

Allen laughed and looked at Agnes.

"Oh, I don't think we'll have any problems in that department, Neil. She's pretty much taken charge of things already."

Agnes bumped Allen's shoulder and laughed.

"You just watch it there, Mister Flaherty. You're going to get yourself in the doghouse before we even have a doghouse."

They all laughed at that, piled into the car, and headed to Smithfield, three young people glad to be alive, glad to be together, after the harrowing years of war. A few days later, on a beautiful Saturday afternoon, Allen and Agnes were married at the Free Methodist Church, and the following Monday, the trio formed a two-car caravan--Allen and Agnes in the Chevy his father had helped him buy, Neil in the old Ford he'd bought as soon as he arrived home--and drove to Washington, where they set up shop in a two-bedroom apartment Agnes had arranged for them.

Time passed quickly, with Neil and Allen putting in long hours at the service station and Agnes keeping the books. The men came home with interesting stories about the people they'd met at the station. For a time, they were the official gas and oil change site for the limousines from the White House. When they weren't working, they enjoyed getting to know their way around Washington, and derived significant satisfaction over their ability to negotiate its arcane and sometimes hectic traffic patterns. Not long after Agnes and Allen celebrated their first anniversary, they welcomed their first child, a happy, healthy little boy. They were all happy in those days. Six months later, tragedy struck.

The elder Neil called to tell them Irene had suffered some sort of attack and it looked very serious. They piled in Neil, Junior's car and raced home. When they reached the hospital, they found Irene lying very still. When she opened her eyes, she smiled at all of them. In a small voice, she asked if she could speak to Agnes alone. The men retreated to the hallway and Agnes sat down by her mother.

"Dearest Agnes, this is very bad. The doctors think I've suffered a cerebral hemorrhage. I don't know if I can survive, and in case I don't, I want you to promise you'll do something for me."

Agnes leaned close to Irene and held her hand.

"Oh, Mom, you're going to make it, I'm sure you will."

"Don't argue with me, Agnes. I want you to promise me."

"Promise what?"

"Promise me that if I die, you will come home and look after Carl. He's getting just old enough to have his own ideas about things and I don't think your father can handle him. Will you do that for me, Agnes? I know it's asking a great deal, but if you don't do it, I don't know who will. Naomi is up there in Wisconsin, struggling to take care of her baby girl and help Cliff keep up with the farm. You're the only person in the family I really trust to do this."

She raised her head to look into Agnes's eyes. Agnes knew she had no choice. She nodded as Irene's head settled back onto the pillow.

"Yes, of course, Mom. We'll come home and help Dad out. But hopefully we won't need to. You need to rest and get better."

Irene pulled her hand free and patted Agnes's hand.

"Thank you, Agnes." She closed her eyes and fell asleep.

Agnes walked to the door and waved the men back into the room. She whispered that Irene was sleeping and they shouldn't wake her up. There were only two chairs in the room. Agnes returned to the one she'd pulled up alongside the bed and Neil sat down in the other, by the window. Allen and Neil, Junior whispered that they'd park themselves in the waiting room. They didn't have long to wait. Two hours later the doctor came in to check on Irene and told them her vital signs were fading. Shortly after that, Agnes noticed that Irene's breathing had become erratic and she noticed a hint of a rattle when she exhaled. She sent her father out to fetch Neil and Allen. Less than five minutes after they stepped into the room, Irene drew a long deep breath, moaned, and was silent. Tears streaming down her face, Agnes ran to the doorway and called down the hall for the nurse, who ran in and checked Irene's pulse. She confirmed what they already knew. Irene was dead, at the age of sixty-two.

After her mother's funeral, which her brothers boycotted to avoid confronting Neil, Agnes stayed at her parents' home with Carl, while Allen and Neil drove to Washington to sell their share of the service station back to Neil's army buddy. Neil decided to use the G-I Bill to get more education. He was soon accepted at West Virginia University in Morgantown. Allen returned to the mines and Agnes stayed home with Carl and baby Glen. The sudden loss of Irene had shaken Agnes and Neil, Junior as much as it had Carl, who was going on twelve. Six months later, Neil rattled them all again when he announced that he was planning to marry their next-door neighbor, Babe Morgan.

Agnes had always thought Neil seemed just a bit too friendly around Babe, but she had never considered it her place to say anything. This news turned her reticence to anger. She confronted Neil soon after his announcement, when he came home from work.

"Dad, I don't think it's appropriate for you to be marrying Babe so soon after Mom's death. It doesn't look very good to the neighbors."

Neil flared up angrily, as he always had when Irene challenged him on his indiscretions.

"Who do you think you are questioning anything I decide to do?"

"I'm your daughter and my mother's child and I just don't think it's right."

"Oh, no? Well, I don't think it's right that you rushed into getting married when you were only twenty-one. And I still don't think you should have married Allen Flaherty. What do you think of that?"

Agnes had inherited her mother's quick wit and sharp tongue. Her mind delivered up a biting retort, but her conscience refused to let her utter it. She closed her mouth and left the room. She would never broach such an issue with Neil again, not even when he shed Babe and moved on to his third and then fourth wife. But she would allude to her opinion of Neil's personal behavior in years to come as she encouraged her own sons to grow into decent, young men. "Your grandfather," she told them, "has no morals." And she meant it, but her sons wouldn't know until many years later exactly what she was referring to.

After Agnes and Allen had been living with Neil for a year or so, Carl started getting involved in some teenaged high jinks. They all decided that the best thing for him would be a stretch on Cliff and Naomi's farm in Wisconsin. He was duly shipped off to the North Country. The Flahertys moved to a house in Green County, not far from the mine and nearer to Allen's family and away from Neil's shenanigans, and soon welcomed their second son, another cherubic baby they named Matt. Life settled into a comfortable routine, with Agnes at home with the boys and Allen plodding off, unenthusiastically, to the mines by day and wedging in some G.I. Bill funded courses at a local business college by night.

Then, in short order, the landscape changed again. Allen headed off to work at the crack of dawn one fateful day, only to return a few hours later, striding energetically toward the house with a huge grin on his face. He informed Agnes that he'd been laid off, which he said left him feeling very good on two counts: one, he hated working in the mines; and two, they could now take Neil , Junior up on his invitation to join him and his new wife in Lancaster County, where he had found work at an electronics plant. A few weeks later, Allen and Agnes were living in a second-floor apartment in a small town east of Lancaster, Dillerville.

Eventually, they both landed jobs with the large farm implement manufacturer headquartered in their borough. Agnes signed on first; the personnel department offered her a position moments after she informed them she had worked for the top-secret Manhattan Project during the war. From that vantage point, Agnes had encouraged Allen to apply for a job opening up in the mail room. He was hired, and soon promoted to second-in-command of the small crew that labored amidst the sorting machines and sacks and sacks of correspondence generated by an international company. They both worked hard, and carved out a middle class life for themselves and the boys.

Other than listing it on her job application, Agnes gave little thought to the Manhattan Project. She kept the wooden "A" pin in her jewelry box, but never wore it. The memory of the Trinitite scare always lurked just beneath the surface of her mind, especially as she awaited the arrival of her sons. But both of them entered the world with the right number of fingers and toes and no apparent physical problems, nothing she might be tempted to blame on radiation.

When her sons brought home Weekly Reader articles about the promising possibilities of peacetime nuclear energy--Atoms for Peace--she mentioned that she had worked with the wartime version of the atomic program, and showed them the diagram she'd kept, with concentric circles recording the range and damage caused by the bomb dropped on Hiroshima. She retrieved the certificate from Secretary Stimson and the signed photograph from Groves from the big box of family pictures and mementos she kept on a shelf in her bedroom closet, and let the boys look at them.

When she did entertain thoughts of the MED and her time in Washington, she continued to tell herself she was one of the lucky ones. Somehow, perhaps by the grace of God, the atomic dragon had not bitten her. But bouts of vertigo that began when she was thirty-five, shook her confidence. The doctor examined her and found nothing physically wrong; in synch with the trend of the sixties, he decided it was probably just nerves, and prescribed Librium. Agnes swallowed the big, red pills faithfully, but the dizziness returned intermittently.

Sometimes it happened on Sunday morning, as she stood in her pew, singing the hymns that meant so much to her. She tried to steady herself so no one would notice, and managed to mask the episodes enough to avoid detection by the other worshippers. But her sons, standing on either side of her, knew. They would feel her suddenly lean into them and see her grasp the back of the pew in front of her with her long, slender fingers, in a grip so tight the blood was forced from her knuckles.

The unpredictable and chronic nature of the dizziness left her fearful that she would one day tip over in public, an embarrassing possibility that her sense of propriety made her determined to avoid. She curtailed her activities, eventually even refraining from attending church, except in rare instances such as Christmas and Easter. But she made sure her boys donned suit and tie every Sunday morning and headed off for their weekly dose of religion.

The rash came later, in her forties. The doctor diagnosed seborrhea and somehow connected it to the nervous condition he'd identified before; he upped her dose of Librium and gave her ointment for the redness. Agnes feared it was something more serious, and would sit at her dressing table rubbing the ointment into her pale skin with tears in her eyes. When her younger son came upon her in a distraught moment, and saw the moistness in her eyes and the ugly, red patches on her arm, he grew concerned and asked what was wrong. Agnes drew in a deep breath and dismissed the whole thing. "Just a rash," she told him. "Dr. Remple gave me some ointment for it. I'm sure it will be gone soon."

Near the end of her forties, Agnes noticed a slight, pricking sensation just below her navel. She couldn't think of any way it might be related to the Trinitite; she knew it couldn't be her appendix, so she ignored it. But it persisted, off and on, over the next few years. Symptoms that could not be overlooked appeared when she reached fifty-five. But they weren't her symptoms; they were Naomi's.

Naomi and Cliff, and their two daughters, had packed up and made a hasty move back to Pennsylvania years before, after Naomi was struck down by a mysterious, debilitating illness. Her doctor, who suspected severe homesickness might be a factor, had told Cliff he'd better get his wife out of Wisconsin and back with her family if he wanted to keep her around. The change of scenery had worked. She had recovered most of her former, lively nature after they joined Agnes and Neil, Junior in Lancaster County. At the age of fifty-seven, she'd gotten sick again, and this time the doctors diagnosed liver cancer.

Agnes, retired by that time from her job in personnel, spent many hours looking after her beloved Naomi. The oncologists removed what they could of the tumor, and put Naomi through chemo and radiation therapy, but to no avail. In less than two years, she was gone. The experts had searched, unsuccessfully, for an explanation, a cause, but found nothing. Naomi did not drink or smoke. She had never worked around hazardous chemicals. The doctors told the family it would remain a mystery, like so many other cancer cases they saw.

Agnes had a theory, but, true to the vow of secrecy she'd taken thirty years ago, she kept it to herself. She remembered Naomi's excitement when she first saw the smooth green rocks Agnes brought home from the office. Naomi had asked a jeweler to mount several of them on the shiny, silver belt that she almost always wore when she really wanted to look snazzy. The Trinitite had not left the red, seeping sores on her that plagued Eleanor and the others, so Naomi had continued to wear the belt for some time after Mrs. O'Leary ordered everyone to dispose of the radioactive rocks. After reading the reports from Japan and the Los Alamos labs, Agnes had insisted that Naomi either have the Trinitite removed from the belt or throw it away. Naomi had finally agreed to get rid of it. What Agnes had learned about the damage radiation could do, combined with her intuition, convinced her Naomi was the latest victim of the bomb. And, she hoped against hope that her name would not be added to the list.

But, in her deeply-disciplined way, she refused to dwell on the negatives. She had too much to live for and too much to do. Neil would need her to continue helping him keep after the house he had bought when he moved to their little town, in retreat from his fourth wife. Vertigo be darned, she had taken on the task of organizing the luncheons the church put on for seniors in the community. And, perhaps most wonderful of all, there were her grandchildren: Karin, the beautiful, blond-haired little girl her younger son and his wife had presented to the family three years ago, and Karin's brother, Jonathan, the adorable, red-headed baby boy, barely three months old when Naomi died. Agnes wanted to spend hours and hours with them, and was especially anxious to see little Karin's eyes the next time they came to visit and she took her into the backyard to show her the cute, little camping trailer she and Allen had just bought. Karin called it the "little house."

There had been a scare a couple of years ago when the accident happened at the Three Mile Island nuclear power plant, twenty miles upwind from where her sweet, six-month old granddaughter lay sleeping peacefully in her crib. Agnes had listened carefully to the reports, waiting to hear how much radiation had escaped. She was relieved, the fifth day after the accident, when Governor Thornburgh told Pennsylvanians there had been a release of radiation, but the experts had determined that it was negligible. People should get on with their lives and not worry about it. Agnes had smiled, thanked God for yet another escape from the nuclear demon, and returned to her reading.

Not that her heart didn't ache sometimes. She worried about her older son, Glen, who had made what she considered an unfortunate choice in a spouse. For the moment, he and she were both on her "Do Not Call" list, after a humiliating encounter she'd had with them while visiting them at their home in Indiana. But she still loved her son, and hated to think of him struggling to make his way in the world with only *that* woman at his side. She felt certain he would need her again one of these days.

And she hurt for Naomi's daughters, too, left motherless just as they stepped out on their own. She had promised Naomi she'd stay close to them; she loved them as dearly as she loved her own boys. She prayed for all of them, confident that God would use her as His instrument to minister to them in good times and bad. And, if she had anything to say about it, there would be far more good times than bad ones.

She had long dreamed of the trips she and Allen would take when she was retired. Their plan was to buy a motor home and gallivant all over the country, seeing the sights, visiting the kids, and enjoying the fruits of their labors over many years. They had made friends in the little town where they lived; she felt a connection there. But she had always told her boys she was a Gypsy at heart, ready to hit the road at the drop of a hat.

The little camping trailer was supposed to be the first step in that direction. Unfortunately, now that they had it, Allen's enthusiasm for the nomadic life had cooled. He was reluctant to hitch up the camper and head out. When he wasn't working, he preferred to play handyman around the house or simply sit in his easy chair in the living room and watch TV. He refused to visit anyone, except for an occasional jaunt to see Neil, Junior and his wife, who were now living in Maryland.

This wasn't the life Agnes had bargained for; she felt the cloud of melancholy descending on her again. She fought to keep it at bay, even breaking out her "rainy day" blouse, the one with the dazzling, multicolored pattern, to brighten her mood and the atmosphere in the house, and stave off the cabin fever that gripped her. At this moment in her life, her intuition failed her, which may have been a blessing in disguise. Had the special sense she and Naomi had inherited from Irene been functioning, she would have known that all the positive thinking in the world could not prevent the events that unfolded next.

When Allen turned fifty-five, the farm implement company, now under new management, forced him and a host of other senior employees to retire, in a cost-cutting move. Allen, who had traded on his business school studies to move into the accounting department, took it hard; he had intended to work another ten years and then live comfortably on his ample pension. He found another job at a local feed mill, but the computer work involved tripped him up, and he left it. His loss would soon become Agnes's gain.

Shortly after she turned fifty-seven, the sharp pain in Agnes's abdomen returned, this time with a vengeance. She thought it might signal a flare-up of the bladder infection that had knocked her off her feet fifteen years earlier. For the first time since the pricking sensation first appeared years ago, she sought the doctor's opinion. He referred her to an internist who ordered tests. When the results came in, the specialist invited Agnes back to his office. She was standing in one of his brightly lit examination rooms when he told her, in words devoid of emotion, what they'd found. Staggered by his pronouncement, Agnes reached out to steady herself on the paper-clad examination table nearby. The doctor took her arm and guided her to a chair along the wall. He gave her a few moments to recover her composure, then had a nurse help her to the waiting room. With tears in her eyes, she told Allen the news.

Two weeks later, she phoned her son Matt to tell him she'd had surgery for cancer. She said the surgeons had removed her gall bladder. When she heard Matt gasp, she hastened to add that the doctors were fairly certain the cancer had been contained in her gall bladder and they had assured her they'd gotten it all. Matt chided her for not telling him about the diagnosis until now. He asked if he and his family should come home to assist her. They were now living in Indiana, where Matt had just taken a teaching job at a small college. Agnes assured him she was going to be fine, she said she was feeling better already, and they needn't interrupt their lives to drag the children back to Pennsylvania. She just wanted to let them know before they heard it from someone else and started to worry. Matt hung up the phone and told his wife, Louise, what Agnes had said. They both had a feeling Agnes, in her perpetual desire to protect those she loved, was putting a positive spin on a story that was not, in reality, nearly so upbeat.

Agnes launched into a cycle of radiation treatments, which necessitated repeated trips to Lancaster. Allen's recent departure from the company worked to their advantage; he was free to drive her to the appointments, at any time of the day. When Matt and his family came home for Christmas, they found a vibrant looking Agnes, fresh from the radiation therapy, perhaps a bit thinner than normal, but showing no signs of illness. She busied herself around the house during their visit, making elaborate meals and playing with Karin and Jonathan.

Shortly after New Year's, the doctors ordered a round of chemo-therapy treatments for Agnes. She again relied on Allen to deliver her to the appointments. Chemo caused side effects Agnes had not experienced with the radiation. Partway through, she had Allen call Matt and Glen and inform them that she was being hospitalized for phlebitis. Matt and Louise packed up the kids and raced to Pennsylvania. They arrived to find a sallow looking Agnes propped up in a hospital bed. She hugged them all, and mustered up a fraction of her radiant smile as she told them she was fine; this was just something that happened when they put you through chemotherapy.

That trip to the hospital was followed by others over the course of the next several months; the chemo was attacking Agnes's blood stream as it sought out errant cancer cells to destroy. Transfusions of healthy blood seemed to pull her around, but she was getting weaker, and losing more weight, as time went by. She didn't report all of this to her sons. She also didn't tell them about the day her oncologist marched into her hospital room to check on her and infuriated Allen by lightly tossing off, in response to Allen's inquiry about what the disease might ultimately do to Agnes, "Well, I'm not sure, exactly, " he'd said, as he breezed out of the room, "but with all of these other complications, it's a sure bet she won't die of cancer." Beside himself with worry, Allen had wanted to throttle the man. Agnes held his hand and calmed him down.

When she returned home from her second round of blood transfusions, Agnes announced that she wanted to visit Matt and Louise in Indiana, and see the home they had recently purchased, and of course, the grandchildren. The trip was quickly arranged, and soon Matt was squiring Agnes around the campus where he and Louise were both working. Matt had commandeered a golf cart from the maintenance department; he and a visibly weakened Agnes rode in the cart with the children, while Allen and Louise tagged along on foot. Agnes was pleased to see the life they were making for themselves. They had struggled along in their early days together, when he was working at low-paying jobs in radio and television news. Their new home was lovely, and they finally had enough money to furnish it nicely. Agnes returned to Pennsylvania satisfied that her son was providing a good life for his family.

A few weeks later, Carl, who was now living in Florida, came to see how Agnes was getting along. When Agnes greeted him at the door, he was shocked and saddened by her condition. When they sat down at the kitchen table to have coffee and cookies, he asked how she was doing. Agnes sighed, tears welling up in her eyes.

"It's not good, Carl. It's just not good."

"Do Matt and Glen know?"

Agnes shook her head.

"No, I haven't told them everything. They're busy with their own families. I don't want to upset them."

"Sis, you have to tell me. I'm your brother, for heaven's sake. Do the doctors know why this happened?"

He expected to hear the same explanation the experts had given for Naomi's illness: "It's a mystery. We'll probably never know." But Agnes's response was very explicit.

"It has to be that Trinitite, in the office, way back during the war."

"What do you mean?"

"Well, when they opened me up they found cancer everywhere."

"Didn't you tell the boys it was just in your gall bladder and they thought they'd gotten all of it?"

Agnes sighed again.

"Yes, of course I did. What good would it do for them to know everything? When the doctors were trying to figure out what caused it, I told them I worked for the Manhattan Project. They told me I have metastatic adenocarcinoma. They said it's similar if not identical to the kind of cancer people developed in Japan after we dropped the bombs. It's caused by exposure to radiation and it can take a long time to develop."

Carl reached out to take her hand, but she pulled it back and bunched both of her hands into fists. Her face flushed with anger.

"Oh, it makes me so darn mad. I never did anything bad. I didn't smoke, I didn't drink. Nothing. I've always tried to be a good, decent person. I've lived a perfectly clean life. It has to be that Trinitite. You know I sat right beside that box of it for weeks. I was there because I wanted to do my duty. And this is the thanks I get."

She buried her face in her hands as the tears washed down her cheeks.

"Oh, Carl, this just isn't fair."

Carl felt his own eyes grow moist and then felt tears streaming down his face. Naomi's death had ripped through him like a jagged knife. Losing Agnes would break his heart in two. He put his hand on her shoulder.

"Is there anything I can do, Sis?"

Agnes looked up at him, her eyes reddened, her fair complexion splotchy with emotion.

"No, Carl, there is nothing anybody can do. Nothing."

"I hear you, Sis. But I'll promise you this. I will stay in touch with your boys and be there for them if they ever need me."

Agnes managed a faint smile.

"Thank you, Carl. You have always been such a loving brother."

Agnes completed her chemotherapy treatments shortly after Carl's visit, but she did not regain her strength as she had after the radiation. Instead, her weight loss accelerated and her strength ebbed even further. Shortly after Easter, Allen called his sons to tell them their mother was not doing well, at all. He said now might be a good time to come see her. Glen and his family came in, but could not stay for long. Matt and Louise arrived, took one look at Agnes, and knew the situation had reached a serious stage.

By this time, Agnes had withdrawn into herself. She sat up for a time, on the deacon's bench in the living room, silently watching her family as the children played and the adults chatted. She closed her eyes and didn't speak, but she seemed determined to stay in their midst. When Matt and his family returned the next day, Agnes was lying in bed, her eyes closed, but not sleeping. Occasionally, she would lift her hand slightly to signal Allen and Matt that she wanted them to moisten her cracked lips with swabs on the nightstand. The day passed with father and son alternating care in the bedroom with conversation and playtime with the grandchildren in the living room. As the hour grew late, Louise and the children said goodnight to Allen and drove to Louise's parents' home, which was nearby. Matt stayed with Allen.

When Agnes seemed to be sleeping soundly, they left the bedroom and walked through the short hallway to the living room. The house was small enough that they could hear Agnes's labored breathing from where they sat. At nine-thirty, they heard a rattling sound from the bedroom. Matt rushed in and watched his mother as she lay on the bed, the covers tucked closely around her withered form to stave off the chill she had felt when she lay down. The rattling sound grew louder; her family physician had said that might happen as her lungs filled with fluid. Agnes tried to lick her lips, but her mouth was too dry for her tongue to accomplish it. Matt picked up a moist swab and gently applied it to the parched tissue around his mother's mouth. When the rattling sound subsided a bit, he returned to the living room.

The two men together without speaking, listening to Agnes's shallow breathing. The doctor had told them she might continue in this condition for some time. And then Allen and Matt realized they weren't hearing anything from the hallway. The breathing had stopped. They raced into the bedroom. Agnes was making no sound at all. She lay perfectly still, her beautiful brown eyes closed, the sagging flesh of her face making her high cheekbones more prominent than ever, her brilliant smile locked behind her cracked lips.

Matt bent down and kissed his mother on the forehead. Her brow felt cold and damp to his lips. Then both men cried. Neither of them could find the strength to speak for several minutes. When they did, it was the normally less-chatty Allen who spoke first.

"I'm sorry, Matt. But your mother is gone."

Matt nodded and wiped away tears. Allen looked down at Agnes and added another thought.

"You know, she told me a couple of weeks ago that she hoped she would live to see another Easter." His shoulders shook as grief took hold of him. "And sure enough, she did. I'm sure she was happy about that."

Matt put his arm around his father and pulled him close.

"Yes, Dad, I'm sure you're right. Thank God she at least got that."

Allen reached down and touched Agnes's face and then walked out of the room. As he went down the hall, he called back to Matt, "Would you call Dr. Kreider and tell her? She said she would come as soon as we told her your mother was gone."

Matt stood and gazed at this wonderful, saintly woman who had given so much to all of them for so many years. "Thank you, Mom," he said softly and then walked to the living room and picked up the phone.

CHAPTER SEVENTEEN

Dozens of people packed the funeral home down the block from the Methodist Church for Agnes's funeral service. Family members were there--the grandchildren, Naomi's daughters, Neil, Junior and his family, and Allen's brother and sisters and their families. Carl was there beside Neil, who slumped in his chair, stunned by the loss of both of his daughters. At one point, he leaned over to Carl and whispered, "Children are supposed to outlive their parents." Allen and his sons knew many of those in attendance, but others they didn't recognize at all.

The young minister from Agnes's church, a man her sparse church attendance had prevented her from coming to know particularly well, eulogized her as a pious Christian woman, devoted to her family, her church and her community. Allen reached repeatedly for the pressed, white handkerchief in his back pocket and wiped away tears that welled up as the minister read the Twenty Third Psalm, and encouraged everyone to be of good cheer; Agnes was with her Father in heaven, he said, reaping the rewards of a life well-lived, a life of loving service to those who crossed her path. Matt struggled to hold back his tears and join in singing Agnes's favorite hymns. Several deep breaths got him most of the way

243

through "The Old Rugged Cross," but he broke down completely on the first verse of "In the Garden," the hymn Agnes had already claimed as her special favorite by the time she packed up for her wartime adventure in Washington. There was no mention of the Manhattan Project, and only a glancing reference to how she died.

When the service ended, many of the unfamiliar mourners waited silently in line for a chance to share with Allen and Glen and Matt how Agnes had touched their lives and what her friendship had meant to them. They all shook their heads and said it was a shame that she had been taken from all of them so soon, only fifty-nine. They said this fine, Christian woman would not be soon forgotten. Even in the depths of their grief, Allen and his sons marveled at the impact Agnes had obviously had on the world around her.

Agnes Jenkins Flaherty died without hearing that, contrary to Governor Thornburgh's reassuring pronouncements in 1979, the Three Mile Island nuclear accident had released as much as 43,000 curies of radioactive krypton into the air that wafted over her son's home twenty miles downwind. She was not alive in the mid-eighties, when a nuclear plant exploded in the Ukraine, killing more than fifty people outright, and spewing radiation for miles that radiation experts predicted would cause anywhere from four thousand to one million more deaths in the months and years to come.

She was already gone when a reporter quoted one of the Trinity test safety officers as saying "...a few people were probably over exposed [after the blast], but they couldn't prove it and we couldn't prove it. So we just assumed we got away with it." She never saw the reports suggesting that radiation from Trinity had shown up as far away as Indiana, and may have fogged photographic film in upstate New York. She was long gone from Washington when investigators found steel barrels filled with pulverized Trinitite buried in a concrete bunker two miles from Ground Zero. She never had a chance to read the CDC study documenting that, in the days and months after Trinity, no one had bothered to examine the soldiers and scientists, not to mention local residents like the Ratliffs, to gauge how much radiation they might have inhaled or ingested as the ruinous rain of fallout from the first test coated their roofs and fence posts like snow. The CDC reported that Los Alamos health officers had explained that they had no facilities for such work.

It was long after her death, and long after America stopped testing atomic bombs above ground, that a U.S. health study concluded that "any person living in the contiguous United States since 1951 has been exposed to radioactive fallout and all organs and tissues of the body have received some radiation exposure." She was not at her desk in Room 5120 to read that the NRC had lowered the standard for safe exposure to radiation from the five roentgens doctors had set before Trinity to .002 roentgens, and some scientists said they didn't know if any dose could be declared safe.

The last war Agnes knew anything about before she died was Vietnam. She never talked about it very much, but when her older son, Glen, lost his college deferment and the draft was closing in, she made sure he enlisted in the Air Force so he could serve his country in England rather than on the front lines in Southeast Asia. And when her younger son, Matt, vowed to move to Canada rather than fight in 'Nam, she didn't lecture him on his duty to God and country; she told him she'd come visit him in Canada.

She didn't live long enough to hear about the "dirty" bombs her country dropped on Iraq and Afghanistan late in the twentieth century, depleted uranium bombs, that threw up radioactive particles as fine as gas that drifted through villages where men, women and children inhaled them. Classifying and filing the disturbing reports predicting that the lethal clouds would cause thousands of cancer deaths in Iraq was no longer her responsibility. The Corps of Engineers was not charged with building an ultimate weapon to end those wars.

The moratorium on American nuclear plant construction, put in place after T.M.I., had not yet been declared when Agnes died. She lived long enough to see the first Arab oil embargo, but never saw the nuclear industry's decades-long public relations campaign for a recommitment to the power of the atom. And she didn't hear the culmination of that crusade, a call-- by a young, liberal, black president--for more nuke plants to replace the dwindling supply of fuel oil needed for power plants.

Agnes Jenkins Flaherty, the bright, country girl from western Pennsylvania, might not have minded missing many of the events that transpired as the world lurched into a new millennium. Her motto was, after all: *If you can't say something nice, don't say anything.* And the corollary was: *Never talk politics or religion in public.* She died as dedicated to her country as she had lived. It's likely, had she known about the deception surrounding the rest of the nation's nuclear experimentation, the half-truths perpetrated after T.M.I., she would have understood. No one, not her parents or Allen or her boys, had ever known the weight of secret responsibility she had borne in those exciting and terrifying days in D.C. It was her duty. Chances are she would have done it all again, although she might have been a bit more careful around that Trinitite. She was saddened to leave her family, especially her beautiful grandchildren, so soon. But she never expressed a single regret for taking the job in Washington.

It was, after all, the first job she'd ever had. At the age of eighteen, she'd been offered an opportunity and a responsibility most ordinary people never come close to. And, as her sons would tell people for decades, in resentful tones, that opportunity, the rain of ruin let loose by Roosevelt, Truman, Stimson, Groves, and Oppenheimer, killed her.

[end of draft]

CHAPTER EIGHTEEN

As Ben typed the last sentence of Agnes Jenkins Flaherty's story, an overwhelming sadness rushed over him. He clicked the "Save" button on his computer and pushed it back on the small table in the kitchenette where he did his writing. Slowly, he lowered his elbows onto the table, buried his face in his hands, and wept; the tears coming in great, racking sobs. In an apartment as small as theirs, the sound of his crying carried quickly to the living room, where Sarah was reading. She laid down her book and walked into the kitchen.

The sight of Ben, his head down, his shoulders shaking, first alarmed her, then sent a pain through her heart as she realized he was in the grip of an emotional reaction, not a physical one. She stepped behind him, put her arms around his neck, and planted a gentle kiss on top of his head.

"Ben, what is it? Did something happen to the manuscript?" She took a risk with her next comment, hoping to lighten his mood. "The computer didn't eat your book, did it?"

Ben tilted his head back to look up at her. The light from the desk lamp reflected on the wet tracks left by tears as they ran down his face. He didn't speak, but from her vantage point above him, she could see the pain on his face.

"What is it, Ben?" She leaned down and put her arm around him. "What is it, sweetie?"

Ben finally calmed down enough to speak.

"I'm okay, honey. It's just that," he stopped and took a shuddering breath, "it's just that I've never been so affected by someone's story before." He paused and wiped away tears that were still trickling down his cheeks. "I mean, you know better than anyone how many stories I've written, touching stories, revelations of the human condition. But no story has ever hit me like this one."

Sarah pulled up the other kitchen chair and sat down. Ben had shared parts of the book with her as he wrote, but mostly he had just pounded away, night after night. She knew few details of Agnes Jenkins Flaherty's life.

"Maybe you're just exhausted from all the writing. You've been staying up too late, especially the last couple of weeks, getting it done."

Ben shook his head, drew in a deep breath, and ran his fingers through his already disheveled hair. He patted Sarah on the knee.

"Thanks for the sympathy, but I'm not crying for me. I'm weeping for this incredible woman whose life I've been living in for the past six months."

Sarah raised her eyebrows.

"I don't mean to be disrespectful, but in what sense is she incredible? I mean, I know she died as a result of her work with the bomb project. But she wasn't Oppenheimer or what's his name-- Groves--or any of the other famous scientists who created the thing. She was just a secretary and a file clerk."

Ben took both of her hands in his and squeezed them. He spoke with an intensity Sarah had rarely seen.

"But that's just it, Sarah. She was *just* a file clerk, but a file clerk who found herself at the heart of the most cataclysmic development in the history of human civilization."

Sarah wasn't catching his drift.

"But she didn't do it, she didn't build the bomb. She just typed letters and filed paperwork. And she had some bad timing in her job search process. I don't understand why that makes you so sad."

"Sarah, Sarah, Sarah, always so pragmatic."

He turned and pointed to the computer screen.

"I want you to read this, every word of it, and then we'll have the rest of this conversation, okay?"

Sarah agreed.

"But you're going to have to print it out, I hate reading long stuff on a computer screen."

Ben's smile had returned. He extended his hand. She took it and gave it a firm shake.

"Deal?"

"Deal."

Ben lugged their old HP-940C printer from the hallway closet and attached the cables. In a few seconds it was cranking out page after page of his book. Sarah returned to the living room and curled up in her reading chair. When the printer pushed the title page onto the stack, Ben picked up the manuscript and carried it to her.

"You can put that thriller away for a night or two." He plopped the printed pages onto her lap. "Happy reading, my love."

Sarah put aside the Dan Brown novel she had in her hand and picked up the first page of Ben's manuscript. As she laid the title page on the end table by her chair, she looked up at him.

"Just one more question before I get into this: Do you still think it'll make a good movie?"

Ben pondered a moment before answering.

"We can discuss that, too, when you're finished. I'm not sure how I feel about that, at this point."

"Why don't you want to make a movie anymore?"

"I didn't say that, my dear. I said we should talk about it when you're finished." He pointed to the stack of paper on Sarah's lap. "Now, read."

Sarah tucked her leg under her and settled in. Ben sank into his reading chair across the small living room, switched on the floor lamp behind the chair, and watched his wife. She had always been his best critic, his best editor and biggest cheerleader. He readily admitted to all of their friends that she was the woman behind the curtain, his one and only muse. He wanted her to like his book and he wanted her to feel Agnes's story as deeply as he had.

When she'd been reading for only five minutes, she reached for the pencil she kept by her reading lamp. Ben leaned forward anxiously.

"What? What's wrong?"

Sarah laughed and waved him off.

"Nothing's wrong, Mr. Creativity. I'm allowed to mark things I have questions about, right?"

Ben nodded, an anxious expression on his face.

"Okay, then, that's all I'm doing. Why don't you find something to do while I'm doing this? I don't want you staring at me like a hawk the whole time."

Ben threw up his hands in surrender and pulled a copy of *New Yorker* from the magazine rack by his chair. He opened it with a flourish and busied himself with the cartoons, and then the articles. Sarah continued reading for another hour, then brought the manuscript to bed with her when they turned in shortly after eleven. She kissed Ben goodnight, pulled her knees up under the covers, and propped the manuscript against them. She was still reading when Ben drifted off to sleep. At two in the morning, she laid the manuscript on the floor by the bed, and switched off the light. She resumed reading the next night, after supper, and finished shortly before midnight. Ben was sitting across the room pretending to be interested in a Sarah Paretsky novel he'd bought recently, but he kept peering over the top edge of his book to see how far Sarah was. He was very sleepy but still there when Sarah finished the last page and sighed.

She looked at Ben, then stood and walked into the kitchenette. She came back holding the carved wooden "A"; Ben had kept it on the kitchen table for inspiration as he wrote. She sat down without speaking, gazing at the A-pin cradled in the palm of her hand. Ben waited anxiously for her reaction. After a long, silent moment, Sarah raised her head and looked across the room at him. She held up the wooden pin.

"Do you think we should return this to Agnes's family?"

Ben was puzzled by the question. This wasn't where he expected Sarah to begin her critique.

"Why do you ask that?"

Sarah responded with another question.

"Are you surprised, now that you know Agnes Flaherty's story, that her family would let someone have this?"

Ben shrugged his shoulders.

"I don't know. I haven't thought of it that way. They were so pleased that someone was finally going to tell Agnes's story, I think they wanted me to have it to inspire me to keep going with the project."

"You don't think any of them felt attached to it?" She held the "A" in her hand and stroked its smooth finish with her fingertip. "Did it inspire you?"

"Yes, it did. I kept thinking about what it meant to Agnes. When I held it in my hand, it conjured up that day in Groves's office when O'Leary presented it to her, and it made me think about what was going through her mind over the years when she reached into her jewelry box for earrings or a necklace, and saw the "A" lying in its little, felt-lined compartment. It's become a sort of talisman for me.

It's the closest connection I've ever had to someone I was writing about."

"You said she never wore it. In the story you link it to the Trinitite business, but do you really think that was why she didn't put it on?"

Ben scratched his head and looked perplexed.

"That's sort of what her son and her granddaughter suggested was the reason, so I went with that. But who really knows? She didn't talk about it."

Sarah looked at the pin, closed her fingers around it and squeezed.

"Maybe if we hold this tight enough," she said, more to herself than to Ben," we can connect with her spirit, wherever she is, and she'll tell us what she was thinking."

"Are you serious? You don't believe in that sort of mumbo-jumbo. Why are you asking all of these questions? I just want to know what you thought of the book."

Sarah looked up at him, the pin gripped tightly in her fist.

"I am telling you what I thought of the book, Ben. I'm telling you that you really connected with me. You made me care what happened to this woman. You made me wish I could sit and talk with her, and ask questions like the ones I'm asking you."

Ben breathed a sigh of relief.

"So you liked it."

"Yes, Ben, I liked it. But more than that, it really makes me think. I worried for a while that you might be getting too involved with the a-bomb issue and ending up with a polemic rather than a good story."

"But you don't think that now?"

"No, I don't. I think you've raised the nuclear issue in a very good way, but you've also created a very moving story, about a young woman who always tried to do the right thing--the good thing--and was ruined, nonetheless, by the tragic events that swirled around her. And the fact that they were real events--horribly real--makes the whole story even more powerful."

A broad smile spread across Ben's face.

"I'm glad you liked it."

Sarah raised her hand to interrupt him.

"I'm not finished. I understand, now, why you were so upset the other night when you finished writing. You allowed yourself to get very involved in Agnes's story. It's a personal story, and I think it works on that level. But I don't think everyone who reads it needs to be reduced to tears by the last page."

Ben broke in to protest.

"I wasn't going for that. I wasn't trying to write a tear-jerker. But I did hope people would feel Agnes's pain, at least a little bit."

Sarah took over.

"I don't think you have to worry about that. It's a touching account. But that's not what I see as your greatest accomplishment with this book."

"Really? What would that be?"

"As I was reading, I thought back to our conversation in the car on the way home from Pennsylvania. You said you wanted to expose the awfulness of the whole nuclear misadventure, which I, of course, agree with. But you also said you saw Agnes Flaherty as a sort of Everyman character, which should probably be revised to Everyperson here in the twenty-first century." She paused and smiled. "But a character who stands for all of us. Right? You remember you said that?"

Ben nodded.

"Well, I wasn't sure a file clerk was the right candidate to represent all of humankind. But I think you did it. I think it's sad that Agnes Jenkins Flaherty didn't get a chance to live out her dreams."

Sarah was speaking more rapidly now, her eyes flashed with intensity and she raised the fist holding the pin into the air.

"But more than a sensitive story of an unfortunate woman, Ben, I think you've written a novel of protest."

She rushed on, her tone passionate, her thoughts tumbling out.

"Agnes Flaherty saw herself as a patriotic American doing her duty for her country. She may not have worn a uniform, but she was every bit as faithful a soldier as her brother, Neil, or her sister's beloved Franklin or even General Groves."

" As I was reading, I imagined her standing quietly, her vow of secrecy clutched against her breast, in an endless line of human beings of all nationalities, their heads filled with nationalistic rhetoric and promises of opportunity from the time they learn to walk, who march off unquestioningly to do the bidding of the rich and powerful in time of war and stand by mutely in other times as those same movers and shakers expose them to the deadly aftereffects of their lucrative investments in military aggression, atomic bombs, nuclear power plants, and chemicals."

"I didn't cry for Agnes Jenkins Flaherty when I finished your book. But your story made me ache for all of the people of the world, whose simple lives are so thoughtlessly sacrificed for the greater gain and glory of the ruling class. Agnes Jenkins Flaherty probably didn't see herself that way, but for me, she *is* the embodiment of Everyperson."

Sarah finished speaking and sank back in her chair, the pin still in her hand. Ben walked over to her, pulled her to her feet and wrapped his arms around her.

"Sarah, you are amazing. I love you--body and soul--more than I can say. Thank you for caring so much about what I wrote."

Sarah kissed him and collapsed back into her chair. Ben retreated to the other side of the room.

"I have to admit, I wasn't going for that strong an Everyperson message, but if you found it there, that's great. But you are an exceptional person. Do you think other people will react that way?"

Sarah sat up, her eyes still bright.

"I sure hope so." She opened her fist.

"So what do you think? If this pin and your story can affect somebody as much as they did me, don't you think we should at least offer to give it back to Agnes's son or her grandchildren?"

"Boy, that's an even tougher question now than when you asked me before. Everything you've said makes me want to hold onto that direct connection to Agnes. She's really become part of my consciousness."

"Are you going to show Matt Flaherty the manuscript?"

"I was thinking I would, since he helped me so much with the research."

"Okay, so maybe you can decide what to do with this," she looked down at the pin lying in the palm of her hand, "after you see his reaction to the book."

Despite the hour, Ben felt wide awake and energized by Sarah's reaction. He rubbed his hands together.

"All right, I'll call my agent first thing tomorrow to see if we can sell this thing."

Sarah held up her hand.

"Not so fast, Mister."

"What?"

Sarah opened the pin attached to the wooden "A" and attached it to her sweater, just over her heart. She parked her ever-present pencil behind one ear, grasped the manuscript in both hands and stood up.

"Let's go out to the table. I want to go over some stuff in here while it's fresh in my mind."

Ben moaned.

"Sarah, it's after midnight. Can't it wait until tomorrow?"

Sarah pointed toward the hallway and then headed to the kitchenette. When he saw the light come on, Ben shrugged his shoulders, smiled, and trudged after her.

Mark Kelley

ABOUT THE AUTHOR

Mark Kelley is a veteran of more than 20 years in broadcast news, both radio and television. He has worked as a news producer, reporter, and until June, 1999, he served as main anchor for WNDU-TV in South Bend, IN. He attended Houghton College, graduated with a BA from the State University of New York at Geneseo, and later earned an MS in Telecommunications and a Ph.D. in Mass Communications from the S.I. Newhouse School of Public Communications at Syracuse University. Kelley has taught at Goshen College in Indiana, Syracuse University, the University of Maine in Orono, and is currently Director of Journalism at the New England School of Communications in Bangor, ME.

He is the author of three books: a novel, *Berman's Lament* (2000, available from the author), a non-fiction book, *Engaging News Media: A Practical Guide for People of Faith* (2006, available from Amazon), and *Rain of Ruin* (2011, available from Amazon Books, the Husson University Bookstore in Bangor, ME 04401, and from the author—contact info below).

Contact the author: kelleym@nescom.edu,

207-866-5772

21 Myrtle Street, Orono, ME 04473

Rain of Ruin

Made in the USA
Lexington, KY
21 March 2012